EILEEN PATRICIA CURRAN

was born in Massachusetts and spent much of her childhood in Connecticut. She attended the University of Texas at Dallas (BA, Economics and Finance, *summa cum laude*), Boston College (MBA, Finance and Marketing), and The New York School of Interior Design. She currently resides in Florida, the land of weirdness, where she hangs by the pool and tends to her gardens. If you've read something you absolutely love, feel free to let her know at hello@eileenpatriciacurran.com. She's always looking for her next great read.

eileenpatriciacurran.com
Instagram: @eileenpatriciacurran

HUNGRY HILL

First published in 2021 by Kinsale Press

For more information visit
www.eileenpatriciacurran.com

ISBN: 978-1-7360752-2-7
eISBN: 978-1-7360752-1-0

This is a work of fiction. All of the
characters, events, and location details
are either products of the author's
imagination or are used fictitiously.

Jacket Design: Sarah Brody
Interior Design: Euan Monaghan
Author Photograph: David Lawrence

Hungry Hill

EILEEN PATRICIA CURRAN

Kinsale Press

For Sonny and the women who raised him in Hungry Hill

later that evening

EXHAUSTED AND SORE, I headed to my room on the second floor of my great-aunt Maggie's house, stripped off my clothes, and crawled into bed. The sheets were soft from decades of use and smelled like unwashed socks. The pillow was lumpy, the mattress slumped in the middle, and the wool blanket emitted a heavy mothball funk.

I imagined how Michael would engage in some good-natured teasing about my sleeping in this bed: it was good for the soul to rough it every now and then; it would help me appreciate all the luxury I'd had in my life. He would even come up with some silly name for the type of décor Maggie had fashioned for the room. Gothic Granny Minimalism. Old Lady Penitentiary.

I would have smiled at the thought, but it was still much too easy for me to conjure my late husband's spirit. I kept hoping for some relief, some small fading of the memory of him, but I could still feel his exact touch. Smell his warm skin. Hear his voice whispering to me in the dark. My eyes were closed; I knew if I just had enough courage, I could reach out and brush my fingers against him.

PULSING RED LIGHTS played off of the ceiling in the bedroom, and muffled voices spoke in serious tones out in the hallway. I panicked when I couldn't make out details in the room, so I frantically tried to move toward the door. I couldn't find it.

A large brown bear balanced on a wire in the space between my bed and the swimming pool.

It took that and a few seconds of subterranean thought for me to realize I was dreaming. Ellen, my Irish wolfhound, was sleeping on the floor next to my bed. Her gentle snoring broke through my sleep-induced haze, and the taillights of a car passing the house on Cleveland Street disappeared from view.

Once awake, my conscious mind took over and started sorting through the debris banging around in its dark corners. It scuttled to a scene from five weeks earlier at the veterinarian's office.

Vertigo, my husband's inseparable companion, was a wolfhound like Ellen—taller, but just as sweet. It had taken two technicians and me to carry him into the clinic. The massive tumor in his abdomen was killing him, and I couldn't bear to see him suffer any longer.

Michael's big, old soldier forgave me while the vet injected him with poison. He watched me with his chocolate brown eyes, trusting me. I knew he thought he would get a treat and a hug when it was all over, but all he got was the hug. I spooned with his sleeping body for an hour afterward. When I couldn't bear to feel him grow any colder, I slid his enormous collar off and whispered a good-bye.

Out in the parking lot, the driver of a Range Rover honked at me furiously because I almost hit him with my pickup truck as I tried to back out. Tears blurred my vision, so I pulled back in to gather my wits.

As I lay in my bed in the dark, I could feel the cold steering wheel of the pickup truck in my hands, and I began to get angry. The memory of the Rover's horn sung in my head, and I now wished that I had continued backing out—hard—into its pristine, stupid side. I squeezed my eyes shut, and hot tears streamed down my face. My heart beat in my ears, and each breath I took burned in my throat.

I shouldn't have had to deal with Vertigo by myself.

1

road trip

I TURNED UP the volume on my BMW 750's sound system and cruised the Hungry Hill section of Springfield, Massachusetts, scanning the intersecting streets for my next turn.

The boom-boom of thumping bass calmed me, even though the seventies hard rock I was streaming wasn't usually my thing. The raucous music was a balm, though, a steady stream of anthems for my brave new world. The weather was an ally as well—it was a gorgeous New England morning: warm, sunny, and green. It had been a bitter winter; the sun entombed in a lead-colored sky that had mirrored my mood. Spring had arrived late, so I took the clear heavens as a good omen, which was optimistic of me lately.

I hadn't been in the area for years, and while the neighborhood was still familiar, a seismic shift had occurred while I was away and altered the place. Some structures remained intact while others had been obliterated, as though an urban tornado had spun violently through the streets. Most of the old trees were gone, hit hard by Dutch elm disease. *Ulmus Americana*: another victim of inadequate public funds. The few remaining trees were maples with many severed limbs and small buds struggling to open.

As I drove through the neighborhood, I experienced moments of nostalgia (the little pocket park where my cousins and I used to play appeared, intact, on my left), followed closely by dismay (an entire block of homes had been flattened and replaced with a strip mall; a sign out front advised that bankruptcy loomed). I hadn't expected everything to remain the same, but I was unprepared for how much everything had changed. I tried to gauge how much of the neighborhood's apparent decline was simply the result of my altered perspective—I had lived in towns full of pricey real estate for a long time—but quickly decided my memory wasn't failing me. The neighborhood had experienced a downward trajectory.

A sliver of apprehension quietly bore its way into my gut, and even Mick Jagger couldn't distract me from the feeling that I was about to take on something I wasn't the least bit prepared for.

As I continued to drive, I saw that the surviving commercial enterprises were basic: a few bars, a used clothing store, and a 7-Eleven competing with a couple of small grocery stores. Some of the storefronts were neatly maintained, but most were sorely in need of new landscaping and a coat of fresh paint. In addition to the physical changes that had taken place in the neighborhood, it had also become more culturally diverse since I last visited—the bodega and hair-braiding salon in one block were testament to that change.

When I last visited Hungry Hill, it was still an Irish-Catholic, blue-collar neighborhood. Its many bars bore Celtic names and all the faces were white; a few of the inhabitants were of French or Italian descent, but they were in the minority, and only tolerated because of shared orthodoxy.

I knew how dug-in my Irish forebears had been here, how important it had been for them to carve out a place of their own in this city, and how many generations had been born within a few square blocks of where I drove. I wondered if their exodus to the suburbs had taken place with resignation or relief. No one had ever talked to me about it; addresses had just changed over the years and I hadn't given it a thought until now.

My sister Emily's oldest son, Cormac, was right behind me driving my two dogs in the little Nissan cube I had just bought. Cormac had offered his services without prompt when he found out the dogs were joining me, and I wanted to bring a second car.

Emily had always encouraged her two sons to treat me like an extension of herself; she respected my decision to remain childless as an adult but was generous in sharing the benefits of motherhood. I adored her sons, and they adored me. I was especially close to Cormac because he had been born prematurely, and I had spent three weeks helping Emily with her new little bundle. He and I had built a strong bond over three a.m. feedings and Seinfeld reruns.

Cormac drove the cube because I denied my pets access to the Beemer and its leather seats; they had a tendency to shed hair, slobber, or worse—hurl, if they became carsick. I had sold my old Ford pickup the prior week and traded it for the cube because I was tired of looking like a contractor with a pet fetish. Besides, I was down to just a pair of canines now and didn't need the truck anymore.

Ellen took up the entire back seat of the cube. She sat sideways, her gaze directed stoically forward, her head lowered and hulking like a gentle chimera protecting my stuff piled high behind her in the cargo area. She may have been bred to guard the huts of villagers against marauders and wolves, but it was her sweet and

7

tolerant nature that made me feel safe. Stogie, my rescue mutt, rode shotgun next to Cormac, which explained the canine graffiti on the cube's front passenger window. They made an amusing picture, the three of them stuffed inside the little asymmetrical car as though the circus had come to town. Just looking at them in my rearview mirror made me smile, and in spite of my growing apprehension regarding our journey, it felt good to know they had my back.

Cormac had followed me in the cube from Greenwich, Connecticut, a town I had called home for many years. The drive was only two hours, but we might as well have been traveling from one planet to the next. The tony stretch of avenue in Greenwich where I owned a house was Hungry Hill's polar opposite. The only threat to existing real estate in Greenwich was the desire for newer and bigger, and our elms received frequent injections of fungicide from attentive arborists.

While we were driving in tandem to our destination, I'd had plenty of time to think. I wasn't sure how I felt about my current predicament. My great-aunt Maggie Reilly had called me three weeks earlier because she desperately needed my help, but she had caught me at a bad time. I wasn't ready to deal with someone else's problems—not even close. Still, she managed to talk me into a stint at her place, so here I was, back in my hometown.

Maggie had existed at the perimeter of my life since I was born. My family had lived in Agawam when I was growing up, a suburb of Springfield, and she had been a colorful fixture at family gatherings. She always showed up in one of her inexplicable outfits (once, I counted three different plaids), and made a habit of obsessing over everyone's footwear. She also usually managed to get wasted on her cocktail of choice—bourbon and seltzer—and loved to tell bawdy jokes once she had achieved a state of bliss. Sometimes, she would open up her purse, pull out her wallet, and distribute its contents to us children. A spoil sport adult—usually my mother—would follow Maggie around, retrieve the bills, and slip them back into her purse.

Maggie and I shared the same birthday in August, and when I was a child, we occasionally celebrated together over fully-loaded ice cream sundaes at Friendly's. She never learned to drive, so it was always a treat when she arrived by cab to pick me up in Agawam so we could share our passion for anything with a cherry on top.

She had never married or borne children, and, as a result, acted as though all of her grandnieces and nephews were her responsibility. For most of her adult life, Maggie had worked as a salesclerk at Morse & Haynes, a shoe store in downtown Springfield, and felt it was her duty to see that we were all well shod. Each of us made annual pilgrimages to the store where she fitted us with a pair of good shoes; there were fifteen of us—nine girls and six boys—and I imagine that the only way she could afford the expense was the result of a generous employee discount.

We usually ended up with Buster Brown-type oxfords with solid orthotics, but sometimes Maggie chose something more fashionable. A few times, she allowed me to pick out my own. My favorites were a pair of black patent leather Mary Janes she bought me for Easter when I was six years old. I still remember the pure joy I felt when I walked on our driveway with the hard, shiny bottoms of the shoes tapping away. Sometimes, I imagine myself in a pink dress with crinolines and those new shoes and escape briefly into my childhood where my priorities were simple.

Sadly, I could not remember the last time I had seen Maggie, and I wondered how she had fared. Once I left for UCLA at eighteen, we exchanged an occasional note and Christmas cards, but our connection had grown tenuous. She had been relegated to the stuff of childhood lore—the quirky great aunt who now operated at the margins of my life, threatened with extinction.

ALTHOUGH MANY OF the familiar landmarks in Hungry Hill had disappeared, I still felt the tug of recognition. I consulted my internal GPS, found Cleveland Street, and hung a left with Cormac tailing. The cube's front grille followed me like a bulldog wearing shades.

The houses all looked similar, but I had no trouble picking out Maggie's old brownstone. I pulled into the cracked and scarred driveway, shifted the Beemer into park, and grabbed a moment for myself.

Maggie's house had fallen into disrepair. Peeling paint curled on windowsills, and the ancient asphalt shingles on the roof were faded. The lawn had not fared well. Patches of thinning grass barely covered the dirt. Although a modest house in a blue-collar neighborhood, Maggie had always kept it well maintained. I hadn't expected such a drastic change, and my apprehension about seeing Maggie in a similar state kept me from getting out of the car.

I glanced in my rearview mirror, and the expression on my nephew's face suggested that he also questioned my decision to come to Springfield. After a minute, though, he got out of the cube and walked up to my window. I hit the button and it whispered down.

"Hey, Cor," I said, pulling down my shades and eyeing him coolly.

"Nice *bass*, Aunt *Grace!*" he replied loudly, using his right index finger to give me a casual salute. His determined silliness under the circumstances made me smile. I turned down the volume on the car's stereo while I racked my brain for a response.

Cormac was a second-year English major at Northeastern in Boston—the first fledgling to leave Emily's nest. Somehow, during the course of packing, lunch, and travel, we had started to play a game that had gotten ridiculous, piling on adverbs to modify our adjectives. Once we had grown bored with that tremendously, hopelessly tedious game, we had switched to rhyming. Our conversations had turned very competitive. I was a few points ahead, but Cormac was closing in on me.

Before I could respond, he returned to the cube and released the dogs, and they immediately began yard patrol. Ellen took a dignified tour of the small patch of lawn bisected by a cracked concrete walkway. With a quick lift of his leg, Stogie focused his attention on several leggy azaleas near the house, telegraphing a simple message: *mine.*

I opened the door of the Beemer and slipped out, avoiding a large fissure in the asphalt driveway. With the dogs in tow, I climbed the steps of screened front porch that ran the width of the house. I didn't find a doorbell, so I knocked on the porch door. I waited before knocking again. Ellen and Stogie sat politely behind me, mouths open, tongues lolling. Cormac remained on the sidewalk, wanting to make certain we were at the right place. Maggie hadn't bothered to remind me of the street number, but I trusted my memory even if he didn't.

It soon appeared more polite knocking wasn't going to get me anywhere, so I tried the door and found it unlocked. Ellen and Stogie followed me inside the porch. Floorboards creaked with our weight, and a few cluster flies bounced around in a lazy attempt at escape. I found a doorbell on the interior door and pushed. I knocked as well in case the bell wasn't working.

Just as I was about to ring the doorbell again, I heard a voice yell out, "*Jesus, Mary and Joseph!* You don't have to take the door down—hold your goddamn horses!"

I glanced about. The voice seemed to come from outside. I looked at Cormac, and he pointed straight up. I left the dogs in the porch and stepped back from the house, my eyes following the direction of Cormac's finger. Maggie was on the upper floor, leaning out of a window.

"Maggie, what the heck are you doing!" I called as craned my neck and shielded my eyes from the bright sun. Maggie's face was in shadow, but I could tell she was smiling. I didn't know what I had expected, exactly, but I was relieved she appeared happy to see me. I realized I was happy to see her, as well, regardless of the circumstances.

"What the hell does it look like I'm doing—having an audience with the Pope?" Maggie shook a rag and a bottle of Windex at me and smiled broadly. Her gray hair was tied in a bright orange scarf, and her pale, flabby arms poked from the sleeves of a thin blue dress sprinkled with faded flowers. She wore a man's suit vest over the dress; I assumed her objective was to protect the old dress while she worked. My great aunt made an amusing picture, especially given her fashion choices.

"Aren't you a little old to be hanging out of second floor windows?" I called out, happy to find Maggie her usual feisty self.

"I'll give you old, young lady!" she hollered back, giving me a little wave. "Come on in Gracie, the door's open. And grab the bag of rags from the kitchen counter on your way up." She paused and added, "Cormac, what the hell's with the shoes?"

Cormac looked down at his red high-top sneakers with their neon green laces and shrugged.

I reentered the porch. The door to the inside was unlocked but stuck. Stogie stood on his short hind legs and offered assistance, leaving more of his signature graffiti. After several hip checks, it finally opened.

"Aunt Grace, I'm going to start unloading the cars," Cormac called as Stogie, Ellen, and I headed into the house. Both vehicles were loaded to the gills.

"Just put everything in the front hallway," I instructed as I headed inside, relieved that our verbal sparring had ceased.

I stood in the hallway. I hadn't been there since the eighties, and I had forgotten how small and dark it was. Other than that, the house was exactly as I remembered, right down to the ticking clock in the hallway and the faint smell of mothballs. Lace curtains fluttered in the windows, and a plum-colored runner edged in faded pink roses stretched down the hall.

A memory surfaced: darkened rooms, flatware clinking on china, gentle laughter wafting down the hall from the kitchen. I was sixteen, standing in the hallway, thrilled with the purple maxi dress I was wearing, a gift from my crazy great aunt. She had insisted I try it on, show it off, and I was both proud and embarrassed at the in-your-face style of the dress.

The memory receded, and once again I was standing in the hall in my expensive dark wash jeans and crisp white Derek Lam shirt.

I knew Maggie had been born in an upstairs bedroom. She had grown up in the house, living with her parents until they were gone, staying on afterward. Eighty-six years on Cleveland Street. I, on the other hand, had moved seven times since I'd turned twenty. I redecorated every time I moved; only a few key pieces of furniture survived each new home. Artwork changed and my aesthetic evolved. My taste in decorating was decades and dollar signs ahead of my elderly great aunt.

It would be a challenge living here. I appreciated the house's history—it was family, too—but I craved space and light. I had spent most of my adult life spoiled by beautiful homes filled with beautiful things—exquisitely furnished, comfortable, and well-maintained sanctuaries. And now I feared I would regret my commitment to come and stay with Maggie. But it was too late to change my mind. Cormac was already filling the porch with my belongings, and Maggie was upstairs waiting for me.

I PUT MY leather tote on a small table in the hallway and headed to the kitchen to get the rags. My fearless wolfhound joined me, doing a thorough security check as we passed the living room on the right, and a closet and half bath on the left.

The kitchen was in the back of the house; when I entered it, my trainers screeched on yellowing linoleum. The room was filled with the smell of canned vegetable soup, and faded wallpaper bore the outlines of objects and pictures rearranged over the years, a ghostly nod to the room's history. The refrigerator—a model from the fifties or sixties—hummed noisily.

As I looked about for Maggie's rags, Ellen walked up to a counter and surveyed a row of items hidden under crocheted covers. I looked at the mystery items, shrugged, and said, "You got me..."

Just as I reached for the rags on the kitchen counter, I heard a high-pitched yelp. It was immediately followed by "What the hell! What are you!—get your dirty little!—*GRACE!*"

I grabbed the rags and sprinted back down the hallway to the stairs. The treads were painted dark brown and covered with a tattered rubber runner pieced together with black adhesive tape. I vaulted up the steps, following the sound of Maggie's voice.

I found her in the front bedroom. She was perched at the top of a short stepladder, Stogie on the bed next to her, his teeth locked on the opposite end of her cleaning rag. They were in a fierce tug-o-war, and it looked as though Stogie had the advantage. Folds in the bedspread bunched around his paws, providing traction.

"Get this goddamn mutt...!" Maggie sputtered as she clung to her end of the rag. "I didn't know what the hell it was, shook my rag at it, and it grabbed on! Won't let go! I suppose it's *yours?*"

"Ahh—yes, *he's* mine, and I guess I forgot to mention him. So sorry—hope it's not a problem."

"What's its name?" Maggie gave the rag a tug.

"Stogie." Stogie rolled his eyes in my direction at the sound of his name.

"Like the cigar?"

Stogie looked back and forth between us and braced himself again for battle.

"Well, just look at him."

Stogie continued to use his fat little brown body as leverage against the rag.

"Must have some rat-dog in him, the way he likes to pull," Maggie said. "We used to have a dog when I was a kid. Killed rats, buried them in the backyard."

I looked at Stogie and tried to imagine him in a different, more useful era.

"Any more surprises?" Maggie asked.

"Well . . ." I felt a slight tic forming in the left side of my face. If Stogie was a problem, I couldn't imagine her reaction to Ellen.

"What the hell does that mean?" Maggie finally relinquished the rag and started down the ladder. "Take the damn thing," she said to Stogie. "When you're done playing, you can finish cleaning the windows."

Before Maggie had a chance to turn and face me, Ellen entered the room quietly and sat, blocking the sunlight that streamed through a window. Maggie's gaze shifted from Stogie to the wall as Ellen's shadow enveloped it and climbed to the ceiling, bending at the shoulders. I held my breath as Maggie followed the apparition, hoping she would return her attention to her little sparring partner, but her eyes widened and she pointed and hollered, "Oh, my God—*what the hell is that!?*"

IT TOOK MY great aunt a few long seconds to recover from the invasion of her home, but once she had, she shifted gears, crossed the room, gave Ellen a wide berth, and offered me a big hug. She was a tall woman, her body all hard angles covered with soft patches of flesh; I held her tightly for a few seconds before releasing her. She took my hand and searched my face, smiling tentatively. I smiled back. Maybe living with Maggie was going to be hard, but at the moment it felt good to be here for her. I took a quick inventory and noted how much she had aged since I had seen her last. Her clothes hung on her, and her hair was a thin, white cloud hovering above a lined face and pale blue eyes.

"I know. I'm old," she said. "Long ride?"

"Not bad," I replied, smiling at her candor. "Just under two hours. Cormac's unloading stuff. I had to bring two cars because of the dogs."

"I'd think you'd need a moving van just for that one," she said, motioning to Ellen. "Jesus Christ—she's enormous."

While Cormac unloaded my clothes and boxes, Maggie and I finished the windows in the other bedrooms. I offered to clean them later once I had settled in, but she obviously didn't trust me to handle the task unsupervised. I quickly learned that there was no use in arguing with her.

Cormac walked the dogs as we worked, drove out for a burger at a nearby McDonalds, and waited for his girlfriend Natalie to pick him up. She was a junior at UConn, forty-five minutes away, and Cormac was looking forward to spending the weekend with her in her small apartment near the campus. I had only met her once, but Natalie seemed to be a good match for my favorite nephew: smart, energetic, and personable. Cormac adored her, and I could see the attraction beyond her blond good looks and enviable young body.

Natalie arrived mid-afternoon, and Cormac said his good-byes. "See you later, alligator," he called from the driveway and gave me a wide smile.

"Now that's just lame!" I called back. "I'm not even sure it counts."

"Don't be a sore loser," he said, and added, "Have fun," before he climbed into Natalie's car.

An hour later the upstairs windows sparkled, and Maggie announced it was time for cocktails. I checked my Cartier watch, thought it a bit early at only four o'clock, but what did I know? My once-clean shirt and jeans wore a layer of dirt and grime. My chestnut-colored hair was a mess, falling out of a hastily tied ponytail.

Maggie and I made our way down the stairs and into the kitchen, where she disappeared into a pantry tucked in a corner. She reappeared with a bottle of bourbon—Jameson—a cheap Irish brand that she had always favored and pulled two glasses from a cabinet over the sink. After setting them on the counter, she went to the ancient refrigerator and pulled out a liter-sized bottle of seltzer and an old aluminum ice tray. Its lever was frozen solid. "Christ!" she muttered, and banged it several times against the counter. Finally, the cubes popped out, and she grabbed at them as they scattered.

She carefully poured two fingers of bourbon into each glass and topped them off with seltzer. "Here, Gracie girl, join me in a little celebration," she said, and handed me one. I eyed the concoction and thought longingly of my wine cellar in Greenwich.

We carried our glasses into the parlor through a two-way door on squeaky hinges, and sat in a pair of overstuffed vintage chairs. They were covered in green fabric worn shiny with age, old crocheted doilies on each arm. When I sat, my chair made a sharp popping noise. I looked at Maggie with alarm, but she seemed to not have noticed. The dogs had followed us, and Ellen sprawled on the threadbare rug while Stogie explored the room.

Maggie offered a toast. "So—here's to being roomies."

"To being roomies." I raised my glass to our little collaboration. It was hardly a cause for celebration, but it was nice to be together again after so many years. I sipped carefully.

"Sorry again that I couldn't make it to the funeral, Grace."

"It's okay—really."

"I should have been there." Maggie looked at me, her expression pained.

"You were sick," I reminded her. "Just out of the hospital. I'm sorry I didn't visit you." I didn't want to talk about Michael's funeral.

"It was just a little chest cold," she said.

"Yeah, like it was just a little funeral."

WE SAT QUIETLY while the late afternoon turned to evening.

Ellen continued her nap on the floor, exhausted from watching us clean. Stogie cruised the parlor and adjacent living room, stopping to admire a bowl of petrified Christmas ribbon candy.

"You pathetic mutts," Maggie finally said, breaking the silence. "You haven't had a thing to eat since you got here. I'm sure I have something for you in the kitchen."

"I can feed them later, they're fine," I said.

"Nonsense." She struggled out of her chair and went back into the kitchen. Stogie padded behind her, the swinging door barely missing his backside. I heard the sound of running water, humming, cabinet doors banging. Munching. Noisy lapping. I didn't want to know what she was feeding the boy, not that it mattered much to him.

"Go ahead, El, it's all right," I said to Ellen, since she was obviously interested in the kitchen clatter. She hauled herself upright and pushed her way through the door.

"Jesus, Mary and Joseph, you're a big girl!" I heard Maggie exclaim. "We big-boned gals need to stick together, eh? Let's see if I have a leg of lamb in here somewhere. Or a side of beef."

After a few more noisy minutes in the kitchen, Maggie returned to the living room, sat down, and sighed heavily. "Housework takes it out of me these days. I usually have everything done as soon as the last snow is gone. Here it is almost June." She looked at me a moment before turning away to stare out a window.

"We'll get it all done," I assured her. Maggie nodded, took a sip of her drink, and absently fingered the doily on the arm of her chair.

"Damn!" she suddenly exclaimed, interrupting the quiet. "I forgot to have Cormac help you move a dresser from the basement to your bedroom! It's too heavy for you to move by yourself, and I can't be much help." She was noticeably upset. "There's nowhere to put your clothes."

"Not a problem, Maggie. I can just live out of my suitcases until I get someone to help me. I don't mind. Really."

"Nonsense." I could see her mentally working on the problem. "There's a nice young man, lives next door—Quinn—he'll help."

"Quinn?"

"Cullen's his first name, but everyone calls him Quinn. I told him you were coming."

I didn't need a dresser right that minute, but, again, Maggie was accustomed to having the final word. I considered freshening up but figured it would be a waste of time since I would only gather more dirt and grime helping Everyone-Calls-Him-Quinn bring the dresser up from the basement.

MAGGIE SENT ME next door to a brownstone that was almost identical to hers. I stepped inside the porch and rang the doorbell.

A young man with damp tousled hair answered after the first ring. Towel draped around his neck. Gym shorts below. He was standing a few inches above me and was tall and athletic-looking. My line of vision hit well below his face, so I had to look up at him. The dark, heavy-framed glasses he wore didn't detract from intelligent blue eyes that looked back at me. He appeared to be in his late twenties. Probably young enough to be my son, but cute enough to make me wish I had cleaned up before coming over. As all of this ran through my mind, a whisper of guilt hissed through my brain and I attempted to push it aside.

Neither of us spoke for an awkward moment, and then I braced myself and said, "Hi, I'm Gracie Cavanaugh. I'm looking for Quinn."

He looked down at me and smiled. "You must be Maggie's niece."

"Actually, I'm her great-niece. Or grandniece. Never could figure out which was right—maybe both." I tried to stop talking but rambled on nervously. "I would have come by sooner, but I decided to wait until I could get myself all gussied up. You know—first impressions and all?"

He just looked at me.

"That was meant to be a joke. It's not my best material, but I'm having to think on my feet, so to speak." I took a deep breath, shrugged and pushed a stray strand of hair from my eyes, trying to regain my composure. I hated being so unsettled.

"Oh. Sorry—don't mean to be rude, come on in," he finally said. "Quinn's in the basement playing pool with friends."

I hesitated. "I don't want to impose. If he's busy, I can come back later." I was often uncomfortable in social situations in recent months, but hated being rude to this young, attractive, polite stranger. So, I decided not to turn and run. Also, call it wishful thinking, but upon closer inspection, I was not convinced that I was old enough to be his mother after all. I chided myself for going there and blamed it on Maggie's bourbon.

"You're not imposing. I'll get him." He held the door for me with one hand and pushed his glasses up on his nose with the other. I moved in, touching his chest briefly with my shoulder. He smelled of soap and a woodsy aftershave.

"Have a seat in the living room. I'll be right back." He turned and padded down the hall in his bare feet.

I couldn't help it—my eyes slid to his backside. *Very nice*, I thought.

He disappeared around a corner. A door opened, and I heard the muffled sound of his steps going down to the basement. Music drifted up—the Beatles singing the tale of Eleanor Rigby to the baroque beat of a cello.

The house was a duplicate of Maggie's inside, just reversed. I stood in the living room, quickly readjusting my shirt, finger-combing my hair, and wishing it hadn't been months since my last cut. I checked my breath in my cupped hand. It smelled faintly of bourbon. Great. The preferred aperitif of old ladies.

After a minute or two my new neighbor reappeared. "Gracie, he says go right on down. The stairs are just around the corner in the kitchen." He motioned for me to follow him, and when we walked into the kitchen he pointed to an open door.

"I'm not interrupting?"

"No, but he has ten bucks riding on this game, wants to finish it."

"Thanks for your help—um—I never did get your name."

"Matt. Matt Quinn," he replied. "Cullen's—Quinn's—brother."

"Nice to meet you, Matt." I tried not to breathe on him.

I went to the top of the stairs leading to the basement and looked down. The area was dark, the only light coming from below. I started down, following the sound of cracking pool balls, and had almost made it to the bottom when I slipped off

the edge of a step and ended up taking the last four on my der-
rière. My elbow slammed against the wall, sending a shockwave
of pain through my funny bone. It yowled back at me and was in
the midst of a full-blown temper tantrum when I scraped my left
Achilles tendon—losing a couple of layers of skin in the process—
as I tried to right myself. I loudly mouthed a four-letter word.

On the plus side, it was over within seconds, but I was left
half sprawled on the floor, staring up at three strange men, their
mouths gaping. I closed my eyes and wished the moment away,
but I was still on the floor when I opened them. The men were
still motionless and slack-jawed. Their pity and my embarrass-
ment hung silently in the air. Without a word, I pulled myself to
my feet and did an about-face, hobbling up the stairs.

Matt stood at the top in the doorway.

"What the hell happened!" he exclaimed as I limped into the
kitchen, pulled out a chair, and sat down delicately. I looked at
him and suppressed the urge to add to the one-sided dialogue I'd
initiated with the stairs moments ago. Instead, I rubbed my elbow
and stayed silent. I winced as Matt gently pulled up my sleeve.
"Damn—that looks like it hurts," he said.

"You *think?*" I inhaled sharply and took a mental inventory of
my pain. My mind and body agreed that my tumble had left no
area unscathed. Everything hurt.

Matt hurried to the refrigerator, grabbed a handful of ice
from the freezer, stuffed it in his towel, and pressed it gently to
my elbow. I raised my leg and examined it.

"Wow, that looks bad," he said. "You're lucky you didn't break
something."

I gave a huge sigh. I had never understood why people felt
obliged to use that phrase. Had I really been lucky, I would have

made it down the stairs on two feet instead of bounding down like a human soccer ball, utterly humiliated.

"Yes, that's me," I said. "Luck just follows me everywhere I go." I groaned as I straightened my leg, and then froze when I heard several pairs of footsteps climbing the basement stairs. I thought about fleeing the scene, but I couldn't have limped away fast enough.

The three men filed into the kitchen. One of them, a lanky redhead with freckles tattooed across his pale face was the first to speak. "Dang, lady—are you all right?" he asked. "That was pretty spectacular."

A pleasant-looking guy with a shaved head and tight black T-shirt stood next to him. "From the sound of her language, she's no lady," he said and grinned.

"Truck driver, possibly," the third man said. "The dialect sounds familiar. I think I work with some members of your tribe." He was well over six feet tall, slightly beefy, with a head full of dark curly hair. "We've had a 'friendly' chat with the stairs. I don't think they'll be bothering you again."

I noted his big smile, lots of white teeth, and nice green eyes. He resembled Matt.

"You must be Quinn," I said, finding it hard not to smile back. "I'm Gracie—Maggie's great-niece."

"I heard you were coming," he said. "Didn't think it would involve so much drama. Should I call for an ambulance?"

"No need," I replied. "Maggie has something for the pain."

THE REST OF the evening was an improvement over what we all referred to as "The Incident."

Matt and Quinn followed me back to Maggie's and moved the dresser from the basement to my bedroom, and then hauled my luggage upstairs while I watched. I tried to help with my belongings, but they preferred having me in a supervisory role—or maybe they just weren't ready to see me navigate stairs again. I felt a little guilty allowing two total strangers handle a task I could've managed on my own, but they were so sweet about it I had to be gracious. Besides, there was nothing to complain about regarding the view from the bottom of the stairs.

Once the brothers completed their chores, they shared a drink with Maggie, and when it got late, Maggie insisted on making us dinner even though we all protested. We dined on overcooked meatloaf and mashed potatoes, with a side of pale canned carrots. Maggie just picked at her meal and filled the dogs' bowl with the remainder. Stogie devoured the meatloaf and begged for more, turning his nose up at the conventional dog food I pushed on him as an alternative.

We sat around the kitchen table, with Maggie and the men trading stories about the neighborhood. Matt and Quinn had grown up in the house next door and had many fond memories. A lot had changed in the past few years, though. They, and most of their childhood friends, had moved on to new jobs and cities to find opportunities elsewhere.

Five months earlier, Quinn had moved back to Springfield from Los Angeles, shortly after their parents had died within a few months of each other. He was working as a mechanical engineer at a nearby manufacturing facility that specialized in fabricating machinery for industrial use. Matt had just moved back as well, taking a summer break from MIT where he was working on a doctorate in applied mathematics.

They weren't ready to part with the house, and clearly missed their parents. Maggie missed them as well. "You would have liked Eleanor," she told me. "She was a peach. Never needed a fence for her to be a good neighbor. She kept the boys in line, kept her house neat as a pin. Real hard worker. Casey was a hard worker, too. Set a good example for these boys. He was so handy. Used to fix things for me all the time."

Quinn was twelve years older than Matt and it was obvious that he enjoyed the role of big brother. Matt's arrival had come as a surprise to their parents who'd given up on having more children. The two men had not actually grown up together, but they had obviously forged a strong bond in spite of their age difference.

Quinn spent the evening teasing Matt about everything from his hair to his taste in women. He had his fun with me, too, referring to me as "Grace" at every opportunity, using my name as a double entendre.

Whenever the conversation was directed at me, I kept my story simple, explaining that I was just moving out of an apartment in Greenwich when Maggie had called and invited me to Springfield. I talked a bit about my career as an architect when we were all discussing education and jobs, but I created a very minimalist version of my life for the two men. I had become skilled at maneuvering around certain subjects. I never talked about Michael. I couldn't anticipate where my emotions would take me, and it was simply too risky.

Besides, I assumed that Maggie had filled them in about my late husband, because she never mentioned him while we were talking. She went along with the neatly edited version I gave of my life, never bringing him up, and I, in turn, pretended that my trip to Springfield was nothing more than a friendly visit. Quinn and Matt politely avoided asking any pointed questions; the four of us simply talked around the obvious: Maggie needed me here for a reason, and I had left more behind in Greenwich than an apartment.

Before long, Maggie excused herself and told us she was going to bed. "Can I help you upstairs?" I asked. I didn't want to offend her, but she looked exhausted.

"Good Lord! Do I look like I need help? I've gotten myself to bed for over eighty years, I think I can manage one more night." She heaved from her chair, navigated the hall, and made her way up the stairs, with Stogie in tow. She lectured him, her voice fading as she reached the second floor. "Now listen here you little mutt—don't think you're spending the night with me. I sleep alone, thank you. Damn, you're a pest!"

Once we heard her door close, Quinn turned to me. "How's Maggie doing, anyway?" he asked. "We've been worried about her. She won't tell us exactly what's going on, but we know something is wrong. I didn't want to bring it up in front of her, but I have to know."

I took a deep breath.

"Maggie has metastatic breast cancer. She found out two months ago when she went to her doctor complaining of abdominal pain. He ordered an MRI. They found spots on her liver and pancreas. It's not good."

The men were silent.

"I figured it was serious," Quinn said finally, sighing. "It's not Maggie's nature to look to anyone for help, and that's the only reason I can imagine she would have you move in with her. Damn."

"I'm sure it was hard for Maggie to ask," I said. "I think one of her parish priests pressured her into making the call. She said he was being a real pain in the ass."

Quinn smiled briefly and said, "That has to be Father Brian—and yes, he can be relentless. He straightened me out a time or two when I was younger. He's pretty old, sort of retired, but he still works at the parish."

"Still, it was a lot to ask of you," said Matt.

"My mom leaned on me when she found out about Maggie's illness," I said. "She and Maggie are close, but my parents are spending several months traveling in Europe. They've been planning it for years, and Maggie threatened to pull the mother of all fits if they cut their trip short because of her."

I felt that they were both waiting for more—wanting to know about Michael—but I wasn't ready to share.

"Is there anything they can do for her?" Matt asked. "I mean, can't she have surgery or something? Chemo?"

I wished I had some good news to offer them, but I didn't. "Her doctor says it's far too advanced. All they can do is help manage her pain, which will probably get pretty bad over time."

"Sonofabitch," Quinn said sadly, shaking his head. "That is no way to go. Our mom had cancer, and it was awful. All of it."

"I hate to ask this," Matt said, "but how long do they give her?"

"They don't know. She could last as long as six months, but it's not likely given her age. Her heart isn't great, so they're concerned that will become a factor before long."

"So, you're here for the duration?"

"As long as she's well enough to stay at home. More than anything, she's afraid of being alone and cared for by strangers. I'm going to try to do what I can to make it easier for her."

"Maggie is lucky to have you," Quinn said. "There aren't many people who would drop everything and move in to care for a sick relative."

"Yeah, well, I didn't have much keeping me in Greenwich. All I had to do was pack up the dogs, some clothes, and a few pair of shoes." I chose my words carefully, ready to change the subject if necessary.

"A few? Try several dozen. Remember, I just hauled your stuff upstairs. I know *you* don't travel light." Quinn pointed an accusing finger at me and smiled.

Before he could say anything else, I got up from the table and picked up my plate, but he stopped me. "You've had a long day. Matt and I will get this."

Quinn and Matt began clearing the dirty dishes from the table, but I insisted on taking care of the rest. Despite being tired, I knew I wouldn't rest until I gave Maggie's kitchen a good scrubbing. I walked them to the door, said goodnight, and went to work.

When the kitchen was as clean as I could get it, I took Ellen out for a quick spin in the front yard, minus Stogie, who had disappeared with Maggie.

Finally, I went upstairs to my new bedroom. Ellen followed me and sprawled on an ugly rag rug near the bed. I looked at the rug and tried to figure out what color it was, but given its age and the grime, it was impossible to tell.

I grabbed my toiletry kit from my overnight bag and headed to the bathroom to clean up. There was a tub, but no shower, and I was too tired for a bath. I filled the sink with water and washed my hands and face, drying them on a threadbare towel. I brushed my teeth over the sink, ignoring the green stains trailing down the sides of the basin. Tomorrow was another day.

2

expresso

I AWOKE AT eight the next morning to a quiet house.

I pulled a short silk robe from my overnight bag and headed to the bathroom. My body ached and dark purple bruises had taken up residence on my elbow and right buttock. I poked at the bruises gingerly, trying to gauge the extent of the damage. My elbow still buzzed, and my injured behind was tender to the touch. Back in my room, when I tried pulling on jeans it hurt, so I dug out a pair of sweatpants.

As I went down the stairs, I heard the patter of Stogie's feet in the hallway heading toward me. His nails made a clacking sound that came and went with the scatter rugs and runner.

"You little traitor! Slept with Maggie instead of me, huh?" I accused him as he bounded up the stairs and met me halfway, joining me in my descent.

I headed toward the kitchen and called out for Maggie. She didn't answer, but I heard a scratching noise through the screen door in the back of the kitchen and went to investigate. I found her digging in a flowerbed that ran along the side of the garage; Ellen was nearby keeping a sober eye on things as she lay on a patch of grass lit with gold from the sun.

"Maggie, good morning!" I called. "Looks like a pretty day!"

"Well, well, look who's up—it's Sleeping Beauty." Maggie struggled to her feet and wiped dirt from her gloved hands. She wore an old apron over a yellow housecoat, her hair tucked beneath a man's plaid rain hat. "Sun's been up for hours!" She stabbed a gloved finger at the sky.

"Maybe for some of us," I replied, yawning. "Nice outfit."

"The dogs don't mind my outfit. At least I got up, got dressed, and let them out this morning at a reasonable hour."

"They're accustomed to sleeping in with me. It's fine with them."

"That's not what they told me," she quipped.

"The little bastards are talking about me behind my back again." I patted Stogie fondly on his traitorous little head.

"Now that you're finally up, do you drink coffee or tea in the morning?" she asked, tucking a stray hair under her hat.

"Coffee."

"I only have tea, so I guess you're out of luck."

"No problem. I don't go anywhere without my espresso maker. It's in a box in the front hall." I shielded my eyes from the bright morning sun.

"*Expresso*—well excuse all of us!" Maggie waved a trowel in Ellen's direction, looking for an ally.

"It *makes* espresso, but I only use it to make coffee," I informed her as I surveyed her little garden. It was a chaotic collection of irises, day lilies, and hostas—looking very much like a sort of wartime orphanage, everyone huddled together just happy to be alive, trying to make sense of their circumstances. I took a moment to mentally rearrange it.

"So why don't you have a *coffee* maker?" she asked.

"You never know when you'll want espresso," I replied.

Stogie was following the conversation and didn't seem to have a problem with the logic, but Maggie was still working on it.

"So, do you ever drink expresso?"

"Not really, but if I wanted it, I could make it—and it's a very cool-looking machine."

Ellen refused to get involved and was more engrossed with a bug that was slowly crawling up the side of her face. Her big, brown eyes followed it as it moved along her nose.

Maggie squinted at me from under the brim of the plaid rain hat. "I don't get it." She waved the trowel in her hand from side to side, right elbow resting in her left hand, trying to work it out. "I just don't get it."

"So, what are you doing out here working away at the crack of dawn," I said, changing the subject. "You should be inside taking it easy, sipping tea, watching Jeopardy or something." I knew as soon as the words left my mouth, Maggie would take exception.

"Good grief! It's a pretty day outside and my irises need tending. Besides, the dawn cracked hours ago, and Jeopardy isn't on until seven tonight."

"Maggie, if something needs to be done, I can do it. I don't want you doing more than you should." I yawned.

"Nonsense! I'm more than able to do the usual around here— I'll let you know when that changes. Go make yourself some coffee in that expresso maker of yours and let me get back to my flowers." Maggie waved a gloved hand at me and turned back to her gardening.

I WENT BACK into the house, began plowing through my boxes in the front hall, and struck pay dirt on the fourth box. I pulled out my state-of-the-art espresso machine with the affection archeologists reserve for special artifacts, and went upstairs to dig out a bag of pre-ground coffee beans from my overnight bag. Stogie followed me and observed me from the comfort of the rag rug. When it was obvious that I was happy with my findings, he clawed vigorously into the rug while lying on his side to help me celebrate.

We headed back downstairs with our loot, and I cleared a spot on the kitchen counter. The espresso machine looked startlingly out of place, like a small alien spaceship mistakenly diverted to the planet of *The Honeymooners*. I filled its carafe with cold water, hoping the flavor of the chlorine-doused city water would not ruin the taste of my coffee, and added extra ground beans to the usual beans-to-water ratio in an attempt to compensate.

Finally, I pressed "Start" and pulled out a vinyl and chrome chair from its matching table and sat. Stogie rode shotgun, and I scratched his head while the wonderful sound and smell of brewing coffee filled the kitchen.

Two cups later, I felt like a new woman. I was ready to rumble.

I went upstairs and bathed in the old stained porcelain-tub-minus-a-showerhead and decided to hire a plumber to install one after I hit my head on the faucet several times rinsing shampoo from my hair. I made a mental list of what the bathroom needed, which included a toothbrush-style scrubbing and fresh paint. Once I had a showerhead installed, I would need a shower curtain, too. And matching window treatment. And maybe one of those little fabric skirts for the sink so I could put all my girl stuff in a basket underneath. And new towels, since I didn't bring any with me. Nice fluffy ones. And maybe new tile on the floor—the old tile was scary.

After my bath, I dried my hair and made my face up, and went back in the bedroom where I put on clean shorts and a T-shirt. I stripped the old linens off the bed, dug through more boxes, and found my king-sized Frette sheets. The mattress was a double, so I had to improvise with my fitted sheet by tucking it under on one side. The top sheet hung to the floor, so I crammed it under the mattress.

Once I had the fresh sheets on, everything else looked even more pathetic. I attempted to style the bed by folding my pretty linens back over the old wool blanket and bedspread. I fluffed the flat, thin pillow. Twice. I patted it carefully into place to avoid deflating it and stepped back to appraise my efforts. The old chenille bedspread was a grayed-out shade of white with fluffy pastel flowers all over it, and no amount of styling was going to help. I looked around the room, sighed, and made more mental notes involving bedspreads and throw rugs and curtains and paint. I verbalized some of the more interesting points so Stogie could visualize the dramatic changes that would take place—yes!—in this very room.

He just looked at me and yawned.

"You are so jaded," I said.

When we returned downstairs, Stogie signaled his desire for a walk by planting himself by the front door. I tried to bribe him into the kitchen by pretending to pull a fake treat out of a pocket in my shorts, but it was an old trick and he didn't fall for it.

"Aw, c'mon, you've already been out with Maggie. Do we really need to do this?" He wouldn't budge. In Greenwich, the morning walk was a ritual set in stone. Michael and I lived in a large house in town on a small lot, so we didn't have much yard for the dogs. To give them adequate exercise, we took daily walks to a park at the end of our street. Stogie loved the social aspects of a stroll and appeared unwilling to alter his routine.

I informed Maggie that we'd be gone for a few minutes and called Ellen to join us. After grabbing their leashes from where I had put them on the newel post, we saddled up and rode off. Stogie decided on the direction, and we followed.

His little scrub brush body plowed down the street past the Quinn's, brown eyes peeking out from unruly bangs. He stopped frequently to divine secret information from shrubs and walls, his nose bent on discovery and decoding. Figuring out the lay of the land, I suspected. It seemed the data was endless. I assumed it was stuff like how many dogs lived on the street, and pertinent male/female indicators, their usual routes, relevant territories, and so forth. Occasionally Stogie would add to the data. (*Hi—new dog now residing on the street: male, single, neutered, fond of long walks and table scraps, enjoys a good belly rub.*)

We continued on, passing one brownstone after another, all bearing a strong resemblance, the only variation being the degree of care or neglect. Most appeared as though they still housed their original occupants; like Maggie, they had reached an age where they had trouble keeping up. A few had fresh paint on front doors and trim, and flowers peeking from window boxes. I assumed these houses had made their way into younger hands.

The dogs and I reached the end of the street. We turned left onto the main road, Elm Street—the name now a misnomer—and walked to the next side street running perpendicular to Cleveland. This one, named Jefferson, implied that Cleveland Street was named after the president, not the city. As we made our way down Jefferson, I saw an elderly couple raking debris from the previous fall from their front yard. The grass beneath the leaves was anemic from lack of sunlight; shrubs concealing the foundation of the house were overgrown and leggy like those in front of Maggie's.

The couple saw Stogie and Ellen and joined us on the sidewalk. They eagerly rubbed the dogs' heads and complimented their manners.

"What's this big girl's name?" the woman asked.

"Ellen."

"Must be hard to keep her in kibbles."

I nodded in agreement. If she only knew.

"And what a nice little doggie you are," the man said to Stogie.

"Yes, a nice little doggie," his wife added. Stogie sat like a gentleman; tail wagging, brown eyes gleaming through his fringe of bangs.

"What kind of doggie are you?" the man asked.

"I don't know, exactly," I said on Stogie's behalf. "Little bit of terrier, little bit of something short and fat. Some kind of hunting dog, likes to chase things," I added when Stogie appeared offended.

"Haven't seen you before," the man said. "Do you live around here?"

"I just moved in on Cleveland Street. I'm keeping my great aunt company."

"Well, welcome to the neighborhood," the woman said. "Nice to have another young person around."

"Yes, especially a pretty young lady," the man added.

"Oh, now Herbert, you're such a flirt," the woman chided, delivering a gentle elbow to her husband's middle.

Maybe living among the elderly wouldn't be so bad. I could develop a reputation for being a hot young chick. Have Herbert and all of his geriatric buddies drooling over me during the weekly group viewing of Ed Sullivan reruns or something. "Hey, Milt, did ya see the little outfit that Cavanaugh babe had on last week?" Stuff like that.

Back at Maggie's, the dogs headed down the hall to the kitchen and the water bowl that she had put out for them. I brought a bag of dog food from the front hall and made them breakfast. After throwing out the spent coffee grinds, I washed out the espresso decanter, and spent a few minutes scrubbing the kitchen countertop. A good dose of elbow grease removed a number of stains from the big porcelain sink. I hoped Maggie wouldn't catch me working on her kitchen.

I was hungry from the walk and checked out the old refrigerator for something edible. It didn't look promising. I found canned peaches in a bowl, a small container of milk, eggs, and gray-looking canned vegetables in a clear plastic tub. At the very back, a stack of margarine containers suggested more leftovers. Two soft-looking grapefruit and an apple shared space in a lower drawer. It was clear some serious shopping was in order.

I figured a couple of eggs wouldn't kill me, and found bread in the pantry, so breakfast ended up being a strange fried-egg-and-toast sandwich. Lots of salt, a little ketchup. Not exactly the breakfast of champions, but it wasn't bad.

Maggie came through the back door as I was finishing up the last bite. She removed her gloves and sat down.

"I hate being old," she said wearily. "It's a pain in the ass. I was starting to lose steam even before I got sick, but now I just get so damn tired." She removed the plaid rain hat from her head and adjusted her flattened perm with thick fingers.

I just nodded, hesitant to pick up the thread of conversation with comments of my own. I knew what it felt like to be so exhausted by life that you just wanted to crawl into bed and call it a day. I admired Maggie for simply getting up in the morning. That alone was an accomplishment.

"I'm supposed to visit the doctor this week—Friday—you know," she continued. "Don't expect you'd want to come?"

From the way she asked the question, I couldn't tell if she was simply asking me to give her a ride or wanting to know how involved I wanted to be. I wasn't certain what I had signed up for. Maggie was stubbornly independent, and I didn't want to assume anything. Maybe she wanted me along, maybe she didn't.

"I could drive you," I said, trying to feel her out. "Get reacquainted with the area with you as my navigator."

"That'd be easier, you know, than taking the bus or a taxi. You don't have to come into the doctor's office with me if you don't want to, but I wouldn't want you hanging around bored or anything." Maggie carefully folded her hat and placed it in her lap.

I sensed that Maggie was looking for more than a ride, but I didn't want her making herself more vulnerable than necessary. "Maybe I should stay with you and avoid confusion about where and when to meet," I said. Maggie didn't have a cell phone, so it was a convenient excuse for me to meet her doctor.

"Yes—it's a big place, that hospital. Wouldn't want to lose track of each other." Maggie finished arranging her thin, gray curls. Her fair Celtic complexion was a pale background for slightly ruddy cheeks.

I met her eyes briefly and smiled. "It's settled then. Maybe

Stogie and Ellen would like to come along. It's cool enough this week to leave them in the car with the windows down."

I picked up my plate and walked to the sink. It would be fun living without a dishwasher. Maybe kitchen remodeling was in my future, if I could talk Maggie into it. My architect's mind was already working on major changes for the house—I couldn't help myself. It was completely impractical, though, given her situation.

"Oh, yes, the mutts might want to join us." Maggie directed the comment to Stogie, and he came over to her, pushing his face into her extended hand. "What a wet little nose you have there, you little beggar," she said as she scratched behind his ears. "Don't suppose you'd like a little something to hold you over until lunch?"

I DECIDED TO do my shopping early in the day so I could make a nice dinner. I considered inviting my handsome neighbors over for a bit of atmosphere and put the idea on the back burner for a little slow cooking.

There was a small grocery store within walking distance, but I had a long list in my head, so I fired up the Beemer and drove the fifty yards.

The store was tidy but small. A half-dozen neat rows of boxed and canned goods filled its center, and on one wall there was a small refrigerated area with diary and meat products. In the back there was a produce section with a limited selection of vegetables. I spent a few minutes filling up my cart with food for dinner and then added a few essentials to get me through the week.

As I hadn't thought to inventory Maggie's pantry before heading out, I searched the little store for basic supplies. I doubted she was into extra virgin olive oil, sea salt, and other items I considered necessary. There wasn't much to select from, but I made do. As I was checking out, the storeowner recommended a few bottles of wine, which would hold me over until I could find a decent wine shop.

An older Hispanic man helped me load the bags in my car. I tipped him with a five-dollar bill, and he looked at it for a moment before tucking it in his shirt pocket. He nodded politely and went back into the store.

Matt was cleaning his car—a late-model Subaru—in his driveway when I drove up with the groceries. He helped me unload them and carry them into the kitchen. He was rather fetching in torn jeans and a vintage Aerosmith T-shirt. I decided having the guys over would be worth the effort of cooking a bigger meal.

"So, Matt, if you and The Big Guy don't have any plans this evening for dinner, you could join Maggie and me," I said. "I'm cooking." I was having difficulty deciding on the seating arrangement: maybe me in the middle of all of that testosterone, and Maggie with a TV tray in the other room.

"That would be great," he said, "and your timing is perfect since it's my turn to cook tonight. I don't exactly excel in that area."

I just nodded, but figured any guy who looked that good in jeans probably didn't need to know a spatula from a whisk. We settled on a time, and I took note of his backside as he left.

MY CULINARY FORTE has always been speed-dialing a good restaurant, although I'm not completely useless in the kitchen. I just lack experience. I don't cook often, although I've taken quite a few culinary courses. Not out of any real passion for cooking—they were all gifts from Michael, who had his own agenda. Since I chose a simple menu, I would do fine.

I focused on the chicken and side dishes and started preparing them carefully. The salad and veggies would be easy—I never screwed them up. I didn't bring a vegetable steamer with me, though. Maggie just barked a laugh when I asked where hers was, so I had to carefully cook the green beans in an old unlined aluminum pot that was part of a set Maggie had inherited from her mother. I imagined the brain damage we would all suffer as a result, but since Maggie's mind was still intact after all these decades, I supposed the damage would be minimal.

The roasted chicken looked delicious when I checked on its progress and the creamy whipped potatoes had me salivating. In spite of a few difficulties finding utensils and serving dishes, I managed to throw together a perfectly edible dinner. Maggie offered her assistance, but she looked tired, so I fixed her a drink and settled her in the parlor. She didn't resist my help, which concerned me. She seemed to have less energy than the day before, and I wondered if she had slept at all the previous night. I felt guilty when I realized that preparing the house for my arrival had probably cost her dearly.

I had told Matt and Quinn to come over early since I figured Maggie wouldn't last long. When they arrived, we went into the parlor for a cocktail. The men joined Maggie in her bourbon fix, and I had a glass of a New Zealand sauvignon blanc recommended by the corner grocer.

Quinn told us about his day at the plant, amusing us with the antics of his co-workers who sounded like children in need of a daily dose of Ritalin. He looked great in a clean pair of jeans and a freshly starched shirt in a pretty shade of pale blue. I couldn't take my eyes off the dark triangle of chest hair peeking out from where he left the shirt unbuttoned. I was a sucker for contrast and had to try very hard to pay attention to everything he said. Talk about needing a dose of Ritalin.

Matt had made an effort to look good, too, and had actually changed his T-shirt to a clean one with a different band logo. Some alternative rock band named Mean Creek I had never heard of. Quinn had fun with Matt's hair, which was long and slightly messy on top, and shorter on the sides and back. It was definitely more Boston than Springfield. Matt was quick to point out to his older brother that at least he still had all of his. Quinn feigned great offense as he ran his fingers through his thick, short curls and gently patted a small crescent of exposed skin on the crown of his head. His laugh was contagious, so he had all of us in a cheery mood, even Maggie, as we went into the kitchen for dinner.

The good-natured teasing and storytelling continued around the table after we finished eating. Quinn harassed Matt, wondering where he had gone wrong in providing a role model for his younger brother. "Who knew my knuckle-headed little bro would turn out to be such a geek?"

"You're just jealous because I'm going to be the next Steve Jobs," Matt shot back. "Besides, you bowed to my geekness when I helped you solve that sorting problem at your plant with my nifty little differential equation."

"You just played into my hand, bro. Right here in front of witnesses: *Geek*."

Quinn then made a minor concession to his younger brother's superior intellect but argued that he was better looking. He tried to draw me into the argument, but I thought they were both adorable and refused to take sides.

I enjoyed the evening, but kept thinking Michael would have enjoyed it, too, and probably joined in on the gentle teasing. I imagined he would have given me an earful later, as well, about my wandering eyes when we were finally alone in bed. I was certain he had always known, though, as soon as he ran his hands over my body, everything and everyone else faded away.

After the men had gone home, and Maggie was in bed and the lights were out, my body ached for him.

I DREAMED ABOUT my grandparents' farm that night. It must have been the fresh vegetables I had for dinner that propelled me back decades to their farm in Connecticut. Nana and Pop were my father's parents, and every summer I spent a week with them as a special treat—no sisters or cousins.

At night, if I had trouble sleeping alone, I would gaze out the second story window of the old farmhouse. A small mountain fell away from the farm in a gentle curve, and the side that remained invisible to me inspired my fantasies. It was where the wolves howled, gold was discovered, and cliffs disappeared into pale fog shadows.

I knew, of course, a big hay meadow stretched out from the base of the little shale-covered mountain on an adjacent farm, but my child's mind created a place for adventure and mystery. Even as an adult, I often dream of that space—it offers so many possibilities.

That night, it sent me on a voyage across a raging ocean, on a galleon full of stolen loot. I hung out on the quarterdeck, casually observing a large schooner that was attacking us. When it was obvious the schooner was about to sink my ship, I conveniently woke up.

"Hey, El—want to hear about my weird farm dream?" I asked Ellen, who was snoring on the rag rug beside my bed. She raised her head, tried to look like she cared, but I knew her heart wasn't in it.

"I'd listen to *your* dreams if you bothered to tell me about them."

She rolled her eyes at me, pitched her massive frame upright, and lurched gracelessly to a standing position. She then stretched out her front legs, pulled her haunches back and up into the air, and yawned.

"Nice down dog," I said.

She came over to the bed and planted a heavy paw on my stomach. I exhaled, grabbed her leg, and held it as she licked my face.

It was early, substantially so for me, but I rolled out of bed anyway. The house was quiet, and Maggie's gentle snoring worked its way down the hall. I crept downstairs and used the little powder room. Next on my agenda was a pot of coffee. I went to the kitchen and my espresso machine and picked up its carafe by the handle. We had a scintillating conversation as I made little talking-back motions with it by popping the lid up and down with my thumb.

"So, how's it going?" (Me.)

"Not bad. I can barely see your lips moving." (The carafe.)

"Pretty cool, huh?" (Me.)

"Don't quit your day job." (Carafe, mocking me.)

I went to the old sink to fill the carafe with the cold, chlorinated water and noticed a small pink plastic tub on the edge of the sink. Maggie's dentures were having a little bath, white teeth sticking out of bright pink gums. Ellen had followed me into the kitchen and ventured over to have a look.

"Don't ask—" I said.

3

goin' for a ride

THURSDAY ARRIVED, AND it was a beautiful morning. Even Cleveland Street looked good. The trees along the sidewalk sported fresh green buds ready to burst into leaves. Hedges and lawns were filling out with new growth. A walk with the dogs was a pleasure in the sun-dappled morning.

I hadn't finished unpacking, but I wasn't in the mood to tackle the job on such a fine day. If I spent another minute in the old house, I would have to start tearing it apart. The gypsy spirit struck me, as it often did, and I decided that Maggie and I could use a little diversion before her doctor's appointment the next day. I love to explore new places and visit old, sentimental ones, so a long car drive is always a good form of therapy for me.

Maggie woke up late, bleary-eyed, and moving slowly. When she finally made her way down to the kitchen, I asked her how she slept, and she mumbled an "Ehh..." while making a so-so gesture with her hand. I wasn't surprised she offered resistance when I suggested we pack a lunch and go for a drive.

"Come on, Maggie, it's a beautiful day, and the road is a-calling," I implored.

Maggie's response was a tired grumble. "Tell the road it's got the wrong number. I don't plan on moving from this house today." I wasn't willing to take no for an answer, so I got a little rough with her. "You're going to really disappoint someone," I said, crossing my arms and looking at Stogie sitting by her side. "Will you be upset if we don't go-for-a-ride, Stog?" I asked. He immediately stood and raced for the front door, nails clacking and ears flying.

Maggie continued to sit in her chair in the kitchen, muttering about my not playing fair while Stogie waited at the door. Ellen made her way gracefully down the hall to join him. Frowning, Maggie finally stood up and went to the pantry. She emerged with an old brown picnic basket and placed it on the kitchen table.

An hour later, Maggie sat in the passenger's seat of the cube, gray curls wrapped in a pink chiffon scarf, purse in her ample lap. I had talked her into wearing an old pair of green polyester pants her sister had given her years ago, but she was having a hard time getting used to them. My outfit consisted of cotton cargo shorts, a white T-shirt, and a Yankees baseball cap, and I wore red Havaiana flip-flops that shared the floor with Maggie's sensible brown oxfords. Maggie didn't understand my choice of footwear, but I explained to her that flip-flops were "in," that all the celebrities in L.A. wore them, even out to dinner. The fashion comment earned a muttered "Christ" from Maggie as she turned her head to look out the window.

I had put the rear seat of the cube down to provide a large cargo area for the two dogs, and Stogie bounced from side-to-side around Ellen, who ignored him. She shared his passion for travel but didn't wear it on her sleeve. Stogie's black nose made translucent smudges in the huge wraparound rear window as we drove through the neighborhood to the main drag. Cleveland Street was less than half-a-mile away from a connector to the highway—the faint drone of traffic was audible from Maggie's front yard.

Once we reached the highway, I started singing like I always do when I'm on the road. This time it was the traveling song, *Goin' for a Ride*, composed especially for Stogie:

> *"Goin' for a ride,*
> *Yeah, we're goin' for a r-i-d-e,*
> *Yes, we're goin' for a ride,*
> *We'll be goin' for a r-i-d-e,*
> *They'll all be goin' for a ride,*
> *Yes, they're goin' for a r-i-d-e,*
> *Yeah, we're goin' for a r-i-d-e..."*

Maggie stopped me as I headed into the second verse, which involved more riding, and asked me to sing something else.

"Good God, if you have to sing, at least make it interesting. *Goin' for a Ride*. Silliest goddamn thing I've ever heard," she said.

"It's a song for Stogie," I informed her.

"So?"

"He only understands so many words. Knows what goin' for a ride means. It allows him to get into the spirit of the song."

"Christ." Maggie rolled her eyes.

Stogie watched us both intently from the back, obviously waiting for the second verse. He waited briefly, and then went back to a window.

"Now look what you've done." I flicked the cube's blinker and switched lanes, speeding up.

"I didn't do anything." Maggie looked back at Stogie.

"He's lost interest. It's your fault," I said.

"Then sing another song. One with *words.*"

"*Goin' has* words."

"More words. Different words."

"Fine. How about *The Nose Song?*" It takes a degree of talent to compose something offensive on the fly, but I figured I was up to the task.

"If it's more than just 'nose, nose, nose,'" Maggie replied.

"Of course it is."

"All right, then."

"*Oh yeah, it's dark in there, and there's a lot of hair...*"

"*JEE-SUS*, Mary and Joseph!" Maggie cried.

"*Oh yeah, it's dark in there, and there's boogers everywhere...*"

"Pull this goddamn car over, I can't stand it!" Maggie put her hand on the cube's passenger door handle, testing it.

"*Oh yeah, it's dark in there, and I don't mean to stare...*"

WE HEADED NORTH from Springfield with no particular destination in mind. It was a perfect, perfect spring day, and just driving through it was magical after the harsh New England winter. Friends of mine in L.A. often asked me why Michael and I settled back in New England after living on the West Coast where every day was beautiful, and it was hard to describe to them just how wonderful days could feel when they were this rare and precious. It was as if your life was beginning all over again, clean and new.

Died and gone to heaven, baby. When we lived in L.A., there were days when I prayed for rain, dark clouds—anything to relieve the monotony of perfect weather.

After heading out to the vast woodlands north of the Mass Pike, we eventually came within striking distance of the Quabbin Reservoir and decided it would make a perfect destination. We arrived at noon; sunlight bounced and glimmered on the silvery water. Although I hadn't spent any time there since childhood, little had changed.

My parents often took my younger sisters and me to the reservoir for picnics on warm summer days, and we used to imagine all of the little villages with their houses that existed before the area was flooded in the 1930s. Emily, Laura, and I would pretend we could see little cottages sitting like ghosts just under the surface of the deeper coves. We loved to imagine there were bodies under there, too, wide-eyed and rotting.

Maggie and I found a meadow overlooking a broad section of deep blue water, and we set up camp in the dappled shade of a large copper beech. I laid out an old Hudson Bay blanket I kept in the cube, and we ate a peaceful lunch while Ellen and Stogie took turns sprawling in the grass and begging for scraps of our sandwiches. Maggie and I didn't talk much. She napped in a patch of sunlight while I read; her gentle snoring blended with the small lapping sounds of the waves moving to the reservoir's shore. We spent the entire day like that, just enjoying the sunshine, fresh air, and each other's undemanding company.

The sun finally worked its way west and away from sight, leaving gray woods and a soft glow on the water's surface. I packed up our belongings, but had a hard time dragging Maggie away from the peace and quiet of the darkening water. When we started the drive back from the reservoir, our headlights picked out details from the shadows. White-tailed deer appeared and disappeared like spirits at the edge of the road as we rounded curves. We finally made it back to Cleveland Street where streetlights illuminated Maggie's driveway. I let the dogs out, and they circled the front yard checking the perimeter for cats and nocturnal squirrels. Maggie was sleeping soundly, so I took great care in waking her and helping her out of the cube. She was all arms and legs, and I wasn't big enough to provide any real leverage for her—even with Maggie's recent weight loss, she still had at least forty pounds on me. I ended up putting a foot on the cube's running board to steady myself, while Maggie held on as if her life depended on it.

"Thank God I'm wearing these damn pants, or my dress would be up around my neck!" Maggie struggled to keep a grip on me. "And they're so slippery!"

"You never know when polyester will come in handy." I pulled Maggie into a standing position, and we shared an embarrassed laugh. We linked arms, and I helped her up the sidewalk to the front steps. Ellen and Stogie stood in the yard watching our progress with neutral expressions, but I knew they would talk about us later.

Once in the house, we went straight to the parlor for drinks. I fed the dogs while Maggie sipped her bourbon, and I joined her for a few minutes before making dinner. I had enjoyed the day and tried not to think while boiling pasta and making a salad. Thinking just got me into trouble; got me missing my old life. I didn't want to ruin the pleasure of our little outing.

My strategy was to pretend that the excursion had been nothing more than a pleasant day with an elderly aunt. Maggie was fine, and my old life was waiting for me back in Greenwich. All I had to do to was put the pups in the car and drive home. Michael would be there waiting for us, and I would tell him all about our little adventure.

I NEVER ATTENDED grief counseling or joined a support group after Michael died. I figured they would just tell me I was breaking all the rules and kick me out of the club. I never knew what all the rules were, but several well-intended friends told me Rule Number One was to not make any major changes in my life or do anything impulsive for a full year.

I knew they meant well, but everything was *already* changed, leaving my world in shambles. Nothing remained the same. Even my toothbrush sitting next to Michael's on the bathroom vanity became something else. If your toothbrush betrays you, isn't it time to move on?

I put our house on the market exactly one month after I put Michael in the ground, and I slept with his best friend Rick two months later. Michael would have been fine with both moves—he was that kind of guy. In twenty-two years of marriage he never once said, "Gracie, don't." I never got anything but free passes from him.

Being alone in our house in Greenwich with Michael's stuff everywhere was unbearable, so I rented an apartment on Greenwich Avenue and grieved in a strange, small, and unloved space. When I was feeling particularly bent, I would torture myself and the dogs by going to the house and weeping on the sofa in Michael's study. Vertigo would lie on the floor as close to me as possible, put his beautiful face next to mine, and make great sighing sounds. He was Michael's dog, but he loved me, too.

I'm sure Rick figured I slept with him because he was a warm body attached to a familiar face. I suppose he also thought I pretended he was Michael for the night—they were so much alike—but I couldn't even bear trying. I simply needed to be warm and naked against a man. The only pretending I did was to imagine I was eighteen again, and I hadn't yet met Michael. My whole life was still ahead of me, waiting like a winter moon in the western sky.

THE NEXT MORNING, we all piled into the cube again, but the mood was more reflective as we drove to Baystate Medical Center for Maggie's appointment. It was the first day of June, but the sky wore a gauzy layer of clouds, and the air had a bite to it. Yesterday had been beautiful, but today it was hard to believe that summer was just around the corner. Typical New England weather.

I spared Maggie more road trip songs, although I caught her glimpsing my way now and then, as though bracing herself. When she caught me watching her, we both smiled briefly. I opened my mouth a couple of times and inhaled as though I was about to start singing, and then laughed at her expression.

"No, Maggie, I'm not going to favor you with one of my little tunes." I glanced at her again and smiled.

"I sure as hell hope not! I'm a sick woman, and I don't need the stress. I'm sure Dr. Kevorkian is going to insist on taking my blood pressure, and I don't want him checking me into the hospital today because it looks like I'm about to blow a gasket."

"We can't have that, now, can we?"

"Certainly not. I'll be checking in soon enough without your helping me along."

I wanted to keep the mood light but couldn't think of a clever response. I didn't want to talk about illness and death. I couldn't reassure her; tell her everything was going to be all right. It wasn't—it was going to be awful. I felt heart sick, and told myself, not for the first time, that I had made a terrible mistake by agreeing to go through this with Maggie. I didn't have any emotional reserves; they had been all used up. I had nothing to offer her. Every day I kept it together by getting through that one day, by staying in the moment, by pretending that Michael wasn't gone.

"Are we having fun yet?" I asked, uncomfortable with the silence that told me we were both lost in our own thoughts.

"Not really, Grace," Maggie said and sighed.

"We'll get through today, then there's always bourbon and seltzer tonight." I tried to sound optimistic.

"Well, that's something to cling to," Maggie said.

"DR. KEVORKIAN" TURNED out to be a handsome man in his late forties who had a charming and gentle manner. He met us in the hallway on the second floor of a professional wing lined with physicians' private offices. He asked a young male nurse to get us coffee and tea after we sat down on a sofa in his office.

The space was comfortable and personal, and I was impressed. Large windows overlooked a terrace, and potted plants shared space on his desk and credenza with pictures of his children and wife. He had two girls who favored their mother; she was slender and blond with intelligent blue eyes. I was glad he had a nice family waiting for him at the end of the day given his line of work.

"So, Mrs. Cavanaugh, it's nice to meet you after talking with you on the phone." Dr. Cunningham directed the comment to me, but his eyes were on Maggie. "I'm glad you came today."

"It's nice to put a face with the name. Please call me Grace."

"Grace it is. Maggie, how are you feeling?" He watched Maggie closely, and I saw concern in his expression. "Looks like you've lost a bit more weight. Is Grace feeding you properly, or is she as bad a cook as I am?"

"Well, if she wasn't sitting right here, I might be a bit more candid—I'm not big on biting the hand that feeds me." Maggie cracked a smile, so I knew she was just teasing, but I still felt like a kid in the principal's office.

I launched an articulate defense of my cooking. "Umm, hey..."

"Don't worry, Gracie," Maggie said. "You're a perfectly good cook." She turned her head slightly towards Dr. Cunningham and rolled her eyes.

"I saw that," I said. "Behave—both of you. I know people who know people who know other people. A *lot* of other people," I added.

Dr. Cunningham smiled. "Sounds like you two are made for each other. Maggie, let's send you down the hall for blood work." He opened her file and quickly scanned it. "I want to see how things are going." He picked up his phone and called the nurse, who came in immediately.

"Sam, please take Miss Reilly to the lab, then settle her in the lobby," he said, and turned to Maggie. "I'll have Grace meet you down there. Be nice to the nurses this time."

Maggie struggled from the sofa, and she and Sam headed out

the door. I heard a "good grief" from Maggie over something Sam must have said.

"She's a pistol, that one." Dr. Cunningham smiled briefly as he watched them disappear.

"More like a bazooka, if you ask me. She's lost a lot of weight?" I worried that I wasn't watching her closely enough.

"They'll weigh her when they take blood, but I'm guessing she's down eight or ten pounds from three weeks ago. She's a big woman but losing weight that rapidly is never a good sign."

"She just picks at her meals."

He picked up his pen, twirled it between his fingers, and gently tapped it on her file, as if the information it contained confirmed his opinion. "Her digestive tract is at risk from the cancer, and her poor appetite is not a good sign."

"What should I do?"

"I'll get you a supply of a liquid dietary supplement that she should be able to drink without any discomfort. Make sure she drinks at least sixteen ounces a day. Try to get her to drink a few glasses of water every day, too. She'll feel better if she stays properly hydrated." He flicked a bit of lint from his dark trousers as he crossed his legs.

"How about her level of activity? I may be pushing her too hard to get out of the house, but I'm afraid she'll become depressed if she stays inside all of time." I worried that I wouldn't get things right. I might be doing too much of one thing—or too little of another.

"Taking her for a drive or outing won't do her any harm. It might do some good. Just understand that there may be days that she just doesn't feel like doing anything. Try not to take it personally. Her energy level will definitely decline, probably pretty quickly." He made a small adjustment to his tie and added, "You might want to rent a wheelchair."

I thought about asking more questions, but I wasn't sure I wanted any answers. I decided, at least for the time being, to maintain my present strategy in dealing with Maggie's problems: take it one day at a time, stay in the moment, and pretend that everything was all right.

"I'll give you a refill on her codeine. Please try to monitor how much she's taking," Dr. Cunningham said. "She'll probably need stronger medication soon, but I'd like to keep her on this as long as possible since there are fewer negative side effects." He picked up a manila folder, opened it, and wrote briefly. "Maggie doesn't like to complain, so keep an eye on her. Be sure to touch base with me to let me know how she's doing. I'll call if I find anything new from her blood work."

My experience with doctors was limited, but I found that they were not big on expansive dialogue. If you didn't press for information, you didn't have to deal with unwanted answers. Dr. Cunningham didn't do anything to dispel any possible misconceptions. He made a few more notes, looked up and smiled, nodded, and thanked me for stopping in with Maggie.

She wasn't in the lobby when I stepped off the elevator, so I decided to check on the pups. We went for a quick walk, exploring the limited landscaping in the parking lot.

When I returned to the hospital lobby, I found Maggie waiting. She was having a conversation with another elderly woman, probably exchanging war stories about the blood lab. They had pulled up the sleeves of their dresses and were comparing puncture wounds and bruised flesh. It looked like Maggie had a slight advantage. She looked old and fragile sitting there with her big purse and her paper-thin skin.

"Hey, Maggie, are you ready to roll?" I asked gently as I approached. "The dogs are waiting for us."

"Gracie girl, I was about to give up on you," she said as I helped her out of her chair. "Dr. Kevorkian is kind of cute, eh?"

"Not bad," I admitted.

"He's a looker, all right," she confided to her new friend. "Looks like a young Paul Newman."

"Someone could have mentioned it," I said. "I would have spent a little more time on the visuals."

"You *could* use a haircut," she replied.

4

ground zero

MICHAEL AND I met my second year at UCLA at the School of the Arts and Architecture. He taught a class in photography, and I was his student.

My parents had given me a Nikon camera for my birthday just before the start of the school year, and I was determined to master the alchemy of a dark room. I wanted to photograph the architecture of L.A.—mid-century modern, Craftsman bungalow, Spanish revival—the city was eye candy to me. As a budding architect, I wanted to take it all in and document it in black and white.

Michael was a graduate student in art, and he taught photography classes to help pay his tuition. He was a big guy—tall and muscular—but carried himself with the grace of an athlete. He had a disarming smile, amused green eyes, and a gentle sense of humor. I was immediately attracted to him and teased him relentlessly during the first few classes until he learned to arrive "armed and mildly dangerous" as he liked to put it. He learned to put me in my place with his quick wit and even quicker intellect.

We discovered that we were both from the East Coast, and Michael invited me out for a cup of coffee in late September so we could compare notes. I missed my family, and he missed his. It was nice to share our misery. When Michael learned of my interest in architecture, he offered to drive me to the Pacific Palisades to photograph Case Study homes by Charles and Ray Eames and Eero Saarinen. We went the following week, and I took several rolls of film while Michael supervised. I was anxious to see the results of my work, so we drove back to the dark room on campus and he developed my film and showed me how to make my first prints. I fell in love with photography and Michael, and never looked back.

By the end of the semester, we were inseparable. We were both supposed to return home for the summer, but we decided to stay in sunny California. We moved into a small apartment in the Hollywood hills, and started planning our life together.

Shortly after we graduated, we moved from our apartment to a small house in Venice near the beach. A year later, we married in Santa Barbara, where our immediate families joined us. Emily and Laura were my bridesmaids and looked so beautiful I cried. It was the first time our parents met, but it was as if they had known each other forever. They laughed and danced together the entire afternoon, and by the end of the evening the Cavanaughs had decided to join my parents on their next cruise.

Michael and I slipped away from the party and made out in the garden behind the beautiful old house where we had our reception and promised to be together forever. I can think of many other perfect moments in my life, but they were all before Michael died, and none of them as sweet to me as that day.

Not long after our wedding, science became a stronger pull for Michael than art, so he went back to UCLA to get combined master's degrees in computer science and business. He'd always had an ability to clearly visualize things the rest of us couldn't begin to imagine, and he began a series of successful companies almost as soon as he graduated, just shy of thirty.

We moved from our little house in Venice to a much bigger place in the Palisades after Michael sold his first software venture. I pursued a career in architecture by designing condominiums in Manhattan Beach and Hermosa, and Michael put his creative energy into building his second company. We talked about starting a family, but never got around to it. Our friends joked that it was the only way Michael and I ever attempted to manage our carbon footprint, but the reality was we didn't need much but each other.

We might have stayed in California forever if it wasn't for the perfect weather, and I wonder if things would have worked out differently if we had.

IT WAS MID-JUNE and my third week with Maggie when I realized I'd had my fill of Springfield. I needed a break. A day trip to Greenwich would do a girl a world of good. Goodbye, Sears. Hello, Saks Fifth Avenue and Richards.

I don't know why, but I didn't think it through, didn't consider how hard it might be to go back so soon. A part of me pretended I had never had a life there—the part that excelled at being in denial—and I was just going to visit.

I would have left Maggie behind, but she was acting out of sorts that morning and I knew I would feel guilty leaving her. Taking her with me would limit what I could do, but I thought she needed a break, too. From her life, if not Springfield.

"Maggie, I don't suppose you've ever been to Greenwich, have you?" I broached the subject while I washed breakfast dishes. The only relatives who had visited me there were my sisters with their families, my parents, and the occasional first cousin. I briefly amused myself by imagining Maggie traveling to Greenwich to check out shoe store competition on the Avenue. Morse & Haynes never carried Manolo Blanik, Chanel or Gucci. They would have all been foreign names to Maggie.

She glanced up. "No, why do you ask?"

"We could drive there for lunch—it's pretty once you get to the parkway."

"What—are you going to pull the *goin'* thing on me again?" Maggie eyed me suspiciously.

"No, it's too hot to leave the dogs in the car. I'll ask Matt to keep an eye on them."

"Good plan," Maggie said. "In that case, *I'll* stay home with the dogs and that good-looking boy, and *you* can high-tail it to Greenwich."

"Come on, Mags—it'll be fun."

"*Mags?* You have one hell of a nerve getting overly familiar with me like that," she replied, wagging a finger at me and trying to hide her amusement. She talked tough, but I knew better.

"Hey, I've seen you in your old lady underwear."

"You have not!"

"Stogie pushed the door open at a critical moment this morning," I informed her.

"Jesus, Mary and Joseph—that dog is a pain in the ass!" Maggie rolled her eyes heavenward and crossed herself.

"You don't look half bad for a woman of your advanced years, but you could use some new old lady underwear."

"Mind your own damn business. Next thing I know, you'll try to talk me into underwear that disappear between my cheeks. And I don't mean these cheeks." She gently slapped her face with both hands, looked at me and gave me wane smile.

"Have you been reading my *In Style* magazines again, Mags?" I asked.

"Quit with the 'Mags,' damn it!"

"If you go to Greenwich with me, I'll refer to you as 'Madame' all day, and I'll buy you a nice lunch at a French restaurant." I smiled at her sweetly.

Maggie was silent for a moment, and finally said, "If you insist."

"I do." I was surprised she had given in so easily.

"All right, then, but I'm not wearing those damn polyester pants."

"No problemo." I picked up our plates and carried them to the kitchen sink.

"And we're not shopping for underwear."

"No problemo." I turned on the water and started scrubbing.

"And you're going to stop with the Spanish thing since I'm making the rules, and there will be absolutely *no* singing."

"You're no fun." I flicked bubbles and water in her direction.

"And you're a regular barrel of monkeys." Maggie ducked too late.

"Hey—I know a great monkey song, you sure you don't want to hear it?"

"Don't even try that one on me," Maggie said. "I'm sure the song involves things monkeys do that I don't even want to know about."

The two-hour drive to Greenwich was uneventful with the exception of heavy traffic on the Merritt Parkway as we went through Fairfield. Thanks to Matt, who had kindly agreed to look after the dogs, we were able to take the Beemer. Even though my request for a sitter had been short notice, I'm fairly certain Matt applauded my efforts to get Maggie out of the house. Maggie commented on how comfortable the Beemer was versus the cube.

"You *should* be comfortable for eighty thousand dollars," I told her.

"Jesus, Mary and Joseph!" she exclaimed. "I didn't know you could spend that much money on a car!"

"You can spend a lot more."

"Or buy a small island and name it after yourself," she muttered.

We took the North Street exit off the Merritt and drove down through the mansions, McMansions, and stately old homes that lined the road. Maggie was quiet as we drove along the endless stonewalls, hedges and manicured landscapes.

"Reminds me of Cleveland Street," she finally said.

I didn't respond, but when I looked over at her, she hooted a laugh. "If I'm going to spend the day here, maybe I *do* need some new underwear," she said.

"They'll never know, and I won't tell them." I gave Maggie a conspiratorial smile.

We neared the end of North Street, where the houses were closer together and mostly antique, and turned onto Putnam Avenue at the old Second Congregational Church. We had missed the incredible display of purple and yellow crocuses that made an annual spring appearance across the street from the church. Someone had already mowed the patch of greenery where they grew, and the grass was taking over again.

I slowly cruised down Greenwich Avenue, identifying favorite haunts for Maggie. She commented on the painfully slow crawl of traffic, and the aggressive competition for the rare parking space. Halfway down the Avenue we finally found a place to park across the street from Saks Fifth Avenue, in front of the only Catholic church anywhere near the heart of Greenwich. Maggie crossed herself when she got out of the car, and stood staring at the church for a moment. I was really hoping she wasn't going to try to catch a service or confess to a bad underwear day.

It was a short walk to an intersection, where we had to wait for a neatly dressed police officer to order pedestrians to "Walk!" while locals glared at the uninitiated who tried to step off the curb without an invitation. Maggie was immediately in love with the military precision and rules and regulations put upon pedestrians and motorists. "Now we are talking!" she said as we walked—invited—across the avenue with a group of impeccably dressed matrons and tattooed teenagers with designer T-shirts and backpacks.

Halfway up the block again, on the other side of the street, we entered Saks and walked around the clothing department on the main level. Maggie looked at the occasional price tag and muttered to herself. A few times, she audibly gasped. I downplayed my excitement when I found a Prada skirt I really liked, and refused to let Maggie see its tag for fear of a "Jesus, Mary, and Joseph!" meltdown in the couture department.

"Where're the shoes?" Maggie finally asked, after we had wandered around for a few minutes.

"Lower level. Want to see them?"

"Since when do shoes belong in the basement?"

"Since they needed a lot of room," I explained.

I headed to the staircase at the back of the store, and Maggie followed. We went down to the shoe department, and I had to put up with a lot of clucking as Maggie randomly picked up shoes and checked prices. She probably hadn't purchased a new pair in twenty years, and I was sure even then they weren't exactly Louboutins. Even I could get a touch of sticker shock at Saks, so Maggie was fun to watch.

Half-an-hour later—yes, I tried a few on—we headed back upstairs. I decided against any purchases since I knew there would be no end to the comments involving six-hundred-dollar shoes. I was sure, way back when, those patent leather Mary Janes were only seven or eight dollars at the most.

I could have shopped in denial all day, but Maggie had her fill and was tiring fast. We finally headed back to the car and continued down the Avenue. We passed the building where I had camped out with the dogs and my grief, and I glanced up at the window overlooking the flow of traffic. I saw the face of a little girl peering out, smiling. I imagined the apartment a happier place now that I was gone.

We stopped at Le Courte Èchelle for lunch; the maître d' kissed me on both cheeks. He told me how beautiful I looked, said that he had missed me, and asked me how Monsieur Cavanaugh was doing. He obviously didn't know my husband had died rather unexpectedly from a tricky little brain aneurysm, and that Madame was living in an alternate reality where that hadn't happened. I had a deer-in-the-headlights moment, and finally mumbled that I would give Michael his regards. He moved on to Maggie, fawned over her a bit after being introduced, and then led us to a booth in the rear where Michael and I always sat. I didn't mention this to Maggie, but I knew she saw me hesitate before sitting. She quietly went over the menu, occasionally looking up and meeting my eyes.

The last time Michael and I had been at the restaurant it

had been Valentine's Day. We had met our good friends, Allison and Will, for dinner. I remembered the evening like it was yesterday, even though it had been almost fifteen months. Michael and I enjoyed our friends' company, because—like us—they were still in love. We didn't need to be alone, even on that special day, because we always had each other.

Michael had held my hand between courses and laughed at my jokes, and I could almost feel the warmth of his fingers running over mine as I sat at the table with Maggie. He had engaged in his wonderful habit of tracing my wrist so it felt like I was wearing a bracelet made of air. We had taken turns pushing my hair behind my ear, and when Michael did it, he would run his thumb down the curve of my chin before removing his hand.

It was later that night, after the wine and the candlelight, that I lost him.

I closed my eyes, shook my head, and wondered what the hell I was doing in Greenwich. I certainly wasn't ready to acknowledge Michael's absence and engage in some form of reminiscing with my great aunt. I still struggled to say Michael's name out loud. I guess a small part of me must have wished that given some time and distance, I could submerge my toes in familiar water and not find it unbearably cold. Instead, though, I found myself in an icy abyss where it was hard to breathe.

Maggie obviously picked up on my discomfort because she was on her best behavior and even offered to pick up the check. She opened her big purse and pulled out her wallet, but I put a firm hand on hers and tried to smile.

"Remember, you're here on my invitation," I said.

"Perhaps, but I'm not sure you enjoyed the lunch," Maggie replied. "Maybe you shouldn't have to pay for it."

"At least the company was good."

"So, you noticed," she said. "Wasn't easy."

HAVING BARELY SURVIVED lunch, I decided to tear off the bandage and rip open my wound on the way out of town. Why bother making good decisions now? I drove a few minutes north and turned into the circular gravel driveway at the house on Lake Avenue. The house I had shared with Michael.

The Realtor's sign was still in front. It had been there for over a year, and I regularly turned down offers from people who had never even seen the interior of the stately white Greek Revival antique, since I wouldn't let anyone inside. The gardens were as lovely as ever, still tended to by Gabriel, my handyman-cum-gardener. Gabriel called me monthly, identifying himself as "Chauncey"—our little Peter Sellers joke. He gave me updates on how well the boxwood behaved while he trimmed them, how gorgeous the tulips looked when they were in full bloom, and always politely inquired about how I was doing in his charming Venezuelan accent. I knew he missed me, and I always felt badly when he called because I never answered.

We sat in the driveway, and I stared at the house. I asked Maggie if she wanted to go inside; I held my breath. She looked at me and smiled when our eyes met.

"I do need to use the facilities," she said, but when she saw the look on my face she added, "Or, maybe not. I can wait. We don't need to go inside if you don't want to."

"Are you sure, Madame?" I asked and slowly exhaled.

"I'm sure," she replied, patting my hand.

I wasn't ready to leave, so we sat briefly while I longingly took in my house—a place of so much love and sadness. I desperately wanted to go in, lie down on the sofa in Michael's study, and absorb what might be left of him. The need to be surrounded by his belongings overwhelmed me, and the desire to feel connected to him swept through me trailing pain in its wake.

"So, Madame, if we could take a pass on this today, you'd be cool with it?" I finally asked. "I know this was a long drive for shoe shopping and lunch, but maybe we should head back to Springfield?"

I tried to hold it together—I really did—but an enormous pressure in my chest and an agonizing lump in my throat finally got the better of me. I willed my tears to stay put, but it only made things worse. Before Maggie could respond, I let out a strangled sob, and then the tears flowed.

Maggie held her hand out and grasped mine, and then she was crying, too. After a few minutes, she took a wad of tissues out of her purse, split the bundle, and handed me half.

"Well, that was fun," she said.

INSTEAD OF DRIVING back through town, I took a shortcut to the Merritt by driving north on Lake Avenue. I had done enough damage for one day, and—surprisingly—I just wanted to get back to Springfield.

I couldn't continue to live in a world divided between pain and pretense, and I needed to figure out where to go from here. Part of me wanted the pain and couldn't live without it because it was all I had left of Michael, but it competed with another part of me that couldn't bear it any longer. When Maggie asked me to move to Hungry Hill, I realized I didn't do it to save her. I did it to save myself. I knew that I had to accept Michael's death and move on, but I couldn't do it alone. I needed to process it with someone who felt as close to death as I did, and Maggie had that to offer me in return for my company.

Maggie was humming an old tune when we joined the rush hour traffic crawling through the woods of Stamford and New Canaan. I turned on the car's audio system, searched through my music app, and played the song for her. It was a nice Cole Porter tune, and we managed a bit of bad karaoke together without the benefit of lyric video. When the song was done, Maggie asked me to play it again, Sam. We did better the second time around.

By the time we reached Fairfield, we had finished singing and Maggie encouraged me to talk about Michael. She had only met him briefly at a family wedding, so she didn't really know him. I told her he was the finest person I had ever met. He wasn't just kind and good—he was smart and attentive, and funny as hell. I always felt like the center of his perfect universe.

"Must be hard living in the real world with the rest of us now," Maggie said, patting me on the arm and shaking her head. "I can't even imagine what it's like being with a man like that, since I'm the world's oldest living virgin." She threw her head back, barked a laugh, and said, "Jesus, Mary and Joseph! Maybe it's the underwear!"

"Maggie, did you ever have a special man in your life?" I asked. "I don't remember ever hearing about one."

"No," she replied, "never any particular man. I dated a boy in high school, but he perished during the Battle of the Bulge along with another boy I knew from Hungry Hill."

"I'm so sorry."

"Well, we never even kissed," she confessed. "It was really just a crush on my part. But I still think of him now and then . . ."

"So—there was never anyone else?"

"Oh, I went on a few dates when I was younger, but it was always one thing or another. I had my job, and I had my family. It was enough."

We continued to move slowly along with the traffic and drove without talking for a while. I spent the time trying to decide if a whole life without Michael would have been easier than only half a life with him.

Losing him sure had been a bitch.

MAGGIE AND I arrived back at the house to find Matt slumped on the sofa watching TV, both dogs snoozing at his feet. I noticed that his toenails were painted.

He followed my gaze. "There are two little girls at the end of the street. When they heard that I was babysitting your dogs, they had to come over and meet them. We had a manly-paddy party, or something like that."

"Nice," I said.

"Thanks. Any idea how to get this stuff off?"

"Sure, come on upstairs and I'll take care of you." I paused. "Um—I didn't mean that the way it sounded."

Matt stood, pressed both hands to his heart and gave a sigh. "My loss," he said.

"Oh, please," I replied. "Save it for some sweet young thing." I tried to sound casual, but the truth was I enjoyed the teasing.

We went upstairs to the bathroom and I had him sit on the toilet seat. I found my nail polish remover and cotton balls and sat on the tile floor in front of him. He was wearing that woodsy aftershave again and a pair of running shorts, and I had a fine view of his package. *Hello there, gentleman*, I thought, then immediately redirected my attention. If Matt caught me staring at his crotch, I would never hear the end of it. I went to work on the two different colors he had on alternating toes.

"This is kind of a shame, Matt," I said. "It's a good look on you. Emphasizes your nice feet."

"Thanks, but my feet aren't exactly the first thing the ladies notice when they look my way, if you know what I mean." He stretched out his left leg, admiring it. "What do you think, Cavanaugh?"

I suppressed a smile. "They're not bad." That was an understatement. His legs were long and lean, and finely muscled. I would have been hard-pressed to decide what part of his anatomy was most enticing.

"You can put it down now," I said. "I know what your legs look like."

"And?"

"Like I said—not bad. Even we older women enjoy a good set of legs on a man when we see them." I tweaked a freshly nude toe on his right foot.

"You're not *that* much older," he said. "I don't see any crow's feet."

"The lighting in here is really good." I decided not to mention that I'd switched out Maggie's glaring, high-wattage bulbs for softer ones. "But, hey, I'm not one to turn down a compliment. If that's what that was." I released his right foot. "Okay, you're all done here."

"Thanks for restoring my dignity."

"My pleasure," I said, looking up at him. I felt a little thrill of surprise and a dose of discomfort at finding his intense, blue-eyed gaze locked right on me.

"Know what I think, Cavanaugh?" He reached down and lightly brushed stray strands of hair out of my eyes.

"What?" I asked, my eyes looking deeply into his. The skin on my forehead felt hot. I felt hot. I suddenly needed to open a window.

"You could really use a haircut."

"Oh. Gee. Thanks for noticing." I flicked my hair into place and tried to reel myself in. I thought Matt would laugh at my discomfort, but he just helped me gather my tools from the floor.

I put everything away, and we headed downstairs. I invited Matt to join us for drinks, but he declined, saying he had plans for the evening. After wishing Maggie a good night, he asked me to walk him out. He waited until we were on the front porch with the door closed behind us before speaking.

"So, how'd it go in Greenwich?"

"I think Maggie enjoyed getting out," I said. "Not that she would ever admit it."

"I'm not talking about Maggie. I'm asking how it went for you."

The question surprised me, and I wondered, even now, how much Matt and his brother actually knew with regard to my past. They had never pressed for information. "It's true that I have, um, unfinished business there. I'm working on it."

"If there's anything I can do to help, please let me know." Matt moved closer to me and rubbed his warm hands up and down my arms. "You look cold, Grace, maybe you should put on a sweater or something."

"I'm fine," I replied. "It's just cooler here on the porch than it was upstairs."

Matt stepped back and worked his hands into the pockets of his shorts. Glancing down at his bare toes, he wiggled them briefly, and looked up at me again.

"Grace, if I asked you to have dinner with me Saturday night, would you make a big deal about it and find an excuse not to, or would you consider it for a bit before turning me down?"

I was taken by surprise by his invitation and hesitated, but then regrouped and replied teasingly, "Surely you don't get many dates with that approach."

"Not true. Women are drawn to vulnerability—it works every time." Matt smiled at me, adjusted his glasses, and blinked with feigned innocence.

I thought about it briefly before saying, "Okay, as long as *you* don't make a big deal about it. I'm not ready for any big deals."

"Just drinks and dinner—and good conversation."

"I guess I can handle that."

"Great." He gave me a big smile.

"By the way, Matt," I said. "Exactly how old are you?"

"Twenty-nine," he replied. "Why?"

I sighed, and did some quick math. Okay, maybe I *wasn't* old enough to be his mother. "You do realize I'm a tad older than you, right?"

"A *tad?*" He grinned and popped me in the arm. "You wish!"

"Hey—you need to improve on your treatment of the elderly," I chided, suppressing a smile.

"Your age is irrelevant, Cavanaugh," he said. "It's your maturity that concerns me." He turned to leave before I could set him straight. I admired his receding behind and cocked an eyebrow, which probably only proved his point.

〉⟨⟨⟨

IT HAD BEEN Maggie's routine for years to attend Catholic Mass every evening at St. Ann's, which was conveniently located on the street perpendicular to Cleveland and the other presidents on the west side of Hungry Hill. Maggie had walked to St. Ann's almost every day of her life. I couldn't imagine having so indelible a routine. A cup of coffee first thing in the morning, a glass of wine at night: yes. Hanging out in a dark church every evening while a priest droned on? I'd pass, or probably fall asleep.

In spite of Maggie's illness, she was determined to abide by her lifelong tradition when she felt up to it. Most evenings, she still managed to disappear before cocktails and dinner to participate in Mass with her devout neighbors.

Catholic rituals were a mystery to me. I had been raised Protestant by my parents, continuing the tradition of my father's side of the family. As a result, I didn't understand the attraction of a daily Mass, particularly since Maggie told me some the priests at St. Ann's were old school and still occasionally performed the service entirely in Latin.

Attending Mass seemed to be a habitual and social, rather than spiritual exercise for Maggie, although I suspected that spending time with Him had taken on greater significance lately. Maggie and I hadn't really talked about her illness yet—let alone death—but she was a practical person at her core and was probably hedging her bets.

"Gracie girl, why don't you come to Mass with me tonight," she said that evening after Matt had left and we had finished cocktails and dinner. "I don't feel like going by myself."

I was sleepy and comfortable hanging out with the dogs, and

even picking up a good book seemed like it would take too much effort. The day in Greenwich and planning a big date with Matt had completely worn me out. I had no interest at all, and was about to beg off, but the expression on Maggie's face stopped me. "Hey—sounds like fun," I said instead. "You and I can hang out in back and make fun of the priests. They always dress up pretty weird."

"Good grief, Grace—grow up!" Maggie chided.

"Seriously, *that* would be no fun." I groaned and stretched.

The last time I set foot in a church was the day I put Michael in the ground. He was raised Catholic, and even though he was never particularly religious, I knew he would want a traditional Mass for his service. So, he had the whole nine yards. I would have tried to keep it simple for Michael's sake, but I was clueless when it came to reining in the party planners at the local church, and it ended up being a major production.

If it had been entirely up to me, I would have had him cremated. I would have gone down to the beach at Tod's Point with a few close friends and the dogs and tossed his ashes into Long Island Sound. I would have spent the night there, cursing God, and eventually getting booted out by the Greenwich police.

But Michael never shared my sense of the dramatic. He was always a nuts-and-bolts kind of guy, practical to a fault. He would have planned a simple service and found a pleasant little plot in a non-denominational cemetery somewhere convenient. I knew he thought dying wasn't a very big deal; it happened to the best of us. I knew all this, but it didn't help.

So, the last time I was in a Catholic church, my world was falling apart. *Get over it*, I told myself. *You're supposed to be there for Maggie.* The Catholic Church wasn't responsible for Michael's death—it just made it official.

"Maggie, is it all right if I just watch?" I asked. "I don't have to do communion with you or anything, right?" I hauled myself out of the comfortable chair and went to the bathroom to fix my hair and check my face. Maggie trailed behind me and waited in the hall, talking to me while I refined my look.

"I can guarantee you one thing, Gracie girl: the priests at St. Ann's wouldn't even think about giving you the sacraments. You have Protestant written all over you. Just come and keep me company, and I'll be goddamn Catholic enough for the two of us!"

We settled Ellen and Stogie in front of the television with Nat Geo reruns and took off down Cleveland Street to St. Ann's. The first time I had walked by the church with the dogs, unfortunate signage—everything in capital letters and not properly spaced—made me think it was Stan's church. For a moment, I had thought some guy had started his own religion before I finally figured things out. When I had mentioned this to Maggie, she had just looked at me and rolled her eyes.

"Hey, that would be pretty cool," I had muttered to myself.

The evening was a little chilly, so we moved as quickly as Maggie's stiff limbs would allow. We entered the church through the main doors, although I had tried unsuccessfully to talk Maggie into sneaking in from one of the side entrances. Father Brian was standing just inside the vestibule with another, younger priest, and she called out to him.

"Evening, Father! Hope you don't mind, but I brought my niece, Grace, along for the ride. Better be a good Mass, 'cause she's one of them heathen Protestants, and you know how they can be." Maggie grasped my arm and pulled me over to meet her favorite priest. He was tall and gray-haired, with slightly stooped posture, and looked to be approximately the same vintage as Maggie.

"So, this is the infamous Grace," he said in a soft brogue as he held out his hand to greet me. "I've been looking forward ta meetin' ya."

Maggie smiled widely as we shook hands.

"Well, darlin'," he continued, "I'm glad you could make it this evenin', and I'm pleased that you're in town to keep an eye on this one." He motioned toward Maggie with his head.

"All right, enough chit chat," Maggie said. "We better get a seat—the good ones fill up fast!" She took my arm and pulled me away.

"Nice to meet you, Grace," Father Brian called as Maggie directed me down the aisle. We followed a trio of elderly women and found seats in the middle of the nave close to the action in the apse.

The younger priest performed the service—surprisingly, some of it in Latin—and it went uneventfully. Watching Maggie in the near dark with her eyes half-closed was a peaceful experience. She fingered a rosary, and slowly nodded her head to the cadence of his voice.

We sailed on a sea of ancient sounds with our elderly neighbors, and my heartbeat slowed along with my breathing. When it was our turn to take communion, Maggie sat tight, held my hand, and kept me company.

5

sexbomb

My hair was out of control, and close to reaching epic proportions. When it was properly cut, I looked chic and sophisticated. Right now, Stogie and I looked like we shared familial DNA. When I went back to the little grocery store around the corner, the grocer didn't recognize me. He apologized when I mentioned who I was after discussing various wines and asked me if I had "changed something." If I hoped to knock Matt's socks off on Saturday night, I would have to address my hair.

I figured I would have to drive to Boston to find a proper stylist. I certainly wasn't taking any of Maggie's recommendations, since her coiffure reminded me of a geriatric poodle with an oddly blue coat. Matt had his wild thatch cut by a chick that worked out of her apartment downtown, and Quinn cut his own locks with tiny cuticle scissors. He'd offered to cut mine, and I had almost accepted, but the thought of having his big hands running through my hair just wasn't enough to put my mop at risk.

I bought a Boston Magazine and found a slick ad for a salon on Newberry Street, called and scheduled an appointment, and crossed my fingers. I would have had Maggie start a novena for me, but I didn't have the nine days, and I can only imagine the "Christ!" I would have gotten out of that request.

I CRANKED UP the stereo on the Beemer as I headed to Boston doing eighty-five miles-per-hour. Which was no big deal in the state of Mass because neighboring vehicles, including a police cruiser, were passing me left and right.

I exited into the enormous rest stop just east of Sturbridge, gassed up, and fed a handful of quarters into a machine for a contraband Coke. The smell of deep-fried food lured me into a McDonald's on the way out, and I splurged on a rare treat of perfectly cooked French fries loaded with hydrogenated oil, anti-foaming agents, and preservatives—yum! I munched and slurped as I cruised south of Worcester, singing *Sexbomb* and *She's a Lady* along with Tom Jones.

The traffic slowed when I finally made it to downtown Boston, and I immediately found myself hopelessly lost even though I was using my GPS—it guided me to a street dead-ended by Jersey barriers where a gang of homeboys was hanging out. They were amused at my predicament, and playfully pointed me back in the right direction, complimenting me on my choice of wheels. "Got to *bling* those wheels *out*, sister!" one of them yelled as I turned around.

I finally worked my way over to Newberry Street, and drove in heavy traffic looking for the address of the salon. I found it on the second floor of a turn-of-the-century brick building, sitting above an art gallery. There was a cramped parking lot a block away, and I anxiously left the Beemer and my keys with a too-young attendant with purple highlights in his hair, tats covering his arms, and little silver rings through various parts of his facial anatomy. I tipped him ten dollars and promised him bodily harm if there were any dings in the car when I returned. He tossed my keys high up into the air and caught them behind his back.

"Nice trick," I said, and stood with my hands on my hips while I watched him put the keys on a hook in a small booth. "Remember—bodily harm."

The salon was as lovely as its advertisement had promised, and my new stylist, Daniel, was French, thin, and blond, and dressed all in black. He ran his fingers through my mop of hair, frowned, and asked me when I had my last cut. I honestly couldn't remember. "No matter," he said, "Daniel will fix." And fix, Daniel did. Forty-five minutes later I barely recognized myself. Gracie Cavanaugh was gorgeous again, and ready for action.

"Daniel, do you think this cut makes me look hot?" I asked, admiring my new look in the mirror.

"Absolutement!" he replied. "I touch you, and I burn." He pressed a polished finger to my shoulder and made a sizzling "psss" sound. He smirked at his joke and sent me to the cashier. I handed over my credit card and put three twenty-dollar bills in a tip envelope. Money well spent.

I decided to do a little clothes shopping before I headed back to Springfield. Trendy boutiques lined Newberry Street, and I hit the most promising-looking shops. For the next two hours, I flipped through racks of clothing. One store specialized in bohemian chic, and I bought a pretty slate gray blouse in silk with a low keyhole neckline, poet sleeves, and a lovely pin tuck bodice.

Another shop offered an extensive collection of jeans. I found a pair with slim legs that emphasized my narrow hips. They pared my looks down by about five years, although I would have paid extra for ten. I grabbed a few lace panties near the checkout counter, settled up with the cashier, and headed back to my car.

The young parking attendant did a double-take when I returned. He grabbed the car keys and helped me put my bags into the Beemer. "I barely recognized you," he said. "You changed your hair. Cool."

"Thanks," I said, "but you already got your tip."

The drive home was another slice of heaven, and I was surprised to find I was able to be alone and enjoy myself. I was tempted to pull into the rest stop on the way back and get another order of fries, but reminded myself I didn't need the extra cargo if I hoped to fit into my new jeans. Besides, it wouldn't be long before cocktail hour, and I was looking forward to seeing Maggie and the dogs.

It had been a good day: I had spent quality time by myself, gotten a kick-ass haircut, been deemed "hot" by a gay stylist, and earned a look of approval from a tattooed teenager. Okay, so maybe it had been all about the tips, but as I saw it, one had nothing to do with the other, and I was sticking with that theory.

IT WAS SATURDAY, the night of my big date with Matt, and after soaking in the tub with my favorite bath salts, I reached inside the Chanel cosmetics bag beside the tub that held my shaving kit. Only Michael would have thought of ordering a razor handmade by European artisans with a bone handle and accompanying lavender-scented gel. Sadly, the razor had seen little action in recent months, which explained why it took a full ten minutes for me to shave my legs. My bath and shampoo behind me, I dried with an old towel, grabbed my reading glasses and applied the razor to my knees in case I had missed a stray hair. I knew that Matt wouldn't care if I missed a spot—it was supposed to be a harmless dinner for Pete's sake—but for some reason the details seemed important.

Makeup was another challenge, since I was aiming for youthful and casual. I avoided the areas around my eyes when I applied foundation, so I wouldn't end up exaggerating the crop of wrinkles I'd been working on successfully for decades. I kept the eye makeup light, although my eyes were my best facial feature and I didn't want to play them down too much. Was Matt putting in this much effort? I seriously doubted it. He would probably just throw on a clean T-shirt before he picked me up.

Ellen wandered up to my bedroom while I was getting dressed, but didn't offer any opinions or assistance. She regarded me with her typical noble grace and suffered in silence through my tirade about not having quite the right bra for my pretty bohemian top and its keyhole neckline. I had a devil-may-care moment and opted to go braless. Luckily for me, my breasts are still reasonably perky and not big enough to fuss over. I pulled on my fabulous new jeans and slipped on a pair of charcoal leather Jimmy Choo sandals I had brought with me from Greenwich.

I did a little twirl. "Hey, El, what do you think?"

She made a few non-verbal observations and gave me a sweet nudge with her dark, wet nose.

It had been a long time since I'd spent time alone with a man. I felt a quiver of anxiety in the pit of my stomach. I tried on my signature strategy for everything: stay in the moment, pretend everything is okay, and don't think too much. I waited for a sense of calm to kick in. Nothing happened.

"Don't make a big deal about tonight, okay?" I said. "It's just a little date with some guy from the hood."

Ellen sighed, plopped down on the rag rug, and fully extended her impressive body in the wolfhound version of a stretch-and-yawn. I removed one of the Jimmy Choos and gave her belly a good rubbing with my bare foot. She huffed and rolled her eyes.

"All right, wish Momma luck." I slipped the sandal back on and headed for the stairs, popping into the bathroom for one last look at my efforts. My hair and makeup looked great, especially in the low light of the new bulbs I had installed. "El, we need to change more bulbs in the house—Momma's not as young as she used to be," I called in the direction of my bedroom. I could hear her snoring gently, and found it comforting. At least she was being cool about my big night.

I headed downstairs for a cocktail with Maggie. I figured Matt would probably be a little late, what with the time it took to change a T-shirt and all. I poured myself a glass of wine and joined Maggie who was already working on her bourbon in the parlor. Her gaze was fixed on Stogie who was lying on his back, snoring. She was clearly amused. "The little mutt is out cold," she said. "He takes more naps than I do."

"Looks like somebody had a hard day trying to keep up with you," I said.

"It's not easy running with the big dogs." Maggie took a sip of her drink.

"So—what did you two do all day?"

"Mostly watched TV. Took a nap."

"I can see how that would take its toll."

Maggie chuffed a little laugh and looked at me closely. "Well, Gracie girl, aren't you looking special?"

"Do you think Matt is going to appreciate the effort?" I asked.

"He's got to love those shoes."

"To be honest, I'm a little nervous. Have any advice for a chick in her prime who's about to go out with a sweet young thing?"

"Sure as hell do—have fun, and don't be afraid to take advantage of the boy!"

MAGGIE WAS EATING a small salad I had prepared for her, and Ellen and Stogie were supervising at her feet when the doorbell rang at precisely seven o'clock. I went to the door, and both dogs followed. They must have read my anxiety, because they crowded me protectively, and we collected at the door in an awkward little pack. I finally convinced them to back off.

I ran a hand though my hair, braced myself, and opened the door.

Matt was wearing beautifully tailored trousers and a linen shirt with nice accessories—a black belt and matching leather loafers. He had a fresh haircut that was slightly long and slightly messy on top. His hair was still damp, and even though we stood several feet apart I caught a whiff of something spicy. He looked and smelled sexy as hell.

"Hey, I thought we were going *casual*," I said, stepping aside so he could enter. "I'm wearing jeans—I didn't think you owned any big boy pants." As I closed the door, I noted that Ellen and Stogie were watching us closely. I hoped they hadn't picked up on my fashion faux pas and were feeling sorry for me.

"I considered wearing my signature look," Matt said, "but I

figured a beautiful lady like you would be decked out in something, well, classy," he said, eyeing my jeans. "I didn't want to
bring down your game, and I had these clothes left over from a
wedding I attended on the Cape last summer."

"You don't like my outfit?" I asked as I stepped closer to him
and fingered the collar of his shirt. "Maybe we should have compared notes before our date."

Matt gave me a slow smile. "I'm liking it better and better,"
he said as his gaze moved slowly down my body. "I don't think
I've ever seen you in girlie shoes. They're pretty high. Do you
even know how to walk in those things?"

"Can—and will," I replied, moving a little closer. Matt stood
his ground, and we faced each other smiling.

"Hey, enough already!" Maggie barked from the kitchen. "Go
rent a room!" and added, "Come to Auntie Maggie, kids. You're
both a little young for that action in the front hall." She rattled a
box of crackers to get their attention.

"Seriously, Grace, you look great," Matt said. "Doesn't even
matter what *I'm* wearing. No one will be looking at me."

MATT AND I said goodbye to Maggie and the dogs and headed
out the front door. I thought about offering to drive in case Matt
felt self-conscious about squiring me in his beat-up Subaru, but I
decided I was just being a snob. Matt had at least vacuumed and
washed the little bugger, and I teased him about the "new car
scent" air freshener hanging from his rearview mirror.

"Hey," he said, "only the best for you." If he was embarrassed
about his vehicle, he didn't show it.

We headed toward the big city, hopped onto the highway briefly, and exited near the center of downtown Springfield. Matt pulled the Subaru into an enormous parking garage, where he parked the car carefully on an end spot.

"Wouldn't want my baby to get dinged," he said, and laughed when I rolled my eyes.

"How would you tell? Do you have all of the current dings mapped out on a diagram somewhere?"

"Daddy would know, wouldn't he Sheila?" He patted the dashboard fondly.

"Sheila?"

"Named her after an old girlfriend."

"Was she a little past her prime, too?" I teased.

"Lucky for you I like older women."

"Hey—I'm *in* my prime, not *past* it."

"Don't think I didn't notice."

We locked Sheila up nice and tight, and headed for the garage elevator. Matt walked close to me with a protective hand on my shoulder and brushed up against me when he held the elevator door.

My body sent me a dozen conflicting signals all at once—I felt nervous, excited, guilty—and several other emotions that were hard to identify. I must have telegraphed my discomfort to Matt, because in the elevator, he took my hand, turned my palm up, and kissed it gently.

"You doing okay?" he asked. "You looked a little weirded out there for a minute."

"Honestly, this feels *very* weird to me," I admitted. "Nice, but weird. I haven't been on a 'first date' in decades."

Matt took both of my hands in his and gently rubbed the tops of them with his thumbs. He slowly fingered the slim band I still wore on my left hand. "Cavanaugh, you're gorgeous and funny, and I'm really enjoying getting to know you, but we're just here to have a nice dinner together. The pleasure of your company is more than enough…"

When my expression suggested disbelief, he grinned. "Fine. So I'm not a Boy Scout."

I inhaled deeply and tried to return his smile. The elevator door opened, and he dropped my hands.

"Come on, you sweet man," I said, and sighed. "Let's go have dinner. I'm not promising you anything, but don't let your hopes die."

The restaurant was more elegant than I thought possible in downtown Springfield. An ambitious soul from Manhattan had evidently decided the blue-collar city needed a shot of the Big Apple. The place was crowded and busy. The maître'd apologized, said it would take a few minutes to seat us, so Matt and I grabbed a pair of stools at the bar and ordered cocktails. We were on our second round by the time our table was ready.

Café Viande wasn't even close to being a real French restaurant, but the owner had a good sense of humor—viande simply means "meat" in French—and they served a mean steak with *pommes frites*. Matt and I ordered the same meal, since I informed him I wasn't good at sharing, and we both wanted steak. We settled on a nice bottle of cabernet, and had a great time eating and talking. After two cocktails and a glass of wine, I was feeling a lot more comfortable.

"Matt, I'm having a really good time," I told him. "I'm not sure what I expected, but…" I stuffed a carefully arranged forkful of steak and fries into my mouth.

"So—words fail you. With you, I'll take that as a compliment," he said, and reached across the table in an attempt to spear a perfect square of beef off my plate. I always take the time and effort to create a tantalizing tableau with my food, so I really couldn't blame him.

"Hey! I explained the rules of engagement when we ordered," I reminded him. "I don't share—next time you lose a body part, and it's not going to be pretty. My knife is a little dull." I held my fork and knife in a defensive position, and Matt grinned and sat back in his chair with his hands in the air. He looked longingly at the steak he almost succeeded in stealing, and then resumed eating off his own plate.

We spent the rest of our dinner comparing notes about our childhoods, friends and families, and interests. Despite our age difference, Matt and I had a lot in common. We both grew up in close-knit Irish families in Springfield and were close to our siblings. As opposed to Matt, I was the oldest child in my family. Emily and Laura were both younger, but Emily and I were only eleven months apart.

"My father sometimes referred to us affectionately as 'my Irish twins,'" I said. "Although my mother objected to the term. 'Your father and I planned you both very carefully,' she always said."

I described to Matt our occasional grappling for the top position in the familial lineup, although I had always won. Those precious eleven months had been my perennial trump card.

Matt laughed when I listed the benefits of being top dog: my own room, new clothes—not hand-me-downs—best seat in the back of the family station wagon. "That explains a lot about you, Cavanaugh," he commented. "You're definitely a little bossy. Since I'm accustomed to being at the bottom of the pecking order, you and I might actually get along. Or maybe," he added, "we might have to arm wrestle occasionally."

"Only if you accept you're going to lose going into it," I said, and smiled. I really liked it when he called me "Cavanaugh."

He wondered if I stayed in touch with my sisters.

"I confess to keeping them—along with everyone else—at arms' length recently," I admitted.

Matt didn't say anything, just waited for me to continue.

"I don't know what Maggie's told you about me. I assume she's said something, since last week you asked how things went for me in Greenwich."

"She said you lost your husband," he replied gently. "That you've been taking it really hard."

I blew out a long breath. "Yeah, that's a bit of an understatement. I guess I've gone a little crazy since Michael died." It was hard to say the words.

"It's totally understandable."

"I guess. I never thought I would go off the deep end over *anything*."

"So even though you're 'a little crazy,' your sisters let you keep your distance?"

"That's probably why," I replied smiling. "It's not like we don't stay in touch—Emily calls me all the time—but she just calls to check in on me, talk about my nephews and the weather. She never pushes me to go anywhere with her emotionally. She knows me. I don't go anywhere I don't want to."

"I'll keep that in mind." Matt looked at me and smiled. I was concerned that he would pursue the subject of Michael, but he let it drop and I was relieved. It felt like a courtesy, and I was grateful.

His parents had been loving, hard-working, and pragmatic, as were mine. My father had made a good living as an executive at Mass Mutual, though, while Matt's father had worked as an auto mechanic most of his life. My childhood had involved less sacrifice than Matt's, but my parents were always very careful with their money. We lived in a modest house in the suburbs, attended public schools, and watched our pennies.

After getting his three daughters through good colleges, my father had retired, and he and my mother had been able to attack his retirement with a vengeance. They sold our house and moved to a condo in Hilton Head, where my dad played golf every day when they weren't traveling to some exotic destination or on a month-long cruise.

"Cavanaugh, you're damn lucky both of your parents are still alive," Matt said wistfully.

"I'm very grateful," I replied, meaning it. "My parents are still healthy, too. I hope to have them around for a long time."

"Don't take it for granted," Matt cautioned me. "I thought my mom and dad would get to see me marry and have kids—the whole nine yards. But they're gone now, and none of that is going to happen."

"Oh, believe me, I don't take anything for granted," I replied. "You never know when someone you love is going to leave you—and break your heart in the process."

"I'm sure it's been hard for you."

"The hardest part for me—next to losing Michael—has been getting over it enough to move on." I looked at Matt, and he nodded empathetically.

"Well, I don't know much about getting over a broken heart," he said, "but I do know how to find velocity as a function of time using an equation of motion."

"Huh?" I said.

"Pay attention. See, I guess that would apply to matters of the heart, too." Matt picked up a dinner roll, tore it almost in half, and held it over the table. "Here's your broken heart." He let go of the roll and it landed on the table. "As it falls to the table— or, as with your heart, tries to get to a place where it can move on—gravity is the equivalent of your desire to get there. Are you following me so far?"

"Sure. The poor little muffin is suicidal because you made it ugly."

"Okay, you're not paying attention. This is clearly a dinner roll." Matt smiled and continued, "Acceleration to that point is impacted by both your *desire* to get there, and any *resistance* to the idea of moving on—which is the equivalent of air providing resistance to the roll as it falls. Does that make sense to you?"

"My goodness, you really *are* a geek, aren't you?"

Matt ignored my comment. "My point is, I guess the easiest way for you to get over your broken heart—with greater velocity— is to let me be your gravity." He smiled and batted his blue eyes behind his glasses. "I'd like to help in any way I can, Cavanaugh."

"I can only imagine. What if there is some *resistance* to that idea?"

"I think I can do something about that." Matt motioned to our waiter for the check.

WE SHARED THE elevator in the garage with a pair of businessmen in matching charcoal suits, who conversed in hushed tones about another bad day in the markets. They exited on the floor below ours.

When we were alone, Matt turned to me and lifted one of the ends of the small tie on the neck of my blouse and rolled it gently between his fingers. When I didn't move away, he ran his hand down my arm and took my hand in his.

He leaned toward me, whispering in my ear—"Resistance is futile..."—and gently insinuated his fingers between mine.

"I should tell you to behave," I murmured as the elevator door slid open on our floor.

Matt released my hand as we stepped out of the elevator. His hand reappeared at the small of my back as we started across the parking garage. I had forgotten how nice the simple gesture felt.

Sheila had survived her time alone in the garage without incident. Matt led me to her passenger's side, but instead of opening my door, he gently put his hands on my shoulders and turned me to face him. He stared at me intently, slipped his arms around my waist, and stepped close. I wasn't expecting the move and panicked for a moment. I took a step back and bumped up against Sheila.

"Grace, it's all right," he murmured, moving closer. "I just want to know how this feels." His hands moved to my face and he held it gently. Before I could think or move, he pressed his lips to mine. His body felt solid against me—warm and inviting. I opened my mouth, and our tongues met. I let out a muffled moan and was immediately embarrassed.

I pulled away and gave a nervous laugh, but Matt lightly tugged me closer, slid his fingers into my hair, and kissed me again. His hands slid to my hips, and he held me as he pushed his body into mine. He continued kissing me, working my tongue with his and gently biting my lips. His mouth moved to my neck, and then to the hollow of my throat.

He was right. Resistance *was* futile. I grasped the back of his shirt, pulled it from his trousers, and slipped my hands under it. His skin was smooth and warm. Two rows of muscle framed the soft bumps of his spine, and I flattened my hands and moved them up his back. An urgent need moved through my body, and I pressed myself against him.

Just as I was making serious contact, the elevator dinged loudly some twenty feet away, and I jumped, banging Matt's chin with my head. "Sorry!" I yelped, and pulled away, trying to gather my wits about me and catch my breath.

Matt watched with amusement as I ran my fingers through my hair and tugged on my blouse, which had become twisted.

"Hey, you lied," I finally said, pointing an accusing finger at him. "You were going for a whole lot more than a kiss."

"Should I apologize?" He smiled as he tucked in his shirt.

"No—no apology necessary," I said, shaking my head and smiling back, "but we should definitely go before we get arrested."

WE DIDN'T TALK on the drive back, but I was aware each time Matt looked my way.

He put an old Aretha Franklin tape into Sheila's ancient player, and Aretha's gorgeous voice kept us company. When we reached Cleveland Street, Matt pulled into Maggie's driveway. He cut the engine but didn't make a move to get out. "So—are you going to invite me in?" he asked, giving me an innocent look.

"Sorry, but I can only handle so much excitement in one evening. Remember, I'm a *tad* older than you."

"You admit that you were excited?"

"More than enough for one night."

"We need to build up your stamina." He leaned over to kiss me.

"*You* need to behave." I pressed my palm against his chest to stop him.

"Can I at least walk you to the door?"

"I think I can make it on my own."

"Grace, you're breaking my heart." He looked at me longingly. I could see the desire in his eyes, even in the dark, and while I would have enjoyed more of him, I knew it was a bad idea. I wasn't ready.

I leaned over, gave him a quick kiss, and opened the car door before I had a chance to change my mind. He remained in the driveway until I was safely inside, and then he started Sheila's engine and slowly backed out.

)‹‹‹

THE HOUSE WAS quiet.

The clock ticked in the hall, and I could smell the faint scent of mothballs. The ribbon candy glowed on the living room table, reflecting light from the lamp Maggie had left on for me.

I crept up to my bedroom, trying to be as quiet as I could despite the squeaky stairs. I used the bathroom, stripped off my clothing, and crawled into bed. The familiar sag in the mattress hugged my naked body, and the light of the moon found its way through the old drapes.

"I hate to break it to you, Michael," I whispered in the dark, "but the boy is hot."

6

bad hair day

THE SUN WAS streaming through my windows when I awoke the next morning. It was eight thirty, and I could hear Ellen pacing around in the hallway outside my bedroom door. I yawned, stretching my limbs under the sheets and rolling my shoulders. I slipped out of bed and threw on a fresh set of panties, sweats, and T-shirt, and opened the door.

Ellen immediately shoved her face into my hand and turned for the stairs. I heard Stogie shuffling behind Maggie's closed door, so I let him out and peeked in on her. She was snoring loudly, her head thrown back on her pillow and arms outstretched. Her empty mouth was a black hole that made her look curiously alien.

I tiptoed down the stairs with Stogie following closely and used the half bath near the kitchen before letting the dogs out into the backyard. It was a lovely day, and I stayed with them for a few minutes before heading in to make coffee. I was worried about Maggie. It was unusual for her to sleep in, even when she didn't feel well. I wondered if she'd had a tough night and was making up for lost sleep.

I made my coffee as quietly as possible, holding my breath while the espresso maker cheerfully burbled and belched. Ellen and Stogie were ready to come back in, so I prepared their breakfast. They devoured their meal while I mainlined caffeine. When we were done, we went into the parlor to watch the news. I kept the volume low so we wouldn't wake Maggie. After the weekend substitutes for George and Robin finished dishing out their gossip on *Good Morning America*, I put on a baseball cap and sunglasses and took the dogs for a walk.

Quinn and Matt were sitting on their front porch reading the paper, and Matt called to me as we passed, "Looking good, Cavanaugh!"

I laughed, blew them a two-handed kiss, and did a quick imitation of Grace Cavanaugh on the catwalk—cheeks sucked in as I glided down the cracked sidewalk. Just as I was about to execute a complicated runway turn with my sleek pets, I tripped on the edge of a protruding slab of concrete. Quinn chuckled and said, "Nice move, Grace."

I wondered if Matt had mentioned our exploits in the parking garage. When I glanced back at them, they were both staring at me, so I drew my own conclusions. I hoped Matt had included the part about how gorgeous I looked in my cool new outfit, but —bummer—I knew that men rarely gave fashion details.

The dogs and I did the usual tour of the neighborhood, greeted the occasional octogenarian parked on a front stoop, and spent a little time in a small park near Stan's. With the weather as nice as it was, I could have walked all day, but I was driven back to the house by a nagging concern for Maggie. Which was why, even though I would have enjoyed a nice chat with the guys, I just waved as we passed by on our way back home.

I put fresh water out for the dogs, and then headed up the stairs. As I reached the top, I heard the toilet flush. Over the sound of running water, Maggie voiced a loud complaint. "*Deethus, Mawy an Dothus!* Ith it pathible to ave a worth oddamn bad air day?"

I burst out laughing. Maggie opened the bathroom door, bleary-eyed and toothless. "Ta hell ith all uf ou!" she said. And yes, she *was* having a bad hair day.

"Well, look who's up—hmm, Sleeping Beauty doesn't really cover it—look who's finally up," I said, stifling more laughter.

Maggie just gave me a look, scratched her head, made a failed attempt to arrange her hair, and headed downstairs to the kitchen. I figured her mood would improve if I gave her a few minutes alone to get herself together, so I spent some time tidying up my room.

When I finally went down to the kitchen, I found her sitting at the kitchen table sipping tea, waiting for a slice of bread to toast in the little art deco toaster she kept concealed under a crocheted cozy on the kitchen counter.

"Tough night?" I asked and joined her at the table.

"The worst. I stayed up pretty late watching TV with the dogs, thinking I might fall asleep easier if I was really tired, but it didn't do a damn bit of good," she said. "I must have been up half the night. The pest kept getting up and checking on me. I couldn't get comfortable. I can feel the pain in my bones, and those pills don't help. Plus, they give me damn angina."

"I'll call Dr. Cunningham," I said. "He can prescribe stronger medication. I'm sorry you were having such a lousy time when I was having such a good one. Hardly seems fair."

"Fair has nothing to do with it, Grace. I'm glad one of us had a memorable evening." Maggie took a small sip of her tea. "I'd like to hear all about it, but maybe later, okay? I think I'll go back upstairs in a bit and lie down for a while, see if I can get a little sleep."

I grabbed her toast when it popped up, buttered it and set it down in front of her, but she just looked at it. "Thanks, but I don't feel like eating," she said and slowly stood. "Don't worry. I'm fine, I'm just a little pooped. Call Dr. Kevorkian for me if you don't mind and let him earn his pay." She turned and headed for the hall.

She passed by Ellen and Stogie, who were napping on the kitchen floor. Stogie opened his eyes at the sound of Maggie's footsteps, stood, and followed.

"Christ—you're a damn pest," Maggie said, her voice growing faint as she neared the top of the stairs. "You didn't get much sleep last night either, eh? Come on, we'll catch ourselves a nap." After a minute, I heard her bedroom door close.

I grabbed my cell phone and called Dr. Cunningham. He wasn't available so I spoke with the on-call oncologist who promised to call Maggie's pharmacy and order a stronger painkiller. I asked him to prescribe a sleep aid as well, but he suggested I take it up with Dr. Cunningham.

"The Vicodin is pretty strong," he said. "We might want to see if that gives her enough relief before adding to it."

I ran out to get the new prescription while Maggie napped. When I returned, I took the bottle of pills and a glass of water to her room and woke her up long enough to give her one.

"Come on, Stog," I said, and tried to talk the little sausage into leaving his charge. "It's okay, she'll be okay," I whispered to him. He hesitated and looked at Maggie.

She raised her head briefly, and said, "Out of here, little man. Go get some sunshine."

⟨⟨⟨

I DIDN'T WANT to leave Maggie for long, but I needed to get out of the house. The brownstone was making me claustrophobic.

I loaded the dogs into the cube and headed briefly south to Springfield College. We explored the campus for a few minutes and took a stroll on the green near the campus union.

The Sunday afternoon summer college crowd was out in full force playing Frisbee and enjoying the sun. It felt good to be surrounded by so many young bodies. Many of the students had never seen a dog Ellen's size so we were stopped repeatedly. She was polite and gentle with everyone, and ignored the fact that Stogie was put out by the lack of attention given him. "It's okay, Stog," I told him, "you may not stand out in a crowd like El, but you have other interesting qualities." As though to prove my point, he made an attempt to show off by chasing a few Frisbees, but eventually gave up. He obviously realized it just wasn't his thing.

Once we had our fill of the green, we stopped for an afternoon latte at a small coffee shop near the campus, and the young barista gave me a plastic bowl with water for the dogs. We hung out there for a while, sharing biscotti, before heading back home.

When we returned, I went upstairs to check on Maggie. She was out cold and snoring, and her facial muscles were completely relaxed so I assumed the Vicodin was doing its job. I allowed Stogie to rejoin her, and he plopped down on her rug, gave a sigh, and closed his eyes.

Downstairs, I sat on the front porch with Ellen and a Dean Koontz novel. I tried to get settled in a wicker chair, but the cushions were so old they were crumbling inside their bark cloth covers. I slowly looked around the porch and the deteriorating furniture and decided I had to make a few changes around Maggie's house.

If I organized everything in advance, I could blow through the house quickly. I wasn't thinking about major renovations, although the house desperately needed updating. But some repairs had to be done before the house totally fell apart. Not to mention, I was tired of living in a time warp, and was itching to bring the place into the twenty-first century. Or at least the twentieth.

Once I made the decision to start a project, my mind went on a rampage. I loved tearing stuff apart and putting it back together again. When I was working with my old architectural firm in Greenwich—Snow & Barton—I gladly took on most of the renovation projects that found their way to our firm, and rarely designed homes from scratch. As land had become increasingly scarce in Fairfield County, more than half of our projects were renovations and I became very adept at the process.

If I could restore an enormous old mansion to perfection, I could certainly update a small urban brownstone.

I went inside for a pad and pen and began making a series of lists. I started with the projects that needed to be addressed, and the various contractors involved in each project. It was a small house, so it took me all of ten minutes. It would be easier to just level the house and start over, but that was completely impractical. I would be here for a while, though, so a few small changes would be better than nothing.

I picked a project from my list and settled on relandscaping the front yard and making the front porch clean and habitable. I could tear up the concrete walkway and put in bluestone pavers and veneer the concrete steps with antique brick. The iron pipe rail was too utilitarian; I would replace it with a slimmer, more sophisticated rail in wrought iron. All of the old rhododendrons and yews needed to be removed and replaced with plants that were smaller in scale. Boxwood and small-leafed holly would be more manageable and tidier, and I could have citron hostas put in between them for a shot of color in the shade of the porch.

After mentally demolishing the front yard, I moved on to the porch. None of the furniture was salvageable. I would replace it with nice vintage reproduction pieces that had weather-resistant cushions. A settee, end tables, and two or three rocking chairs would fit nicely. The floorboards and screened panels of the porch needed replacing, and the entire porch needed a coat of fresh paint.

That was enough project planning for one day, I concluded. I could only imagine how Maggie was going to react to my scheming. I would wait until she had her second cocktail that evening before discussing any of the renovations. I was certain she wouldn't appreciate my suggesting that all of her family's porch furniture from the last three generations be placed in a pile by the side of the road.

Around six that evening, I was in the kitchen making vegetable lasagna and an arugula salad, when I heard Maggie finally wake. She and Stogie puttered around upstairs for a few minutes before heading down. She took her time negotiating the stairs, chatting with Stogie as she went. I could hear him pausing patiently on each tread. They finally reached the lower hall, and then made slow progress to the kitchen.

Maggie pulled out a chair and sat heavily. "Those new pills you got me sure did the trick," she said, "but I feel like I was run over by a truck." She glanced at Stogie, who was sitting by the back door. "I think the pest needs to go out."

I quickly mixed Maggie a cocktail, and then rounded the dogs up for a walk. Daylight was waning, and the evening was peaceful and pleasant. A lone light glowed next door, but Matt's car wasn't in the driveway. I wondered what he was doing.

As we worked our way down the street, the pleasant clatter of home life and the aroma of cooking meals drifted out through open windows. We walked slowly, enjoying the evening. By the time we got back to Maggie's, a few more lights had been turned on next door, and Sheila was sitting in the driveway.

The desire to see Matt tugged at me, and I found it hard to resist.

I dropped the dogs off, told Maggie I would be right back, and crossed the yard to the Quinn's. I hesitated on the front steps, wondering if I should have texted first, but then went into the porch and knocked on the door before I could change my mind. Seconds later, Matt appeared. "Still looking good, Cavanaugh," he said, and leaned in the doorframe. "Just cruising the neighborhood and banging on doors randomly, or were you looking for me?"

"I wasn't banging—I was gently rapping," I informed him. "I need to borrow a cup of sugar."

"Are you honing your culinary skills?" he asked.

"They don't need *honing*—they're *honed*."

"Cooking up something sweet, then?" He crossed his arms and smiled.

"I come over for an innocent cup of sugar, and you have to turn it into something *taw-dry*," I said, using my best southern-girl accent, my hand splayed over my innocent heart.

"Hey, I'm not the one with the dirty mind!" Matt replied and laughed. "I was just hoping for cookies."

He looked particularly fetching in a pair of faded gym shorts with the MIT logo, and an old white T-shirt that had seen better days. I sighed with appreciation and wondered if he noticed I wasn't making a lot of eye contact. I was more focused on his legs.

"Hard not to focus on the legs, I know," he said, "but a little eye contact would be nice."

"Stop reading my mind."

"You *are* a little transparent, Cavanaugh."

"I just came over for a little look-see," I informed him. "I have to get back home. Maggie's not feeling well."

"Sorry to hear it," he said. "How 'bout I come over to keep you company later?"

I hesitated. "Maybe we could make it another night when Maggie feels better. I was just lonely, wanted to see your face."

Matt pressed a kiss to my forehead. "I'm here if you need me."

MAGGIE WAS SITTING quietly in the kitchen when I returned. She had only made it halfway through her cocktail, so my chances of liquoring her up and throwing renovations at her were slim to none.

Ellen and Stogie were sprawled on the floor next to her like a pair of canine throw rugs, snoring in stereo.

"Hey, Gracie girl, how's that Quinn boy doing this evening?" Maggie asked. She must have seen me on his porch.

I pulled out a chair and sat, and pulled out another chair on which I propped my feet. "Very fine, I must say. Gets cuter every time I see him."

"Yeah, I remember when he was hell on wheels, terrorizing Cleveland Street with one of those ugly plastic tricycles." Maggie smiled at the memory. "His mother kept his hair in one of them buzz cuts—you know, like they have in the military—and his ears were bigger than Mickey Mouse's. Hard to believe he's all grown up."

"Yeah, he's definitely all grown up, but, hey—thanks for the imagery."

"So, have the two of you done the nasty yet?" Maggie stuck a finger through her gray curls and scratched.

"Nah, I'm taking my time with him. Need to break him in gently before making my move. You know, him being a kid and all."

"He looks pretty grown up to me. But what do I know, I'm the eighty-six-year-old virgin."

We shared a good laugh.

"I need to put dinner on the table," I said and stood. I reached for Maggie's glass. "Let me freshen your drink."

"You trying to get me liquored up?" Maggie asked.

"Why is everyone reading my mind tonight?" I replied.

I BRIEFLY OUTLINED a few of my renovation ideas to Maggie as I put the finishing touches on dinner and set the table. I made it all sound very simple and quick. A piece of cake. I held my breath as I waited for her response.

"Grace, if you want to spend your time and money on this old wreck of a house, be my guest," she said. "I've had no interest in doing anything to the place in years, and I guess it shows."

"Well, I don't want to get involved in any big projects, but I do have time on my hands, and I'd enjoy the work," I replied. I figured I could get everything done in a couple of weeks if I found the right contractors. "Why don't I get paint chips and fabric samples tomorrow so you can choose what you like?"

"Hell, I don't really care, Grace. You decide." Maggie slowly swirled her drink, watching the pale gold liquid race around her glass.

"Maggie, c'mon, it'll be fun! Once we get the porch fixed up—well, it's so nice out in the evenings this time of year—it would be great to sit out there with our cocktails and gossip about the neighbors." I didn't want to sell the idea too hard, but I wanted to make sure Maggie was on board.

"Maybe."

"You ready for dinner?"

"I'm not really hungry."

"I'll fix you a small plate, eat what you can."

I was glad that I didn't get a lot of resistance from Maggie, but it worried me that she agreed to my plan so readily. I didn't want to create chaos in her life at a critical time, and I suspected that some of my desire for activity was a ruse to ignore one of life's realities. My great aunt was dying, and all the renovations in the world weren't going to change that fact. It didn't seem fair to upset her life just so I could better deal with the situation.

Nonetheless, before Michael died, I had always found that a heightened level of activity was good medicine for whatever ailed me. Since then, I had simply stopped caring about the forward motion of life, and nothing had been able to distract me from my pain. So, my newfound interest in a project took me by surprise. I decided not to question Maggie's acquiescence, and take advantage of the opportunity to distract myself—and in the process provide Maggie with a little distraction, too, that might compensate her for any inconvenience.

Of course, I already had another nice distraction in the form of our handsome neighbor. If I were right about Matt, he would prove to be a whole lot more entertaining than paint chips and fabric swatches. I briefly imagined him in old jeans and a tool belt, ripped T-shirt showing tanned skin, and almost forgot about dinner. I'd refine that story line later, when I was staring at my bedroom ceiling. I thought my little story would involve, at some point, removal of the tool belt.

I turned on Maggie's ancient stereo and found an oldies station, and we had a quiet dinner together with the music playing in the background. She poked at the lasagna and sipped at her bourbon.

"Maggie, can I get you a little ice cream or something? Maybe the lasagna is a bit too heavy for your stomach," I said, not realizing until it was too late that I had just given Maggie an opportunity to tease me about my cooking. It didn't go unnoticed.

"Okay, Grace, you just walked into that one, but I guess I'll give you a pass." Maggie waved her almost-empty glass in the air; melted ice cubes slid around and clinked gently. "Nothing wrong with your cooking, girl, I'm just still a little doped up." She looked at me and gave me a conspiratorial wink.

"How about a liquid meal?" I asked. "I don't think you had one yet today, and you shouldn't go without food if you're taking Vicodin." I stood and went to the refrigerator and pulled out a can of the dietary supplement that Dr. Cunningham had recommended. I shook it before pouring it into a glass and placed it in front of Maggie.

"Is this really necessary?" she said. "I'm already having my liquids." She held her drink in the air again.

I tried to look stern as I pointed at the glass on the table.

"You're no fun," she said, put down her cocktail, and started slowing sipping the liquid meal. "Hey! Chocolate!"

"You don't have to drink it all, Maggie. Just enough to make me happy."

I finished my dinner and started clearing the table. Stogie and Ellen followed my every move. "Since when do you two think you get leftovers?" I lectured, and smiled at Maggie. "Someone is spoiling you."

Maggie glanced behind her, then back at me, and shrugged. "Innocent until proven guilty if you're referring to me," she said, and gave me another wink.

"If you two start losing your figures," I told the dogs, "blame the lady with the chocolate."

Maggie managed to finish most of the drink while folding and refolding her napkin. She struggled to her feet and picked up her glass. I took it from her, wordlessly, and set it in the sink.

"C'mon, old girl, let's get you back upstairs and in bed," I said.

"Old girl! Hell of a nerve!" Maggie exclaimed, and then was silent.

"That's it? That's all I'm getting out of you?"

"Let me get a good night's sleep, and I'll see if I can do better tomorrow," she grumbled.

"I can't wait."

Maggie gave me half a smile, and gently pinched my cheek with arthritic fingers. "You're a fresh one, you are."

I held her arm, and we made our way slowly down the hallway with both dogs in tow. When we reached the staircase, Maggie and I turned and proceeded up the stairs, treading carefully on the ruined black runner. The dogs were right behind us, Stogie navigating the stairs slowly in step with us, and Ellen waiting for more progress before taking four steps at a time.

Maggie paused halfway up, taking a moment to catch her breath as she glanced down at the dogs. Stogie wagged his stump of a tail, and then we continued upward with our awkward little parade.

)≪≪

MAGGIE SLEPT IN late the following morning. She looked more rested when she joined me in the kitchen where I was cooking eggs and bacon.

"Feel like any breakfast, old girl?" I teased, and I could see she thought about taking the bait but reconsidered.

"I wouldn't mind a cup of tea," she replied.

"No problem. The usual?"

"If you don't mind."

"How about toast?" I asked, pulling a faded crocheted cozy off of Maggie's toaster.

"I'll give it a try."

"Feeling any better this morning?"

"A bit. I slept pretty much through the night, had to get up a couple of times to pee. Stepped on Stogie once, thought he was going to have a heart attack." Maggie smiled. "He doesn't seem to be holding a grudge this morning, though."

"He's a good little guy."

"Not bad for a damn pest."

"I have to run a few errands." I put the kettle on the stove and turned on the burner. "I was thinking of taking him with me if you don't mind."

"I guess Ellen and I can hang out," Maggie said. "If I step on *her*, I might not survive the experience, though." She clapped her hands together in Ellen's direction, and Ellen hauled herself up and strolled over.

"Whaddya think, big girl, you want to hang out with Aunt Maggie today and watch TV?" Maggie grabbed Ellen's enormous hairy muzzle in her hands, pulled the obliging dog toward her face, and planted a loud kiss on her head.

I cleaned up after breakfast and made a list of items I wanted to hunt down for my porch project. I did a quick walk through the business pages of Maggie's phone book and thought longingly of using my laptop or phone for searches, but hesitated. The Internet only reminded me that I hadn't checked my email or social media accounts in months. So, I searched the old-fashioned way and found paint and fabric stores in the Springfield area. I was going to enjoy the challenge of doing renovations in unfamiliar territory, and figured that the local shops were probably a gold mine of great deals compared to Fairfield County.

I prepared a small plate of macaroni salad and fruit slices for Maggie's lunch and put it in the refrigerator, and packed up my tote with my notes, snacks, and bottled water for Stogie and me. I went upstairs to check on Maggie and Ellen, and found the girls watching *The View* on the small TV in Maggie's bedroom. Maggie was adding her own commentary, and Ellen was alternating her attention between her and the female babble on the show.

"Yeah—what the hell's wrong with a gay marriage!" Maggie yelled at the TV, apparently siding with a majority of the women. "Everybody's got a right to be happy! Even *married* people." She shook a fist at the world and continued to watch intently. "Some people are just naturally party poopers," she informed Ellen.

"I can see that you're busy," I said, deciding not to elucidate on the term "gay." I could see that Maggie had no idea what the show was referring to. Besides, I agreed with her assessment. "The boy and I are leaving, and your lunch is in the fridge. I plan to ask the hunk next door to check on you a couple of times. I'll leave a key under the 'Welcome' mat."

"Smart girl," Maggie said. "That's the last place a serial rapist would think to look."

"If one shows up, just take out your teeth."

"Smart ass," she said.

"Is that any way to talk to the person who's going to restock the bar?"

Maggie smiled, and made a quick zipping motion across her lips.

I said goodbye, grabbed my purse and tote, motioned for Stogie to follow, and headed next door. Matt was in his driveway detailing Sheila. I snickered when I saw how seriously he was tending to her. "Okay, I'm jealous," I admitted. "You give that old girl a lot of attention. And you've got your hands all over her."

"I like to treat my women well," Matt replied, grinning. "I'd be happy to give your body a good buffing, too, if you'd like."

"I believe the term is 'boffing.'"

"You do seem to think about sex a lot. I was merely offering something along the lines of a good loofah scrub." Matt gave me a long look that said something entirely different. He tossed a large yellow sponge into a bucket and stepped toward me. "Aren't we due for more dinner and conversation?" He plopped a small dollop of soap bubbles on my nose.

"Maybe." I wiped it off.

"What are you doing tonight?"

"I don't have any plans, but I'm going to be out most of the day, and I think I should spend the evening with Maggie. Would you mind looking in on her around lunchtime?"

"No problem. How about dinner tomorrow night?"

I hesitated, sorely tempted but worried about Maggie. "Let's wait and see."

Matt smiled and ran his wet fingers down the side of my face. His fingers stopped on my chin, and I felt a soapy drip work its way down my neck into the front of my tank top. He followed its course with his eyes, wiped his hands on his T-shirt, and gently tucked his fingers into my cleavage to wipe away the water.

"Ah-hem," I said, clearing my throat as a slow burn worked its way through my body. "I have things to do. You're not helping."

"You're sure about tonight?" he asked softly. "Must I beg you, or perhaps compromise my virtue?" He cocked a hip, and slowly pulled off his T-shirt in a silly strip tease while making corny electric *bow-chick-a-wow-wow* guitar sounds. Once he was shirtless and certain he had my full attention, he started a slow bump and grind, picked up the sponge and squeezed it, and sent a cascade of soap and water down his chest and stomach.

"Well, hey—" I said, enjoying the floor show. "I think you've compromised way more than your virtue. I'll try to make it worth it." I dug a dollar bill from my wallet and waved it at him. He danced up to me and I slowly tucked it into the front of his jeans.

There was applause from next door, and I could see Maggie through the screen on her porch. "Give me a minute, and I'll get *my* purse!" she yelled, waving.

"Now look what you've started," I said.

Matt did a couple of quick moves with his hips, grinned,

and removed the dollar. He snapped the bill open, folded it, and shoved it in his pocket.

STOGIE AND I had a lovely afternoon cruising around town in the Beemer getting paint samples and looking for deals on fabric. I decided to let him enjoy the luxury of German engineering after nabbing the Hudson Bay blanket from the cube. I made him swear not to say a word about it to Ellen. "She would only hold it against you," I warned.

I sang every Stogie song I knew, and even made up a new one about shoes called *Got Those (Shoes) Blues*. When I finished singing, the boy and I spent a few minutes howling together. Why bother owning a nice car if you can't have a whole other life in it?

Our first stop was the paint store, which was conveniently located a few blocks from the fabric store. Two older men who owned the pet-friendly shop made a fuss over Stogie and gave him a biscuit when he befriended a grizzled golden retriever that hung out behind their front desk.

They were very helpful once I explained the color I wanted—a custom shade of black-green that I liked using on exterior trim. They patiently mixed a few samples until they got it right. I chose a pale aqua for the porch ceiling and selected a pint sample of a dark gray to test on the new floor of the porch once it was installed.

The fabric store was a messy Mecca of fabrics stacked on long tables and piled high on shelves. There was a section dedicated to outdoor fabrics, and I found a large roll of black and cream ticking that would look great with vintage-styled furniture. I bought the whole roll since they were practically giving it away, and it felt like a major score.

On the way home, I stopped downtown at the only Starbucks I'd seen in all of our wanderings and grabbed a quick cafe latte. Stogie got half a biscotti and fresh water, and we continued home. I swung by a small liquor store a few blocks from Cleveland Street, and purchased an expensive bottle of bourbon for Maggie and wine for me.

Maggie and Ellen were sitting on the porch when we drove up, and I could tell they had missed us. Ellen stood, wagged her tail, and nearly knocked Stogie off his feet in the process.

"Did you ladies enjoy your day together?" I asked.

"We certainly did. Ellen and I bonded over TV and a couple of good naps. She's a great lady—but I have to admit, I missed the pest." Maggie reached for Stogie, and he covered her with canine kisses.

"If my watch is right, I believe it's cocktail hour," she said when Stogie finally settled down. "And don't you worry, I had a decent lunch. You can check with the babysitter."

We formed a funky conga line, and made our way into the house, down the hall, and into the parlor. I made Maggie a fine bourbon and seltzer with the upgraded brand I had purchased and settled down next to her with a glass of wine.

"So, how did your shopping go?" Maggie asked. "Did you manage to get everything done?"

"Yes, my able assistant and I got paint and fabric, and I'm ready to find some capable contractors. I have 'The Vision' in my head. Now I just need help with 'The Execution.'"

"Sounds painful." Maggie grinned at her joke and took a generous sip of her cocktail. "Mmm—I could get used to this." She held her glass out to me, and we toasted the evening.

7

"one" and "two"

MAGGIE SLEPT IN late again on Tuesday. when she failed to make an appearance by 9:00 a.m., I decided to check on her.

I found Stogie on the floor beside her bed. He opened his eyes, greeted me with a yawn, stood and stretched, and wandered from the room toward the staircase.

I gently rearranged Maggie's bedding, and when she stirred, I asked her if she needed anything. She motioned to her dentures, and I handed them over. She worked them into her mouth and smiled faintly.

"Maybe just a pill," she said. "I think I'd feel better if I could sleep a bit longer, but my painkiller has worn off. I feel like I was run over by a train."

"Is that better or worse than a truck?"

"Same pain—it just lasts longer."

I helped Maggie sit, fluffing the pillows behind her to make her more comfortable. Once I gave her a Vicodin and water to wash it down, I eased her beneath the covers again, sat at the foot of her bed, and rubbed her feet until she was snoring gently.

Downstairs, I called Dr. Cunningham's office and scheduled an appointment. I wasn't sure Maggie would be happy about seeing him again so soon, but I needed to know that I was doing everything possible for her.

The dogs were waiting patiently by the front door, so I took them for a walk. It seemed especially quiet on the street. I figured the younger neighbors had gone to work, and the older ones were staying inside since the day was already getting warm. Near the end of the block, a teenage girl seemed intent on teaching a little sprite in pink how to catch a ball. The child couldn't have been more than three years old. I feared Ellen would frighten her as we got closer and considered crossing the street. Instead, the girl gave a shriek of delight and started toward us, but the teenager pulled her back until I assured her that both dogs were harmless. We spent a few minutes hanging out on the sidewalk while the little girl threw some small toys for Stogie to retrieve. He eventually grew bored with the game, so we returned home.

I tiptoed upstairs, Stogie at my heels, and paused outside Maggie's door. I could hear her snores from where I stood so I cracked the door just wide enough to allow Stogie inside the room. "Be quiet," I whispered. He clacked over to the rug by her bed and plopped himself on the floor as I eased the door closed.

Maggie must have sensed his presence. "Is that you, pest?" she said, her voice groggy. "I've missed you. Come give me a hug." I heard Stogie scrambling to get up on the bed and opened the door again to sneak a quick peek; Stogie was already settled blissfully in Maggie's arms.

I spent a good portion of the rest of the morning tracking down contractors for my project. I needed a carpenter and painter to spruce up the porch, and a landscape contractor to manage the walkway, stairs and plants.

My preferred method of handling a project was to hire contractors that had been separated from the chaff and were capable and reliable. Unfortunately, I had no such resources in Springfield, so I was left hoping for the best and expecting the worst. I attacked the Yellow Pages with a vengeance, took names and numbers, and started making phone calls.

The first contractor I reached was an Italian named Vincent Mobilia. I had always had a soft spot in my heart for the Vinnies of the world. I couldn't remember a single time I'd been disappointed by one—it could have been some kind of macho Italian thing that made them want to please a woman—although most of them talked my ear off.

We arranged to meet the following day to discuss the job, after which he would provide an estimate. On impulse, I asked him if he knew any painters or stone contractors, and he grunted a laugh. "Lady, my whole family is related to that Michelangelo guy," he said. "Paint and stone are in our blood. I'll bring a coupla cousins with me." We signed off, and I crossed my fingers.

Just to be safe, I scheduled appointments with a few non-Vinnie contractors, as well as one with a high-end design and contracting firm located in a wealthy suburb of Springfield. I preferred having several quotes to choose from, and I had no problem with paying more for high-quality work. By the time I finished making my calls, Vinnie and his cousins had plenty of competition.

I was going over my notes when I heard movement upstairs and decided to investigate. Maggie was in the bathroom and Stogie stood guard outside. He greeted me with one of his odd little grins, his mouth so wide I could see all of his teeth.

"My goodness, young man, don't you look tanned and rested," I commented.

"He damn well should be!" Maggie said loudly from behind the closed door. "We had one hell of a nap!"

"So—you're feeling better?" I called back, trying not to match Maggie's volume.

"Maybe not better, but at least I'm what they call 'vertical'!"

"In this house, we'll take what we can get."

"How pathetic are we?" she responded loudly.

I BEGAN INTERVIEWING contractors the following day, and most of them had no problem grasping my vision for Maggie's porch and yard. They all appeared competent and their estimates fair and reasonable.

I'll admit to having had a soft spot for Vinnie Mobilia and his two rather hairy cousins, Christian and Christopher, both of whom went by the name Chris.

I told Vinnie I found that a little confusing, but he just shrugged.

"No problem," he said. "You can just refer to them as 'Bonehead One' and 'Bonehead Two.'"

"I think it would be easier to just call them 'One' and 'Two,'" I said.

"Hey, whatever works."

The Mobilias were definitely on my short list, but I felt it would be rude to cancel on the contractors I had yet to interview so I promised to get back to Vinnie by the end of the week.

In the midst of it all, Maggie and I made a trip to the hospital for her appointment. A nurse escorted her to the lab for blood work, and I met with Dr. Cunningham.

"She's not doing well," I informed him.

He didn't seem particularly alarmed as he queried me and jotted down my responses in Maggie's file. When he was finished, he closed the file and put it on his desk, smiled, and straightened his tie. "Any questions?" he asked. He probably assumed I was prepared for what was coming.

"No—no questions," I said, not wanting to disappoint him, acting like it was just business as usual.

I HIRED THE Mobilias for several reasons.

First of all, I could tell they were eager to make me happy. Major points. Secondly, they agreed to a fairly aggressive schedule—two weeks to get the job done—and once I told them my great aunt was ill, they were sympathetic and promised to work as quickly and quietly as possible. Good guys. Lastly, they were an entertaining bunch, and "One" and "Two" were easy on the eyes—nice bonuses that sealed the deal.

When I awoke the following Wednesday, the day before the Mobilias were scheduled to arrive, I surveyed my frumpy little bedroom, and the buzz I experienced from planning the transformation of the porch extended itself to the possibilities that existed throughout the rest of the old house. Because my bedroom was the single most depressing place I'd ever slept, it was an easy target. In particular, it lacked a desk or any other space where I could comfortably use my laptop. I could have used the kitchen table temporarily, but I thought it would be nice to surf the web without Maggie looking over my shoulder. I missed the Internet, even if I was still avoiding my email, and wanted a place to reconnect in peace.

In Greenwich, I had a spacious home office on our second floor, with a lot of surface area for organizing my projects. I had a desktop computer with an enormous monitor, and all of the state-of-the-art devices necessary to a perfectly trick-out office. Michael was my in-house technology consultant, and he made sure everything was always in excellent working order. Call me spoiled.

When I moved out of our house and into the apartment, I took my laptop with me, but never once turned it on. My email wasn't the only thing I was avoiding. I had turned my back on the world, and avoiding social media and email was part of my strategy. But, enough was enough. I figured I could do a little harmless snooping on the information highway without having to make any unwanted social contact.

So, in addition to making some other critical changes to my bedroom, I would add a workspace. The focal point of the space would be a desk of some sort, and I decided to rope Matt into furniture shopping with me since I had been putting him off for a week. Plus, I had tortured myself long enough with "The Handyman Loses Tool Belt" fantasy and wanted to treat myself to some contact with the real thing.

I considered taking one of the dogs with us, but I thought Maggie might need them both. She hadn't slept well again and had woken up more groggy than usual. She promised me that she'd be fine for a couple of hours, but I worried anyway. I made certain she had the portable phone I purchased for her bedroom, my cell phone number, bottled water, and a variety of snacks.

While I was getting everything organized, Maggie looked

from Ellen to Stogie and back at Ellen before giving a sigh. "Is she ever going to leave?" she asked, throwing an impatient hand in my direction.

"Hey, I heard that," I said, just as the doorbell rang, signaling Matt's arrival. "I expect everyone to behave while I'm gone. No shenanigans."

Maggie raised her right hand in a three-fingered salute. "We swear not to have any fun while you're gone." She winked at Ellen and Stogie, and I hesitated before answering the door.

I DROVE THE Beemer.

Matt admired its interior, running a hand over the leather seats and burled wood dashboard. He pulled the owner's manual out of the glove box and whistled at the car's navigational system and wireless technology.

"Not as much personality as Sheila, but I can see how you might get used to this," he said.

"You're a little fickle. Something sweet comes along with a few new bells and whistles, and 'The Classic' just doesn't cut it anymore?"

"We *are* talking about *cars* here—?" Matt rolled his eyes and stuffed the manual back into the glove box.

"Of course. Does Sheila know about this?"

"Don't worry, she can handle it. She's pretty solid emotionally." He leaned over and gently tapped the end of my nose with his finger to emphasis his point. I grabbed his finger with my teeth, doing a quick catch-and-release that made him laugh.

"Well, good," I said after giving up his finger. "I'd hate to see her fall apart. Oh, wait—she already has."

Matt groaned at my joke and turned his attention to the car's GPS. I had brought Maggie's outdated Yellow Pages with us and had decided on an alphabetical approach to shopping that made Matt a little nervous.

"Just begin at 'A' and punch in the first address," I instructed.

"Lots of letters in that pesky little alphabet, Cavanaugh," he pointed out. "Couldn't you just Google these guys on your cell or something? Call them first?"

"Don't be a girl, Matt," I chided. "Think of this as an adventure, like a treasure hunt."

"Wish I *was* a girl right now; I might be enjoying myself more."

"You're shopping with an expert. Pay attention and you might learn something."

Matt processed my advice, and then said, "Well, you *have* been around long enough to know what you're doing."

"Hey—don't be a smart ass just because you're cranky!"

Matt put an index finger on my thigh, traced suggestively, and said, "Maybe we should head back home where you can punish me properly."

It sounded like a great idea, but we had shopping to do, and I had to keep my priorities straight. So, instead, I drove on, but began working on Season 1, Episode 2: "A Proper Spanking from a Proper Lady."

Fortunately for Matt, I got lucky at the second shop and found a nicely proportioned walnut desk from the early 1900s that was in very good condition. I could envision how nice it would look once it was cleaned and waxed, so I bought it and arranged to have it delivered to Cleveland Street.

After I completed the transaction, Matt insisted on buying us a late lunch at the deli next door. We carried our sandwiches to a small table near a window.

"I'm a little disappointed that we found a desk so quickly," I said as I unwrapped my turkey sandwich. "The chase is part of the fun, and I hate when it ends too soon."

"I couldn't disagree with you more," Matt said, and raised an eyebrow.

"I guess we're not talking about shopping anymore—what, you don't view anticipation as part of the fun?" I asked.

"Feels more like the slow and painful death of one's hopes and dreams," Matt said.

"Don't be such a drama queen."

"First I'm a girl, and then I'm a queen. This might explain why I'm not getting anywhere with you."

"Why don't we step back into my office, and I'll straighten you out," I said. "You seem to be suffering from at least one misconception."

"Which is…?

"Step back into my office and find out."

We finished our sandwiches and headed out to the parking lot. I walked over to my car, grabbed the door handle, and the keyless remote in my bag popped the lock. I started to open the door, but Matt put a hand on my shoulder to stop me.

"I'm done being the girl," he said, grasping my wrist and leading me to the passenger's side. He opened the door and motioned me inside. He closed the door, and a moment later slid behind the wheel.

"Okay, Cavanaugh, straighten me out." He leaned over the console and pulled me to him, his hands circling my waist. He slowly slid them up to my breasts and cupped them gently. I stopped breathing while he fanned his thumbs over my nipples.

When he saw he had my undivided attention, he covered my mouth with his and kissed me deeply.

I'm sure I would have climbed on top of him if it weren't for the Beemer's spacious center console, fully equipped with dual cup holders, gearshift, drive mode selector, and media and navigation toggle.

An elderly gentleman walking by the Beemer glanced inside briefly, smiled, gave us a shaky thumbs up, and continued on.

The drive home was delicious torture. Matt drove with one hand on the wheel, the other caressing my inner left thigh. I finally pressed his hand between my legs as it approached home base and let his fingers cup me with a pressure that took my breath away. I put my head back on the headrest, closed my eyes, and laced my fingers between his.

By mutual agreement, we took the party to Matt's place. We managed to make it into his driveway without wrecking the car, where we groped and groaned over the console for a minute before getting out. I met Matt halfway around the car, and we walked quickly to the porch. He unlocked the front door, took my hand, and led me into the hallway.

A cushy beige carpet covered the stairs and muted our footsteps as we made our way to the second floor. Matt's bedroom faced the street; the dappled afternoon light filtered through enormous maples in the front yard and lit the room with a soft glow. The windows were open, and linen curtains framing the window shuddered in the breeze.

Matt excused himself, headed down the hall, and ducked inside the bathroom. I looked about his room. A modern queen-sized bed draped with a dark gray comforter shared space with vintage side tables and a dresser. I caught the faint scent of Matt's aftershave as I studied a framed photo of a smiling older couple, whose resemblance to Matt and his brother was so strong that I had no doubt I was looking at Eleanor and Casey Quinn.

When Matt returned, he was wearing his gorgeous tan and a pair of navy boxer shorts that sat low on his waist. The shorts were tented in front where his erection pushed out from his muscled abdomen in a perfect right angle.

"My-oh-my," I said slowly, and motioned to the front of his shorts. "I haven't seen one of those in years. You are so young and gorgeous." I met Matt's blue eyes, smiled, and beckoned to him with my fingers. "Don't be frightened, young man. Come to the nice lady."

Matt's voice was slightly husky, but he was clearly amused. "I just hope you're not *too* nice, ma'am," he said. "A little naughty would be a good thing right about now."

"I think I can handle that. Come closer, and I'll show you."

As he approached, I reached out, clasped his erection, and pulled him to me. Time slowed to a crawl and then reversed, and everything in my peripheral vision—the walls, the windows, the lamp on his nightstand—fell away, and I just existed in that moment. I was eighteen again, young and very much alive.

Matt covered my mouth with his in a slow, lingering kiss while I explored his body with my hands, savoring the feel of his warm, taut skin. He slipped his tongue past my lips and delved deeper. I closed my eyes as his hands slid down my back and he drew me close.

He finally broke away, took my hand, and led me to his bed.

8

he's a john wayne fan

My desk arrived the next morning. Two deliverymen carried it upstairs to my bedroom, and, per my instructions, placed it between the windows that overlooked the backyard and Maggie's old-fashioned garden.

I sat at the desk, perched on a chair borrowed from the kitchen, with my laptop open, staring at the screen. I had purchased a temporary Wi-Fi hotspot at the neighborhood Radio Shack but couldn't quite make myself click my email icon because my screensaver made my heart ache. Michael had taught Vertigo how to smile on command, and the two of them were hamming it up on the dock of our house on Lake Waramaug.

A momentary battle with guilt made my throat tight and my palms sweaty. The detailed pictures in my mind from the previous afternoon with Matt seemed a betrayal to the handsome man smiling back at me from my laptop screen. I rolled my shoulders and told myself everything was all right, everything was okay: *I'm okay, you're okay, everyone's okay.* I wiped my hands on my sweats and took a sip of cold coffee I had brought upstairs, moved the arrow on my laptop screen to my email icon, and clicked.

Sixteen months of unopened email was not a pretty sight. I thought everyone would simply stop emailing me eventually, and I could quietly disappear from cyberspace. Not so. My little email inbox notification proved that theory wrong with a five-figure number of waiting messages.

While I sat, wallowing in guilt and staring at the screen, Ellen wandered into the room. She looked at the screen and appeared to be perplexed.

"I know, girlfriend, it's not very pretty," I said, rubbing one of her ears between my fingers. It was going to take hours to get through my email, so I decided to edit the junk for my first session. Anything stored under the promotions tab went into the trash. The social tab was a little more complicated. Just handling those emails would take forever, so I went downstairs to the kitchen for a fresh cup of coffee. I returned to my desk, took a sip of the hot brew, and resumed work.

I had really enjoyed the previous afternoon in bed with Matt, but my feelings of guilt persisted. I was hoping—on the plus side—that guilt was taking up some of the room grief had occupied in my head. I wasn't certain I preferred it, but was hopeful the guilt was only temporary, and when it finally disappeared, the grief wouldn't return to fill the void it left behind. Call me a guilt-and-grief-ridden optimist.

I took a break from deleting Facebook, LinkedIn, and Instagram notifications, picked up my cell phone, and called Matt. He answered on the second ring.

"Hey," he said.

I paused for a moment before responding. "Is that how you greet all of your girlfriends?" I finally asked.

"Nah, just the ones who wear me out so that's all I got left to give."

"I thought I was the one who lacked stamina," I said. "And it's 'have' left to give."

"You calling me a wimp who can't speak proper English?"

"Maybe."

"Come over and try calling me that to my face." I could hear the smile in his voice.

"Sure, so you can take advantage of me again? You *bastard*," I said teasingly. "So, I was thinking maybe we should have dinner tonight. You got a whole lot of Cavanaugh yesterday for a lousy submarine sandwich."

"Are you filing a complaint?" asked Matt. "I thought their subs were pretty good."

"Not bad, but you still owe me. Maybe you need to get out your *Suma Katra* and come up with a little something special."

"I believe it's *Kama Sutra*."

"Tomato, toe-mah-toe. You still owe me." I laughed, and my body warmed pleasantly.

We agreed to have a late dinner once I made sure Maggie was settled in for the night, and reluctantly said our good-byes.

I spent the rest of the morning sorting through my social inbox, aggravating old carpel tunnel problems, but finally deleted most of the notifications. I was ready to quit for the day, but Ellen seemed comfortable lying at my feet and I didn't have the heart to disturb her. I made an executive decision and dove into my primary inbox shortly before noon.

I thought going through my emails would be easy enough, but I was wrong. I just assumed my status as a widow would keep people polite and at bay, but everyone seemed hell bent on getting my attention. After scanning over twenty messages from friends, business associates, and clients, I decided on yet another approach. Delete everything and let technological survival of the fittest do its thing. If anyone really wanted to get in touch with me, he or she would hang in there.

Since I didn't have the nerve to execute that plan, I closed my laptop and decided to go downstairs for a sandwich. "To hell with all of them, El!" I grumbled. "I have better things to do with my time. Like eat."

Maggie was sitting in the parlor, watching the thirteen-inch black-and-white TV she kept on a sideboard. I handed her a duplicate of my turkey sandwich and sat down.

"How the hell can you watch that thing?" I asked, squinting at the miserable little set. "It doesn't even have a remote. How do you change channels?"

"I don't, unless I'm feeling feisty. I tried to teach the pest how to move the dial, but he just looked at me like I was an idiot."

I chuckled at the image of her pantomimic efforts to teach the boy to be useful with a television dial. "Can't say I blame him," I said. "I'm sure he's never seen a TV without a remote—probably had no idea what you were trying to get him to do."

"That might explain his resistance. I thought he was just giving me attitude." Maggie grunted a laugh and squeezed one of Stogie's velvet ears. He was lying next to her on the floor, legs kicked out behind him, fully engrossed in the old Western that Maggie had on for their viewing pleasure.

"Are you actually watching this movie, Maggie?" I asked. "Seems a little dull."

"Don't offend the pest," she replied. "He loves the horsies.

Can't get enough of them," she added, giving his ear another tender squeeze.

"Maggie, have you ever heard the terms 'LCD, OLED, flatscreen'?" I asked. "Do you think Stogie might like seeing horsies that weren't in black-and-white, and were a *little* closer to life-size?"

"Don't talk to me like I'm brain-dead, Gracie girl," Maggie replied. "Everyone knows what LC-whatevers are all about. Even the pest here has been going online researching our options."

"Do you have any idea what you're talking about?" I asked, amused.

"None whatsoever. I can only say that I'm watching a lot more of the tube than usual, which in my case has been quite an education."

ONCE I HAD Maggie tucked in for the evening—snug in her room with the dogs and her TV—I headed over to the Quinn's.

Matt answered the door in a towel, explained that he had just showered after a long run, and asked me to amuse myself while he got dressed for dinner. That precipitated a bit of back and forth about how I might "amuse" myself while he was getting dressed, but we agreed to part company after a lengthy oral exchange that involved a little groping under the towel on my part.

I wandered to the kitchen where I could hear Quinn playing pool in the basement, so I made a show of treading slowly and gracefully down the stairs to say hello to him and his friends.

"Well, if it isn't Grace!" Quinn yelled out cheerfully when he saw me coming down the stairs. "Should I hold my breath and put my hands over my ears?"

One of the men playing pool with him was the redhead who had witnessed my previous Humpty-Dumpty-like descent. He hooted loudly, turned to the new guys in the room, and described "The Incident," adding a reenactment of some of its finer moments. The replay concluded with him spread-eagled on the basement floor.

I crossed the room to the pool table. "Get a grip, Red," I growled. "If you don't behave, I'll grab a stick and whoop your—I assume—very *white* ass." Red continued to make fun of me, so I picked up a short cue and said, "You asked for it! Rack 'em up."

The men all bowed after I cleared the table on my first turn (a *little* cheating was involved), and I made my getaway to a hardy round of applause and loud whistles. I went back upstairs and met Matt walking down the hall to the kitchen. He raised a questioning eyebrow.

"Don't worry, I kept my clothes on," I said, "but it was touch and go there for a while—the money was tempting."

"I'm glad that cooler heads prevailed." Matt smiled at my obvious pleasure and led me out the back door to Sheila.

We had a wonderful dinner at a local restaurant, one of the last Italian holdouts in a primarily Hispanic neighborhood a few blocks away. The owners, Tony and Marco, spent a lot of time sitting with us, reminiscing about the good old days. Matt's parents had been regulars at the restaurant for over thirty years, and the Quinns were like family. Dinner was on the house, but Matt left a huge tip for our young waiter.

It was late when we turned into Matt's driveway. Maggie's house was dark, except for the light I had left on in the living room. Matt invited me in, but I figured Quinn was probably home, and I knew the walls were thin on Cleveland Street. I asked Matt if we could just sit in the car and talk.

Matt suggested we find better real estate and move next door to the Beemer. We crossed the two yards hidden in the shadows of the maple trees, where the blue light of the streetlamps disappeared, and the lawn was black. I had the car's remote in my bag, and its door clicked open when I touched the handle. I crawled into the spacious back seat and kicked off my shoes. Matt followed and closed the door.

He waited a minute for the interior lights to go off, and then pulled me to him. I was wearing a short, gathered skirt with a T-shirt, and I lifted the skirt as I climbed on top of Matt and faced him. His jeans were soft and warm against my inner thighs.

Matt slowly rolled my T-shirt inside out, beginning at the waist, and I extended my arms up as it went over my head. Cool air caressed my skin. Matt briefly mouthed each of my breasts through my bra, touched his lips to mine through my shirt, and finished removing it. He unhooked my bra and slipped it off. I returned the favor by removing his T-shirt and tossing it on the seat.

Matt closed his arms around me, and I leaned against him, taking in his clean scent and delighting in the heady sensation of skin against skin. He caressed my naked back, and worked his hands into my hair, his fingers massaging my scalp. We simply sat there, enjoying the quiet of the car and the warmth of our embraced bodies. The windows of the car slowly fogged over, and we were alone in the world.

I don't know how long we sat there, only that I eventually fell asleep, because I woke up in Michael's arms. It took a minute for me to realize where I was, but it wasn't until after my lips had formed his name.

THE MOBILIA GANG arrived Thursday morning at eight to begin the destruction and eventual reconstruction of 101 Cleveland Street. I put a large carafe of coffee and a box of donuts on a card table in the front yard, since I had learned years ago that nothing says "Welcome" and "Stay and Work Long Hours" to contractors more than Dunkin' Donuts.

Even Maggie came out to watch the amazing efficiency of the three men. We sat together on the lawn in two of the decrepit porch chairs, watching Vinnie blow through the removal of the porch floorboards and screened panels as One and Two cleared away the existing landscaping and concrete walkway. By noon, everything that needed to be removed was gone, thrown into a large dumpster that had been delivered shortly after the gang had arrived.

Vinnie made a phone call over a third cup of coffee and a fourth donut, and minutes later a load of lumber arrived. The young Italian delivering the lumber stayed to help cut and install the floorboards. Maggie and I got high on the smell of freshly cut cedar and decided that lunch was in order. We went inside, and I made egg salad sandwiches.

One and Two requested a meeting with me, so I tucked Maggie in bed with the dogs for an afternoon nap and joined them on the front lawn. We went over the landscape plan, and Two headed off to find the plantings I specified while One stayed and helped Vinnie and his young friend finish the porch floor. By the end of the day, most of the floorboards were cut and installed. We said our good-byes, and I headed in for cocktails with Maggie.

It took longer than usual to get Maggie downstairs. Her grip on the rail was unsteady, so I tucked my arm under hers. I barked a "Stay!" to the anxious dogs at the top of the stairs so they wouldn't trip us as we negotiated our descent. Jesus, Mary and Joseph joined us repeatedly on our journey. By the time we reached the bottom step, my neck and shoulders ached from holding Maggie up.

"I apologize for being such a damn pain in the ass," she said when we finally reached the parlor and sat down. "Maybe I'm spending too much time in bed, but those stairs are getting harder on me every day." She had difficulty catching her breath, so I went into the kitchen and got her a glass of water.

The stunned look on her face when she realized the glass was missing her favorite ingredients sent me into a fit of laughter.

"First the damn stairs, now this!" she grumbled. "Is there no end to the indignities? Get me a goddamn bourbon, Gracie girl!" Maggie handed me the offending glass with her right hand and pointed to the kitchen with her left. I took the glass, still laughing, and disappeared.

"What happened to the pest and my big girl?" Maggie asked loudly through the closed kitchen door. I was in the middle of mixing her drink, but set it down on the counter and went down the hall to the staircase. Ellen and Stogie were still sitting at the top, obediently following my instructions. When they saw me, two pairs of ears bobbed up and down.

"Well—aren't you two good little doggies? Okay, at least one of you doesn't qualify as 'little'—but come on down." I motioned for them. "Maggie's waiting for you."

Later that evening, once Maggie had finished pushing her food around on her dinner plate, we, once again, faced the ordeal of getting her back upstairs to her bedroom. I almost called Matt to help, but I knew Maggie would be mortified. I did my best to hold her steady. It was exhausting for both of us, and I knew we couldn't continue doing it much longer. I had to come up with a better solution, the obvious one being to move her bed downstairs. I wasn't sure Maggie would be willing to make that concession to her illness, but it appeared to be our only option.

After a brief protest, I stayed with Maggie while she used the toilet, and helped her to her room to undress and slip on her nightgown.

"We never did get you new underwear, did we?" I commented. "You might want to do me a favor and let me take you shopping."

"What, you don't like these panties? They're my best pair, my favorites."

"That's scary."

"Bought them downtown at Steigers—1992," she said. "Can't get them there anymore since they tore the place down and put up some damn office buildings. I've had to make them last."

"Maggie, your underwear has survived longer than most marriages. I think it's time to give them up. If you don't feel up to shopping, I could buy some for you. Or we could go online and order some."

"Online, my ass! They'd probably send me underwear with a silly little strap in the back, and it would get lost in my butt crack. I would spend all of my time trying to yank it out." Maggie demonstrated, and I laughed. "If that's not a pretty sight," she said, "I don't know what is. Not exactly how I want to be remembered, Grace."

"I promise you won't have to wear a thong," I said as Maggie struggled to straighten her nightgown, which had wrapped itself between her legs during her floorshow. I helped her to tug it into submission. "How about a shopping trip?"

"What would the pest do without me while I was gone, eh? Gracie girl, given my situation, I think I can make these underwear last a while longer." Maggie patted my arm, sat down on the bed, and let me help her move her legs up and under the covers. I tucked her in and gave her a gentle squeeze on her shoulder.

"Grace?" she said.

"Yes?"

"Thanks for staying with me. Don't know what I would have done. I don't want to be alone."

"Neither do I—it's a fair deal." I thought about bringing up the subject of moving her downstairs but decided it could wait until the morning.

"Where's the pest?" she asked.

"I'll send him up after I let him out."

I retrieved her denture dish from the nightstand and handed it to her. "I can soak those for you if you'd like." She removed her dentures, put them in the dish, and handed them back to me.

"Thanths, Gwathie gurl."

"Anytime, Mags." I shut off the light and stood in the dark doorway.

"*Wehl?*" Maggie said in the dark.

"I was just leaving," I replied, and closed the door.

⟩⟨⟨⟨

IT WAS TEN o'clock Friday morning, and Maggie and I were settled in our chairs on the front lawn watching the progress Vinnie was making on the porch. Maggie and I wore oversized straw hats and enormous sunglasses that I had purchased for the event.

Vinnie had finished the floorboards and was getting ready to build new frames for the screened panels that would enclose the porch. One was at a shop ordering the new wrought iron railing for the stairs, and Two was laying the bluestone walkway.

"Maggie, I was thinking about how hard it's getting for you to get up and down the stairs," I said over the din of power tools and loud conversation between Vinnie and Two. "I don't know how you'd feel about it, but we could make you a pretty nice bedroom downstairs in the living room. We could move your bed and dresser down and make the space comfortable. I'll understand if you don't want to leave your bedroom, but it might be a whole lot easier for you."

She seemed to ponder it. "It would also make it easier to be on time for cocktails, wouldn't it?" She smiled at me and patted my arm. "I know I can't stay upstairs, Grace. Just the thought of trying to get up there for my afternoon nap has me worn out. Maybe if we strapped a saddle on Ellen—" We both laughed at the thought of Maggie astride the big girl.

After Maggie had finished a liquid meal for lunch, I helped her out of her chair, and we started for the front porch so I could get her into the house for a nap. She was exhausted by the morning's activities and leaned heavily on me. When Vinnie saw we were having difficulty getting up the first step—the old porch rail was gone—he wasted no time in coming to our aid. He grabbed a clean shirt from his car and changed so he wouldn't get construction dust all over Maggie.

He didn't need my assistance, so I just trailed behind them as they climbed the stairs. Vinnie had a firm grip around Maggie's substantial waist, and she clung to him for dear life. She cursed a blue streak that would have made a sailor blush, but Vinnie only laughed and kept her moving.

"You're doin' great, Mrs. R," he said. "You and I should take this show on the road. It's very entertainin'."

"Entertaining, my Catholic ass!" Maggie cackled, and briefly faltered. For a moment, I thought that she was going to fall back on me, so I quickly put my hands on her hips.

"Do you have her, Vinnie?" I asked. "It's looking a little scary back here."

"No worries, Grace. She's all mine."

Maggie insisted that she could get to her bedroom by herself once they cleared the stairs, but Vinnie held her arm all the way to her room. After she sat down, he carefully removed her shoes. When it was obvious that Maggie couldn't raise her legs high enough for the bed, Vinnie wrapped his big hands around her calves and gently swung her legs up for her. He straightened her dress out when he was done.

"Don't get too personal there, Vincent," Maggie said. "The Church might not approve."

"Don't you worry, Mrs. R, you're talkin' to a good Catholic boy."

I watched from the doorway, touched by Vinnie's kindness, but overwhelmed by the progression of Maggie's illness and my inadequacies. I wasn't sure I could get her back downstairs for dinner; even more daunting was the trip back up for bed. I got a headache just thinking about it.

After Vinnie had done all he could for Maggie, she dismissed him with a wave of her hand. "Get the hell out of here so I can get my beauty sleep," she ordered.

"Yes, ma'am," he said, raising his hand in a salute. He grinned and turned for the door, giving me a wink on his way out.

While Maggie napped, I decided it would be more useful to take action regarding her care instead of sitting around worrying. I knew I could ask Matt for help in a pinch, but I didn't want to complicate my relationship with him by relying on him too much. I needed professional help.

I called Dr. Cunningham's office, spoke with one of the women who worked the front desk, and asked for a referral to a local home health care agency. She promised to have someone contact me as soon as possible. I also requested a call back from Dr. Cunningham and gave her my cell phone number. I needed advice and a sympathetic ear, even if the best I could hope for were silent nods and tie straightening on the other end of the line.

Once I hung up, I tucked my cell phone in my back pocket, roused Ellen and Stogie who were napping in patches of sunlight on the kitchen floor and headed out for a walk.

I looked for signs of Matt as we passed his house, but everything was quiet. I experienced a brief high-school girl moment and was disappointed that he wasn't sitting at home by a window, waiting for me to walk by. I smiled at my silliness and enjoyed the simple pleasure of wanting someone.

We took our time circling the block and sat on the steps in front of Stan's enjoying the fresh air and sunshine. We weren't there for long before Father Brian appeared (hey, maybe *he* was waiting by the window). He was concerned that he hadn't seen Maggie at Mass recently, and I told him she had taken a turn for the worse.

"I'm sorry to hear that, Grace, darlin'," Father Brian said. "Maggie has been one of our most faithful parishioners for years. I can't imagine my flock without her."

"I'm sure she misses being here, Father. I bet your 'flock' is a little less colorful in her absence."

"More than a little, Grace. There are stories I could tell you, but then I'd have to shoot you, darlin', and the Church might frown on it." He laughed pleasantly. "Do you think she would mind a visit from an old priest?"

"I'm sure she would love it. You could join us for cocktails and dinner this evening. She'll get a big kick out of torturing you outside the safety of Stan's."

"Of what?" Father Brian asked.

"Come on, you've never read your sign?"

"I get the feeling that the apple has not fallin' far from the familial tree." He smiled. "I'd love t'see Maggie."

"Cocktails are at five o'clock and dinner is at six."

"It's my turn to perform Mass, so I can't join the two of you for dinner, but I can certainly be there for cocktails."

"Cocktails, it is then." I considered chastising him for roping me into moving in with Maggie but thought better of it. I hadn't decided yet whether or not he had done me a favor, or even if Maggie's story about his insisting she call me held water.

Father Brian smiled broadly and said, "Now that we have that settled, who are these two handsome beasts?" Stogie and Ellen beamed at his attention, and he sat on the stairs with us for a few minutes enjoying the sun and petting the dogs.

"I used t'have a lovely setter, her name was Belle," Father Brian said. "My one great love. She's been gone for years, but I still sometimes expect t'see her waitin' at the door for me at the end of the day." He gave the dogs one last pat, offered me a small salute, and stood.

"See you at five, then, Grace, darlin'."

"We won't start without you."

"Knowin' Maggie Reilly, I'd better be on time then, hadn't I?"

When Maggie finally awoke, it was after four. I gave her pain medication, helped her to the bathroom, and told her Father Brian planned to join us for cocktails. She looked pleased as she opened the door to her closet and rummaged through it for a suitable outfit.

"Is there anything I can do to help?" I asked.

"I'm trying to find something that doesn't show a lot of cleavage," she said. "I would hate to have Father Brian abandon his vows of celibacy." She looked at me. "Why are you grinning?"

"Like I've said before, I've seen your underwear. Women who wear old lady underwear don't own dresses that show their tits."

"Potty mouth," she said.

"Oh, you're one to talk," I replied.

I decided to give Maggie some time alone to get ready for our guest because she seemed to be doing better. I went to check on her after twenty minutes had passed. As I neared the top of the stairs, I heard her humming and talking to Stogie. Obviously, the pain medication had kicked in. I tapped on the door and found her ready to come downstairs and her mood appeared much improved.

She had somehow managed to put on a clean dress and had worked on her hair, although it was decidedly flat on one side. Getting her downstairs was not as difficult as it usually was, but it was still hard work. I got her settled in one of the parlor chairs, and went into the kitchen to make a small tray of cheese and crackers.

It was five o'clock sharp when Father Brian rang the doorbell. Ellen and Stogie raced down the hall to greet him, and he made a great show of being glad to see them. We cut through the living room into the parlor, the dogs on our heels.

"Well, if it isn't my favorite bag of wind," cracked Maggie when she saw Father Brian. "Still putting the neighbors to sleep at Mass?"

"I do my best to hold up to a certain standard of tedium," he shot back with a smile. He crossed the room and laid a gentle hand on her shoulder. "It's good to see you, Maggie. You're a sight for sore eyes."

"More likely I'm *making* your eyes sore."

"With the glaring light of your beauty, lass."

Maggie laughed and invited him to take the seat next to her. I took his drink order and disappeared into the kitchen. I could hear the continued exchange between the two of them, and their equally brazen comments made me smile.

When I returned with a tray of appetizers and Father Brian's cocktail, he and Maggie were recounting the days when the neighborhood was young, and life was full of promise. Father Brian had been assigned to Stan's when he was in his twenties, and then reassigned later in his life, so his history with Maggie went back a long time.

"I remember you and your lovely sisters attending Mass together when you all still lived here on Cleveland Street," he said. "Seems like yesterday."

"Not to me," Maggie said. "Seems like a lifetime ago. I miss them."

"I visited Anne recently, and it was sad t'see her in such a state."

"Still alive, Father, but no one's really home," Maggie replied sadly, tapping her head with a bent finger. "She doesn't know me anymore. Her doctors don't expect she'll be with us much longer."

Maggie's older sister Elizabeth had died over a decade ago, and Anne, also older, had been in a nursing home in West Springfield for the past several years suffering from Alzheimer's. I hadn't seen either of them since I was a teenager; they were matronly by that time, but their beauty and romantic adventures were legendary. As I recalled, Anne had met and married a handsome Irishman from County Cork; and Elizabeth, despite her many suitors, had eventually settled down with a boy she had known since the first grade.

Maggie had always been on the sidelines, living in their shadows, watching them marry and raise families as she continued living with their parents. I could tell from old photographs that Maggie wasn't a homely girl, but she didn't compare favorably to her two older sisters. I could only imagine her self-perception was a bit harsh given the circumstances, but I knew there was probably another reason she never married. Her father died shortly after Elizabeth gave birth to her first son and Anne was newly wed, and their mother feared living alone. I figured Maggie never planned on living with her mother forever; it just worked out that way.

Shortly before six, Father Brian left for Mass, but promised Maggie he'd visit again soon. He let himself out, and Maggie and I remained in the parlor, talking about family history and life in Hungry Hill. I finally got up to start dinner and laughed at Maggie's expression when I asked her if she was done with cocktail hour.

"You'd think I'd have you properly trained by now," she said, waving her glass at me. "Get me another one and feed these poor dogs while you're at it. The pest is starting to look at me a little funny. He's beginning to drool. If Ellen starts wondering what I taste like, I'm finished." When Ellen heard her name, she came over and put her head in Maggie's lap.

I gave the dogs extra kibble and fresh water, and once they finished eating, sent them out the back door. I instructed Ellen to keep Stogie in our yard and out of trouble, but knew it was a lot to ask. There were times I felt guilty for expecting so much of her.

When I returned to the parlor with Maggie's drink, she asked me to go upstairs and get a box of old photos she kept in a closet in the third bedroom. I found it beneath a pile of old clothes and discarded household items, and realized that I would have to sort through decades of clutter once Maggie was gone.

I delivered the box to Maggie, and she motioned for me to sit next to her. She began shuffling through the stack of photos, introducing me to relatives I never heard of, and filling me in on their backgrounds.

In one photo, my great-grandfather was perched on the driver's bench of a horse-drawn fire wagon. He wore a dark cap, white shirt, and dark trousers with suspenders.

"I didn't know my great-grandfather was a fireman," I said.

"For about a week," Maggie told me. "He looked handsome in the uniform, but he wasn't accustomed to horses. He was born in the city and didn't grow up around them. He couldn't seem get the hang of it."

"Too bad. He does look pretty cool."

"Tell me about it. How do you think he met my mother? She took one look at him in that outfit, and it was all over."

In another photo, Maggie and her sisters were very young, wearing white dresses, white stockings, and buttoned Mary Jane's. Maggie stood in the middle, her gaze fixed on her feet.

"So that's where your obsession with shoes began," I observed.

"First pair of new shoes I ever owned." Maggie took the picture from me. "I loved the buttons. I was mad for the buttons. I was born just before the Great Depression, so we never had nice things. I don't know how my parents managed to afford these, but I loved them."

At the bottom of the box were several pictures of my mother, taken when she was a little girl. It was hard for me to imagine her so young.

"Your mother was such a sweet thing," Maggie said. "She was always a favorite of my mother's and mine. I remember the time we took her to Boston for the day. She became so homesick we had to leave early." She chuckled at the memory and pulled out another picture, one that I'd never seen of my sisters and me. We were getting ready to go to a family wedding, all dolled up in dresses, standing on the front steps of the house on Cleveland Street.

"I remember that day, Maggie, but I don't remember having our picture taken. Did my father take it?" I asked.

"No, Gracie girl, I did," Maggie replied, smiling at the memory. "The three of you were pretty as a picture—so I took one."

IT WAS A quiet Saturday morning, the last day of June.

The construction crew was gone for the weekend, and Maggie was napping in her bedroom with the dogs. I took the opportunity to tear my little bedroom apart and clean it from top to bottom, washing all of the woodwork, cleaning the windows again, and vacuuming and scrubbing the old oak floors. I tossed all of my bedding into the washing machine in the basement, and organized my new desk and thoroughly dusted it, as well as the two ancient end tables on each side of the bed and the old dresser.

On impulse, I went online and found several local bedding stores. After numerous calls, I finally found one that carried a king-sized organic latex mattress set. I arranged to have it and a simple bed frame delivered the following Monday. I knew it would barely fit in the small space, but I was willing to live in tight quarters if it meant getting rid of the miserable little mattress I had been sleeping on. When the perplexed salesperson wondered if I might want to stop in and try the mattress out first, I told him anything would be better than what I was sleeping on now. *Anything.*

When I finished ordering my new mattress, I turned to the upstairs bathroom. I scrubbed around the plumbing like a mad woman, using a toothbrush and an old can of powdered cleanser Maggie kept in the bathroom closet. There were no other cleaning products for the tub and toilet, so I made a run to the corner store for a complete supply of cleaners, sponges, and other necessary items. I returned fully loaded and continued cleaning until every surface in the bathroom—almost—glowed.

MAGGIE WOKE FROM her morning nap at noon. I offered to make her a grilled cheese sandwich, but she wasn't interested.

"You're probably tired of soup and sandwiches," I said. "Instead, I could prepare you a nice goose liver paté with lightly crisped toast, followed by an endive salad, and, for an entrée, a tender filet de beouf served with new potatoes and grilled asparagus."

She just looked at me.

"Okay, fine," I said and headed to the kitchen for her liquid dietary supplement. "Don't say I didn't try."

After Maggie struggled through half of the liquid meal, she followed me into the living room, and we sat on the uncomfortable Victorian sofa staring at the fireplace wall. I explained to her how I would have a sixty-five-inch flatscreen TV mounted to it, just above the mantel. I waved my hands in the air as I raved about wireless speakers, subwoofers, and streaming, and described the drama Maggie would experience in that very room from the comfort of her bed.

"You can record all of your favorite shows and movies and watch them whenever you want. On demand. You can stream whatever you're in the mood for. When you want to nap, you nap—when you want to watch TV, you watch TV. You'll be the queen of your little kingdom here. The Diva of Cleveland Street," I told her.

Maggie just sat staring, and I couldn't tell if I had completely lost her, or if she was imagining herself watching Jeopardy at four in the morning.

"We'll put your bed right here, facing the TV and fireplace, and your dresser can go against that wall." I gestured to the wall behind us. "I'll get you a nice big table to use as a nightstand." I pointed to the left and drew a circle with my index finger to indicate where it would go. "You can put everything you want on it."

I gave Maggie a moment to process her excitement before I went on. "I've already ordered blackout shades for these windows, and drapes for the French doors. It should be more comfortable for you to nap during the day in a dark room. Also, it will be much cooler," I added.

Maggie turned her head and briefly looked at the windows.

"So, what do you think?" I asked.

She looked around the room. "Do I get that surround sound?"

"That's what all of the speakers are for," I told her.

"Oh."

"So, what do you think?" I asked again.

"Sounds like it will cost a lot of money."

"Not your problem."

Maggie sighed, and looked around the room. "Grace, I don't want you spending a lot of money on all of this. I may not get to enjoy it for long."

"Maggie, even a long life is too short to spend any time watching a thirteen-inch black-and-white TV."

"Well, I don't mind the lack of color, but a damn remote would be nice since I haven't had any luck training the pest." Maggie smiled briefly and went back to staring at the fireplace wall. "I can record Westerns for the pest?" she asked.

"He'll be able to watch one whenever he wants."

"Great. He's a huge John Wayne fan."

We chatted a while longer, but I could tell Maggie was beginning to fade. I helped her up the stairs, trying to convince her I didn't mind the exercise, even as I struggled to just get her up the next step and the next. I assisted her in the bathroom before tucking her in bed, and called the dogs in to keep her company.

Once I was certain Maggie had all she needed, I decided to drive to the Holyoke Mall and buy myself a carload of good bedding and towels. While I was at it, I'd find a store that sold comfortable area rugs, and then hit an electronics store—I had gone long enough without modern technology.

I called Matt on the way to see if he was free that evening. When he didn't answer his phone, I left a message inviting him over for dinner. I was enjoying my own company, but there was a part of me that felt lonely. Spending time with Matt would be a good antidote, and I knew Maggie wouldn't mind having our handsome young neighbor over for the evening.

The mall's anchor store was having a huge sale in its home goods department, so I cleaned up on bedding and towels. I left my bags with a salesperson and continued shopping, stopping for a slice of cardboard pizza at the food court before moving on. It wasn't Greenwich Avenue, for sure. I didn't recognize many of the low-priced chain stores, probably because there were zoning regulations preventing them from having locations in Fairfield County. Yes, I'm a total snob.

On the way back to my stash of linens, I found a plus-size lingerie store, and decided to shop for old lady underwear to replace Maggie's vintage collection. I described her decrepit underwear to a salesperson, and she led me to a stack of seriously depressing cotton panties that looked perfect for Maggie. I bought half the pile, even as I imagined the scolding I was going to get when I returned home. Maggie needed new bras, too, but I wasn't even going to take a stab at that one. Maybe I could swipe one of her old bras and bring it to a shop with me sometime—or maybe not.

I picked up my bags of linens on the way out and carried everything to the Beemer. I still had plenty of room, so I headed out of the mall parking lot and searched for more stores. My bedroom needed something more inviting than the old rag rug, and the carpet in the living room had seen better days. There was a rug store in a nearby plaza, so I stopped in and searched through several stacks of bound carpets. I picked out a large hand-tufted wool rug with an ivory background and black geometric detail, took off my shoes and walked around on it, and told them to find another one like it, only larger, and have them both delivered to Cleveland Street.

There was a small audio/visual store that shared the plaza with the rug store, so I decided to shop for TVs and audio systems. The manager of the store made a beeline for me the minute I got through the front door. He must have seen me arrive in my Beemer; he was a funny and engaging man, and had me considering an enormous TV and everything to go with it in less than fifteen minutes. I asked if he could find someone local to deliver and install the system for a reasonable price, and if he would cut me a deal on a forty-inch TV. I figured I could put it on top of the dresser in my bedroom. He handed me a card for a reliable service, and gave me a twenty-percent discount on my entire purchase.

I could have had the smaller of the two TVs delivered with everything else, but I needed immediate audio/visual gratification. Two young salesmen at the store removed it from its oversized box and laid it on my back seat.

I was less than a mile from Maggie's when my cell phone rang. It was Matt. I answered with a "Sex Addicts Anonymous" in a nasally drawl.

Matt laughed on the other end of the phone.

"Do you want to describe your problem to me, sir?" I asked. "I'm all ears. Okay, I *do* have other body parts, but I have *enormous* ears. Our conversation is completely confidential, of course, although I may record it for use later this evening."

Matt chuckled and said, "It all started when I met this older woman."

"Older? How much older?"

"It's hard to say. I think she may have had work done."

"Or maybe she's just naturally gorgeous and can't help it," I suggested.

"Thing is, she's leading me down a sinful, lustful path."

"And you have a problem with that?"

Matt laughed. "So what time is dinner?" he asked.

"I'm going to have to reconsider my offer. Bad things happen to men who assume I have to work at being beautiful."

"How bad?"

"Really, really bad."

"I can't wait."

When I got back to Maggie's, Matt met me in the driveway and helped me unload the car. We piled the linens in the front hallway, and Matt hauled my sleek new TV carefully into the house.

"Do you even have a cable hookup in your bedroom to connect this to?" Matt asked.

"Not yet. I plan on putting this in the parlor until I get the big one set up in the living room. Then this thing goes upstairs. I'll have the guy who's doing the living room installation run cable to my bedroom."

Ellen had been napping in the front hall waiting for me to come home, and she gravely surveyed our progress as we carried the new TV down the hall and into the parlor. Matt unplugged the old TV and put it on the floor, and we set the new one on the sideboard. He hooked it up to the cable box and plugged it in while I went back out to the car to get the bag with the owner's manual and remote.

We played around with the new TV and selected a list of favorite channels for Maggie. When I was sure that it was set up properly and ready for show time, I went upstairs to wake her.

9

gotta pee

I GENTLY KNOCKED on Maggie's door and waited for a response. I heard a soft plunk and little clacking noises as Stogie jumped off her bed and headed for the door. When I got no reply from Maggie, I rapped a little louder.

"Good grief!" Maggie grumbled from inside her bedroom. "Who are you, and what are you selling?"

I let myself in, and nearly tripped over Stogie as he scooted into the hall and down the stairs. I stepped back into the hall and called to Matt, asking him to let Stogie out.

Maggie called to me from the room, her voice a dry fingernail rasping on chalkboard. I hurried back, turned on a lamp near her bed, and put my hand on her shoulder.

"You okay, Maggie?" I asked, concerned at her appearance.

"Do I *look* okay?" she croaked.

"Actually, you look a little..." I was at a loss for words. She didn't look good. "Rough nap, huh?"

"Damn right."

"What can I do for you?"

"I really need to pee, but I don't think I can get up." Maggie let out a ragged breath and coughed.

"I bought a bedpan," I said. "I can go get it, or I can help you to the bathroom."

"I don't think I want to use a bedpan," she replied, grimacing.

"Let's get you to the bathroom, then." I folded her covers back, and slowly helped her move her rigid legs to the edge of the bed.

"Do you think you can stand?" I asked. "I can try to help you, but Matt's downstairs if you think we need to call in the cavalry."

Maggie reached for me and wrapped a cold arm around my neck. She pulled me toward her as she tried to lift herself from the bed, and I fell forward. My face ended up in her lap.

"Mags, I'm not sure this is going to work," I said, laughing a little, my voice muffled by fabric and soft thigh. "It's basic physics, not much we can do to fight it. Let me get Matt before we both wind up on the floor." I gently extracted Maggie's grasping arm from around my neck, and promised I'd be back right back. I ran downstairs, looking for Matt. He was just coming into the house through the back door, and I tackled him in the kitchen.

"Maggie needs us right now!" I said and grabbed his arm. "We have a bit of an emergency."

We raced up the stairs, down the hall, and into Maggie's room. Her face was gray; she clutched her blankets. Matt put his arms around her and pulled her into a seated position on the edge of the bed. We each grabbed an arm, pulled her to her feet, and hauled her down the hall toward the bathroom.

"We're almost there," I said. "Hold on!"

"This is almost as embarrassing as farting at Mass when everyone knows it's *you!*" Maggie wailed. "I can't *stand* it!"

We finally got her positioned over the toilet, and I lifted her dress and started tugging on her old lady panties.

"Good Lord, Grace!" Maggie yelled at me. "Can I have a little *privacy?*"

Matt grinned at me, put his hand over his eyes, and quickly exited the bathroom.

"Not that I don't appreciate the help, Matthew," she called out as I lowered her onto the toilet.

WE GOT MAGGIE settled back in bed with a small tumbler of bourbon, per her instructions. I thought about watering it down, but I knew I would never get away with it. As part of our negotiated compromise, she followed the bourbon with a cup of tea for dinner. I tried to push a liquid meal on her, but she wasn't having any part of it. I checked the bottle of Vicodin on her nightstand and realized that she had gone through most of them, and in half the time as her last bottle.

I hurried downstairs and asked Matt to stay with Maggie while I ran out to the pharmacy. I called Dr. Cunningham's service for a refill on the way. I was worried about her drinking and taking so many painkillers, and asked the service to have Dr. Cunningham call me so I could discuss it with him.

While waiting for Maggie's refill, I called the local Chinese restaurant on my cell phone and ordered takeout. On the way home, the smell of lo mein and beef fried rice filled the car, and I realized that I was absolutely starved. The pizza I had eaten at the mall was ancient history as far as my digestive tract was concerned.

I arrived home where I found Matt and the dogs watching the Yankees slam the Red Sox on the new TV. He was obviously a Sox fan, so it was going to be a long night for him. It probably would have been less painful watching the game on the old black and white set.

"You'd think they'd learn," I said, waving at the new TV, referring to the Sox from my position as a Yankees fan. "They should just pack up their little balls and go home." Matt had the top of his hair pulled back in a short ponytail, a silly but oddly cool look on him. I sat down next to him and yanked on it. "Giddy-up, little pony."

"It's only the second inning, you dork," he said. "No one's packin' up anything, and I'm not going to *giddy-up* anywhere. And yeah, I know I need a haircut."

"Just you wait and see." I sighed, resigned to Matt's dismay at the outcome. "The game is only going to get uglier."

He smiled at me and leaned over and kissed me. He took his time, and I gave him points for hanging in there even when the crowd went wild in the background. He finally pulled away, took my hand, and held it to his chest.

"I spent time with Maggie while you were gone," he said. "We talked. I'm worried about her, and I'm worried about you. Please tell me what I can do to help."

I took Matt's little ponytail in my hand again and gently fingered it. "I'm working on it," I said, and told him of my plans to hire someone from a home health care agency.

"You don't have to hire someone, Grace. I'll help." Matt gave my hand a little squeeze.

"I'm not sure either of us is up to bedpans and sponge baths." I returned the squeeze. "And I'm not so sure Maggie would be crazy about the idea of her kid neighbor with the plastic tricycle getting so personal, either."

"The plastic what?"

"You know, the form of transportation you favored prior to Sheila. Big Wheel."

"God, Maggie has a long memory."

"Tell me about it. I could have lived without some of her recollections. I can see you now—big ears, buzz cut, the works." I flicked one of Matt's ears and smiled.

He looked closely at me and studied my face. I got the impression he was trying to imagine me as a little girl.

"Let me make it easy for you," I said, "I was born beautiful, and I never grew out of it."

"Yeah, you've got the attitude of someone who's never known ugly." Matt smiled at me and trailed his finger across my lips. The smile faded and he suddenly looked serious. "Listen, Cavanaugh, I took care of my mom when she was sick. It was hard, but I wouldn't have changed that time we had together for the world. I don't have any commitments until the fall that require me to be in Boston. Just a little consulting work I can do remotely. I want to help with Maggie."

I looked at Matt, and he met and held my eyes.

"It's not going to be pretty, but I guess I don't have to tell you that," I finally said. "I still want to hire a professional, but if you want to pitch in, I can use your help. I don't know how Maggie will feel about it, though."

"Maggie will be fine with my help, I promise. Remember, she and I go way back." Matt grinned at me, probably recalling sunny afternoons on his Big Wheel.

"I guess that settles it."

"Good. I'm glad you're seeing it my way, Cavanaugh. You can be a little stubborn. Let me spend the night over here in case you need me. We'll work out a schedule when you hire a nurse."

"Spend the night, huh?"

"Got to be something in it for me. Did you get Chinese? I smell Chinese." Matt looked expectantly toward the kitchen.

We chowed down on lo mein as the Yankees pummeled the Sox, but then the Sox slowly worked their way back. This led to extra innings that kept Matt's interest, but finally lost mine. I cleaned our plates and chopsticks, checked on Maggie, and crawled onto Matt's lap while the game dragged on late into the evening. I tucked my face into his neck and listened to the comforting sound of the crowd droning on in the background. Matt wrapped his arms around me, and I closed my eyes.

I was happy to be with Matt and comforted by the fact that he wanted to help. I cared about him, too, and looked forward to having him spend the night. But I have to admit, from time to time, when the only noise in the room came from the TV, I pretended that I was in Michael's arms. It wasn't a particularly satisfying fantasy; it had been years since Michael and I had been at the stage in our relationship where I still crawled into his lap, and my body kept reminding me I wasn't home. I think Matt knew I was lost in a different world, looking for familiar terrain, because he didn't say much.

"You're a good sport," I eventually whispered in his ear, knowing that my meaning would be a bit ambiguous given his offer to help with Maggie.

"Whatever it takes," he replied, and I knew by his tone that I wasn't hiding anything.

It was after midnight when the Sox finally succumbed to New York. Matt took the dogs out for a final pee, and the four of us headed upstairs to bed. Stogie wanted in with Maggie, and Ellen decided to join him. I checked on her; she stirred so I offered her a glass of water and another pill.

Once Matt and I crawled into bed, I told him about the king-sized mattress and other comforts that would transform the room the next day. In the meantime, we made do with the ugly old chenille bedspread and mothballed blankets, and our bodies met in the curve in the middle of the mattress. We took our time making love, and eventually fell asleep with our arms and legs entangled as the night quietly stalked the dawn.

OUR ROOM WAS still dark the next morning, the first day of a blistering hot July, when Maggie called for help. I bolted from the bed, checked the clock—5:15 a.m.—and pulled on a T-shirt and shorts as Matt kicked off his side of the covers. I quickly headed down the hall to Maggie's room, with Matt right behind me.

"Gwath, I haf ta get ta da bafroom!" Maggie cried when I opened her door. The dogs were shuffling nervously by the bed.

"We've got you," I told Maggie as Matt followed me in. "It's okay Mags. Everything is going to be okay."

Between the two of us, Matt and I made quick work of getting Maggie out of the bed and to the bathroom. As soon as I had her positioned over the toilet, Matt gave Maggie a quick salute and disappeared.

"Matt, do me a favor and grab Maggie's dentures in the bedroom," I called after him.

I helped Maggie by singing potty songs from my childhood, made up by my sisters and me. After she finished using the toilet,

Matt slipped the dentures through a crack in the door and I handed them to her. She quickly inserted them, and immediately wailed, "Good God! Give an old woman a break! You and your damn songs!"

"You didn't like *Gotta Pee, Pee, Pee?*" I asked.

"I'll give you a goddamn *Gotta Pee!*" she barked.

"It's *Gotta Pee, Pee, Peeee.* Let's get you back into bed," I said, suppressing laughter. "You seem a little grumpy. You okay?"

Maggie managed a small smile. "My head feels like it's going to explode," she said. "I'm sure that's what woke me up, but as soon as I opened my eyes, I couldn't wait to get to the bathroom. My headache's worse since I got up. Can't imagine *why...*"

"Let's get you a painkiller and something to drink." I took Maggie's arm, and led her out of the bathroom. Matt helped me get her into bed again, and I immediately reached for her prescription bottle. I sat with her for a while, lightly stroking her arm, waiting until she and the dogs had settled down. Finally, I returned to my bedroom where I pulled off my T-shirt and shorts and tossed them on a chair.

"At least she didn't freak out when she saw me in my underwear," Matt said from under the covers.

I joined him. "Don't think she didn't notice. You could have given her a heart attack, you gorgeous man. Please keep that in mind in the future." I lifted the covers and sighed at the sight of his six-foot-plus body, slipped my naked leg between his, and rolled over on top of him so our faces met. I kissed his mouth at length, and then gave his neck and chest my attention as I worked my way down his body. When I reached his waist, I slipped my fingers inside the elastic of his boxers, turning them inside out as I peeled them down around his thighs. The elastic had pressed a tan mosaic into his skin, and I fingered it gently.

><<<

EVERYONE SLEPT IN late after the early-morning interruption, including the dogs. I finally woke up at nine when my cell phone rang on the end table. Dr. Cunningham spoke from the other end of the line.

"Grace—is everything all right?" he asked. "I just got your message from yesterday. Sorry it took so long to get back to you."

"No, everything is *not* all right, but I'm not sure what you can do about it," I said, falling back into my pillow, and sending out a digital search party for the comfort of Matt's body. When my fingers met his thigh, and his hand closed around mine, I continued my conversation. "Maggie's losing ground. She's hardly eating, all she wants is her bourbon, and she almost doubled her Vicodin intake this week. I want to make sure I'm taking care of her, but I don't know what to do—I'm completely out of my element."

"My office told me they referred your case to the visiting nurses. Have you heard from anyone?" I heard the faint rustle of paper, a pen scratching, and I could imagine the tie—probably a neat regimental stripe—being straightened by a nicely manicured hand with a gold band on the commitment finger.

"Not yet, but I only spoke with your front desk person on Friday, so I'm not surprised. I'm sure I'll hear something soon."

"I think you've made a wise decision—both for Maggie's sake and yours—by looking into professional care," he said. "A nurse will be able to monitor Maggie's situation and make sure she's getting what she needs." He cleared his throat. I heard background noise.

"I'm sure you're right," I replied. "I hope whoever they send is patient and can hold their own. Maggie's not exactly easy to deal with."

Dr. Cunningham laughed. "Grace, it will be fine," he said. "All of the nurses are quite capable. However, I have a particular nurse in mind for Maggie. He's older, but he will bring a great deal of experience with him. I'll make a call, see if there's any chance he's available."

I processed the "he's-and-him" part of the conversation, thought about it briefly, and said, "I'm not sure Maggie's going to go for a male nurse."

"Grace, you're going to have to trust me on this," Dr. Cunningham said. "Two days into the relationship, Maggie won't care. It will work it out just fine."

I blew out a long, dubious breath and said, "If you say so…"

WHEN WE FINISHED feeding and walking the dogs, Matt and I had a quiet breakfast together. It was nice sitting in the kitchen on a bright Sunday morning with the light streaming in and the sound of newspaper pages turning and snapping into place. Now and then, one of us would look up and comment on an article.

I enjoyed Matt's company and felt we had formed a bond in our shared commitment to Maggie. But, once he headed home after helping me get Maggie up and about, I felt empty and sad. The morning was bittersweet. It reminded me of the life I once had with Michael, when everything felt perfect and whole, and I missed it more than ever. I began to worry that my heart was like a stubborn divining rod, searching for a deep pool of water, refusing to acknowledge the moisture that had managed to accumulate everywhere between the layers of terra firma—moisture that could sustain me if I would only allow it. If that were true, I wondered, how would I ever move on?

AFTER A RELATIVELY quiet weekend, Monday morning arrived like a boisterous relative full of loud jokes and elbow jabs.

Vinnie, One, and Two showed up just before eight o'clock, and at eight-fifteen a truck arrived, loaded with more bluestone pavers for the walkway and antique bricks for the stair façade. Vinnie continued working on the porch panels, and One and Two worked together laying the bluestone in a deep bed of stone dust. They worked quickly, making frequent adjustments to the height of the dust to accommodate the varying depths of the pavers, and then tapping them into place with rubber mallets.

Maggie wasn't up to watching their progress that morning. Matt and I helped her downstairs to the parlor and made her as comfortable as possible in one of the green chairs so she could enjoy the new TV. Matt moved another chair and pillow in front of her and gently propped her legs up.

"This situation is only temporary," I told Maggie. "Matt and I are going to create nirvana for you next door in the living room, and by the end of the day, it will be all yours."

We spent the morning rearranging the living room, moving the overstuffed Victorian sofa into the third bedroom, doing all we could to create space for Maggie's antique mahogany bed. Matt disassembled it, and I helped him carry sections downstairs for reassembly. We positioned it so the footboard was just a few feet away from the fireplace wall, so Maggie would have a good view of the TV that would be installed just above the mantel.

The new window treatments arrived via UPS shortly after Matt and I put fresh sheets and blankets on Maggie's bed. Matt ran next door for a toolbox. We made a good team and had the blackout shades installed in just over an hour. Once finished, we added enormous rods over the two sets of French doors leading to the hallway and the parlor, and hung velvet drapes that I had purchased to provide Maggie with additional privacy.

"Cavanaugh, it looks like a bordello in here now," Matt said, scanning the room. "I'm getting hot and bothered just looking at it."

"Hey, Sport, just imagine Maggie lying in that bed channel surfing with Stogie by her side," I replied. "Bedpans, prescription bottles, the works. Old John Wayne movies instead of adult pay-per-view. Does that help your male mind put things into perspective?" I smiled at Matt's pained expression, and gently poked him in the arm with a knuckle.

"Are you always this much fun?" he asked, "or do you just save it for me?"

I took pity on him. "Just wait until my king-sized latex mattress is delivered this afternoon. You think this room has you all hot and bothered? Imagine 'Cavanaugh World' with all the bells and whistles."

VINNIE FINISHED WITH the new screened panels for the porch by noon, and One and Two completed laying the bluestone pavers. After a quick lunch break, they started on the brick façade, giving the old concrete steps a facelift. Vinnie had hired two more cousins to paint the porch; they would start the following day.

Two had made arrangements for the delivery of the new sod

and plantings on Wednesday, and I was eager to see the finished product. All I had left to do was buy furniture for the porch and have the cushions upholstered in the fabric I had purchased.

Maggie ate a small bowl of soup and took a Vicodin; Matt and I were ready to move her into her new space once she finished. Having watched our progress from the parlor, she was anxious to check out her new bedroom. Although tired and ready for a nap, she seemed genuinely pleased by its arrangement.

"We'll get the TV installed for you tomorrow," I promised. "Until then, we can move you back into the parlor when you're awake."

"Those boys can't see in here, can they?" Maggie asked. "I don't want them watching me sleep."

"Not to worry. These shades have an extra layer, so you can't see in. You have total privacy. You might be able to hear them working, but I'll ask them to keep the noise down."

"Oh, I don't care about the noise, Gracie girl. I'll sleep like the dead after taking one of those pills." Maggie settled back onto her pillow and surveyed the room. "Hey, it looks like a bordello in here!" she said.

Matt heated up leftover Chinese food, and we ate on the back steps. We took turns feeding each other carefully with our chopsticks, and occasionally shared a noodle from either end that ended with a Disney kiss. Michael and I had enjoyed the same playfulness; I was delighted when Matt initiated the silly move.

While we were washing the dishes, a truck arrived with my new mattress. In my opinion, nothing less than a king-sized mattress is worth buying. Even when you're alone in bed, you can appreciate the real estate. You can spread your limbs in all directions, and not feel the suffocating pressure of tucked bedding. On hot summer nights, you can open your bedroom windows, and move from one cool spot to the next if you want to enjoy the night air. When you're in bed with a man, you can have a date in the middle, and then head home to your own peaceful turf after the lovin'. A king-sized bed is a private island in the sea of life, just off the coast of Perfection.

"Cavanaugh, you're just a little thing," Matt said when the enormous mattress was finally set up in Cavanaugh World. "Why on earth do you need such a big bed?"

"Don't even get me started," I replied. "Give me ten minutes to trick this thing out with new sheets and stuff, and I'll let you take a test drive."

Matt retrieved the bags of bedding I had stored in the third bedroom, and I tore open the packages. I began dressing the bed with a fleece mattress cover, added four-hundred-thread-count Egyptian cotton sheets, and a down-filled duvet and cover. I had bought four king-sized down pillows, and, after stuffing them inside their cases, I tossed them against the wall in place of a headboard.

"Okay, Matt, remove all of your clothing, and get into that baby," I instructed.

He pulled off his T-shirt and shorts.

"Lose the boxers," I said. "Otherwise, you're not going to get the full effect."

Matt slipped them off, and we both grinned.

"See, somebody likes it," I said.

Because I have an insatiable desire to name things, we christened my new mattress "Bertha" during a rather spectacular nap together. Matt agreed that bigger *was* better.

After we woke up from the sleeping portion of our nap, Matt headed downstairs to check on Maggie. I heard a brief exchange between the two of them, and they made noises that indicated Matt was helping Maggie to the small bathroom near the kitchen. I heard a door close, and additional muffled conversation. I checked the digital clock on my nightstand—it was 2:15 p.m.— and decided to grab a few more minutes of shut-eye. I awoke twenty minutes later and discovered Matt had crawled back into Bertha with me.

I finally got up and went downstairs. The Mobilia crew had finished early for the day and left the premises. I checked on Maggie to see if she needed anything. She was lying quietly with Stogie by her side and Ellen snoring on the floor. I opened the drapes and cracked the windows, then sat next to her on the bed. Ellen roused herself and joined us, resting her hairy muzzle near Maggie's pillow.

"How do you like your new bedroom?" I asked.

"It's a little strange being down here, but I think I'm going to like the benefits."

"Did you sleep?"

"A little. Did you sleep?"

"A little."

Maggie cracked a smile, and I grinned in return. Matt walked in, and we both looked at him.

"Like the new bed?" Maggie asked him.

"It *rocks*."

"No kidding," she replied.

I could see she was still tired. Matt and I kept her company for a few minutes, and once she dosed off, we coaxed the dogs out for a walk. We checked out the progress on the porch and walk- way, admiring the meticulous new brickwork that covered the concrete stairs. One and Two had transformed them with a lovely herring-bone pattern that worked beautifully with the bluestone walkway and newly-renovated porch.

It was a beautiful late afternoon in July, and the sun still hung industriously in a stretch of blue sky behind the enormous maples lining the street. Flowerbeds blazed with color, the plants heavy with blooms. The scented air reminded me of my gardens on Lake Avenue. My favorite time of year had always been the height of summer, when I opened the windows at night and drifted off to sleep surrounded by the fragrance of my garden wafting into the bedroom.

I thought about Gabriel, my gardener, and decided to return his many calls when I had a chance. My house always looked spectacular in the summer, surrounded by gardens in full bloom, and I wondered if I could see it now and feel something more than loss and longing.

"You're pretty quiet for you," Matt said as we headed past Stan's and turned onto Jefferson Street. "You okay?"

I took his hand and smiled. "I'm okay, you're okay, everyone's okay. Okay, maybe not *everyone*, but, yeah, I'm okay."

Matt smiled at my silliness. "Anyway, you want to talk about anything? To quote a friend: 'I'm all ears.'"

"Lucky for me, you *do* have other body parts." I squeezed his hand to emphasize my point.

"Girl—you have a one-track mind." Matt smiled and squeezed back. "Not that I'm complaining."

"I'm good," I said. "Just enjoying the evening and your exceptional company."

When we arrived back at the house, I checked my cell phone and found a message from the home health care agency. I quickly returned the call, hoping to catch someone before they all left for the day. A pleasant woman named Doris answered the phone, and I waited a minute as she tracked down my file.

"It looks like Henry is available starting next week," Doris said. "You lucked out."

"Who's Henry?" I asked.

"Dr. Cunningham didn't mention Henry to you?"

"Oh, *that* Henry. I'm not sure my elderly aunt is going to agree to a male nurse."

"Henry's the best," she said. "He works with female patients all the time. No one's ever complained."

"You haven't met my great aunt."

Doris chuckled, and I could hear her shuffling paper. "Margaret Reilly. Eighty-six. Cleveland Street. Is that in Hungry Hill?"

"Uh, yeah."

"Oh, he's been there and done that, sweetie."

We agreed on an eight o'clock interview for Henry the following Monday morning. Doris offered to book a temporary nurse, but I assured her I could manage for a few more days. "There's a neighbor, lives next door, who's helping me," I told her. "He's known her forever."

"I hope it's more of a help than an imposition."

"Oh, Doris, if you only knew," I said suggestively, and laughed.

"Well, then," she said. "Don't let me rain on your parade."

I was still having doubts about hiring a male nurse as Matt and I helped Maggie to the bathroom and into one of the chairs in the parlor. Matt left to run a few errands and change into clean clothes. It was close to cocktail hour, so I made Maggie her bourbon and seltzer, and poured myself a glass of wine. We turned on the new TV and surfed for a show, settling on an episode of *Animal Planet* involving the most extreme scavengers. Stogie was immediately enthralled with a family of hyenas devouring something that resembled a hapless water buffalo. I whined a bit about the whole thing, but Maggie insisted that the pest needed to watch an educational program for a change.

"Don't blame me when he starts looking at you like you're a potential meal," I warned. I wanted to change the channel to something a little more civilized. "*I've* tried to protect him from The Dark Side."

"Oh, please!" Maggie responded. "The pest certainly knows the difference between me and a dead carcass." Maggie gave Stogie's wiry bottom a pat.

"You better not sleep too soundly," I said, smiling. "You might be asking for trouble."

"Oh, hell," Maggie said. "Give me the damn remote."

We found a different show, one that didn't involve carnivores and dead bodies, and spent some quiet time watching the new TV. When Maggie finished her drink, I convinced her to have a bowl of chicken soup. She didn't put up a lot of resistance, but I could tell she wasn't hungry. It took her almost an hour to finish it, and then she asked me if I would help her to back into bed.

"The pest and I are worn out," she said.

I helped her to the downstairs bathroom one last time, and left her to manage her nighttime routine with her denture container and a washcloth. When she was done, she called for me. I held her arm as she walked back to the living room, helped her into her nightgown, and got her settled in bed. It was as good a time as any to mention Henry.

"Maggie, I've made an appointment with a nurse to meet you next Monday. I want you to have the best care you can get, and

I think that means we need to get a pro in here to keep an eye on things. Dr. Cunningham recommended this particular nurse himself."

"Ah don know ha comfoble ahm gonna be wif a stanger takin air uf me," she replied.

"The nurse will just be helping us. I'll still be taking care of you. I just think we need to have all of our bases covered, you know, so when Matt isn't available to help, there's someone else around." I was careful not to mention the fact that the nurse was a Henry, since I was pretty sure it wasn't going to be as easy as everyone thought to get Maggie sold on the idea. "Don't worry about it, Maggie. It will be fine. If you're not comfortable, we'll work out something else." I laid a hand on her shoulder, and, on impulse, planted a kiss on her cheek.

MATT RETURNED FROM his errands and came into the kitchen where I was washing dishes. He was carrying a bag of groceries, and Ellen had followed him from her post in the hall. She scrutinized the bag of food and gave Matt a thorough once-over before releasing him to my custody. Matt placed the bag on the counter. "Maggie's in bed?" he asked.

"Yup—she's all tucked in," I said.

"*Yup?*"

"Just experimenting with the English language."

"Slumming in the hood?" Matt smiled at me.

"I told her about Henry. Well, I didn't exactly tell her about *Henry*, per se, but she knows someone is coming to interview on Monday morning."

"So, you didn't want to break the news to her about getting a boy toy?" He pulled a quart of milk out of the bag and walked it over to the refrigerator. "You might have made her day."

"Seriously, don't you think she's going to have a fit when a man walks into the house?" I asked.

"Maggie?"

"Yes—Maggie."

"Right—whom else would we be talking about?" Matt headed back to the bag of groceries.

"*Whom* else?"

"I'm also experimenting with the English language," he said over his shoulder. "Trying to use it properly."

"Don't hurt yourself," I teased, "and, in spite of your best efforts, it's *who* else."

"Now you're a *snob* slumming in the hood."

"Give me a break," I replied.

"Hey, great, we're having our first fight!" he exclaimed. "Can we have makeup sex now?"

I smiled, and Matt grinned and took me in his arms. "So, just for your information," he said, "I don't think Maggie's going to have a problem with having a man around to take care of her."

"She yelled when you stayed in the bathroom," I pointed out.

"We kind of took her by surprise then. If she knows that's the lay of the land, she'll deal," he said.

"I like it when you talk like you're street-smart instead of a geek. Maybe I'll do you just because you're so dope." I lowered my hands down to his waist and pulled him to me.

10

henry bujnarowski

TUESDAY WAS MY favorite day of the week since it involved the installation of the enormous TV in Maggie's room, and moving the smaller one into Cavanaugh World. The two technicians installing the TV over the fireplace had their work cut out for them, but they got creative and managed to do an admirable job without tearing apart the entire wall. They ran a cable line up to my bedroom and placed my TV on top of the dresser.

I had bought a load of throw pillows while shopping for porch furniture, and they came in handy when Maggie wanted to be propped into a sitting position as she watched the new TV. Watching TV with Maggie became a social event that week with everyone lounging on her bed. We celebrated Independence Day with a pajama party, complete with popcorn and sodas, as we watched fireworks on the big screen.

When Maggie finally kicked us out of the living room in the evenings so she could sleep, Matt and I moved to my bedroom. On Thursday, we had a Nora Ephron fest with pay-per-view, and

Matt watched *When Harry Met Sally* and *Sleepless in Seattle* for the first time. I remembered when both movies were released like it was yesterday; Matt was probably just learning how to ride a two-wheeler while Meg Ryan's memorable performance for Billy Crystal was being filmed.

Matt didn't complain that I had roped him into sitting through two chick flicks, and I was in a great mood after watching them. Win-win television.

⟩⟨⟨⟨

VINNIE, ONE, AND two finished the renovation of the porch and completed the new landscaping early in the week. By Thursday afternoon, Vinnie's other cousins had finished painting the porch. (They got a kick out of my calling them "Three" and "Four," even though their names were Jim and Robbie). The dark green paint on the trim and door looked great; the pale aqua ceiling was a nice touch, and the freshly-painted floor looked inviting in its gray lacquered coat.

On Friday evening, Matt brought three kitchen chairs to the porch for cocktails.

"What's next?" asked Maggie as we settled in with our drinks. "I like having you around, Gracie girl. You just can't leave things alone. Not that I'm complaining," she added while taking in the renovated porch.

"I have to admit I'm getting tired of washing the dishes by hand," I said. "I'm not very fond of that upstairs bathroom, either. Not having a shower sucks, and there isn't any counter space. My girl stuff keeps falling off the sink—I've lost a brush and a nail file to the toilet gods, and I almost fried myself when my blow dryer took a dive into the sink. Lucky for me the sink was empty, and I wasn't standing in it, but it was a close call nonetheless."

"So, are you going to be able to leave the kitchen and bathroom alone, or what?" Maggie asked. "Don't rein yourself in on my account—I already miss those nice Italian boys. That Two had a nice caboose, if you know what I mean, and One, well..."

"I know—*One*..." I sighed.

"One what?" asked Matt.

Maggie and I exchanged glances and did a clumsy high-five.

"You two are a pain in the ass," he said.

"So, what's next?" asked Maggie.

I knew that I could tear the little house apart in my sleep and put it back together again in the morning, but I also knew that Maggie needed peace and quiet. She was clearly inching closer to the finish line, and, while I was doing my best to remain outwardly calm and composed, I was struggling.

"I think I'll give us all a break from the chaos for a while," I said. "I can live with dishpan hands and the occasional sacrifice to the toilet gods for a bit longer. Then we'll see..."

I TIPTOED INTO the living room Sunday morning, noted the deep lines of fatigue on Maggie's face, and could tell she'd had a rough night. She didn't put up a fuss when I suggested she use the bedpan. Instead of getting up for lunch, she ordered "room service" in the form of a small bowl of soup, which Matt carefully spoon-fed her.

I was worried that, with her worsening condition, Maggie would resist getting out of bed. So, once she fell asleep, I ran out and bought a comfortable chair and ottoman for her room, cramming them into the back seat of the Beemer.

Matt coaxed Maggie from the bed to the chair when she awakened late that afternoon. She spent an hour sitting in it, but the following day she could only manage a few minutes before her pain drove her back to bed. I knew she would become bedridden at some point; even so, I wasn't prepared. It seemed much too soon.

Matt pulled me from the room after we had helped her from the chair to her bed. "Maggie's in a lot of pain, Grace," he said, keeping his voice low. "If laying down gives her some relief we shouldn't pressure her into getting up or moving around. Just let her be."

His advice didn't sit well with me. I wasn't ready to let her be, but arguing with Matt wasn't going to change the circumstances or the outcome. I moped about, and then tidied up my little room while anxiety made the walls close in around me.

I finally asked Matt to sit with Maggie so I could get out of the house for a while. I didn't want to be alone, so I loaded Ellen into the cube, and drove around aimlessly. We finally ended up at Forest Park in the south end of Springfield, a place my parents had taken my sisters and me several times a year for pony rides and staring contests with lions and polar bears.

The urban park no longer offered pony rides, and the caged wild beasts were gone, replaced with a small petting zoo. The park was populated with families biking and walking, and in its center the flower gardens were as lush and vibrant with color as I remembered. I drove past an Hispanic family celebrating a young girl's birthday at a picnic table; a Justin Bieber piñata hung from the branch of an oak tree.

I parked the cube in an isolated area near one of the ponds near the back of the park, cut the engine, and finally gave into my grief. I cried for Michael, and for the loss of the life we had together. I still missed him so much. I cried for Maggie, because I didn't want to lose her after growing close to her again after so many years. I knew I would miss her as well.

Tears streamed down my face, and I pulled out the Starbucks napkins I had stored in the glove compartment and blew my nose.

Several minutes into my misery a police car pulled over in front of me. An officer climbed out, walked up to the cube, and tapped the glass on the driver's side with a rigid forefinger. I turned on the ignition and lowered the window.

"Hello, officer," I said, sniffling. "Was I speeding?"

"No, ma'am," he said, suppressing a smile. "Your speed was at zero."

"Oh, so that's why the scenery wasn't changing." I was certain I looked pathetic; I wiped at my face with the napkin. "Is everything okay?" I asked.

"Just keeping an eye on things, ma'am. I like knowing who's in my park and what they're up to." Ellen shoved her nose over my headrest and out the window, and he patted her enormous head. "You're not dealing drugs, are you?" he asked. He was young, but cute in a man-in-uniform kind of way.

"I've got a small bottle of Tylenol in my purse. I suppose for the right price..."

He grinned and looked at me, searched my face briefly and asked, "Are you okay?"

"Aside from having people I love dying on me, or attempting to die, I'm pretty good." I blew loudly into the last of my napkins. "Sorry."

"Not a problem," he said, giving Ellen another pat on her head. "You want your privacy back, ma'am?"

"I'm pretty much over the self-pity. I think we'll head back home."

"Okay, then. Drive safely." He rapped the roof of the cube gently with his knuckles, hesitated, turned, and walked quickly to his patrol car without looking back.

It was getting dark when Ellen and I finally returned to Maggie's. As we came through the door, Matt called my name from the second floor, and Ellen made a beeline up the stairs when she heard his voice. I peeked in on Maggie and saw that she was sound asleep with Stogie by her side. I had to bribe the little guy with a cookie to get him to leave Maggie's room and join me in the backyard for a potty break.

Back inside, Stogie went right back to Maggie's room and I headed upstairs to see Matt. He and Ellen were sprawled on Bertha streaming Netflix. When I walked into the room, Ellen looked at Matt, then at me, and quickly jumped off my bed and made a show of settling herself on the rug.

"Mamma leaves you two alone for one minute, and all hell breaks loose," I observed.

"Not her fault, Cavanaugh," Matt said. "It wasn't easy to talk her into climbing on board with me."

I smiled and gave Ellen a rubdown with my sneaker. "It's okay, sweet girl. I should have warned you. He can be a bad influence."

"Hey, I just like spoiling my women," he said.

"Does that include running downstairs to get me a glass of wine? I would like nothing better than to crawl into bed and watch a little TV right now."

"You look like you could use a little downtime. Are you okay?"

"You're the second person who asked me that today," I replied. "I'm just trying to deal with some stuff."

"In that case, can I get you something to eat while I'm down there?" asked Matt.

"I wouldn't mind pasta with my wine." I kicked off my sneakers and started wriggling out of my shorts. "Could you order in from Tony and Marco's?"

"Spaghetti?"

"How about *penne al arrabiata?*"

"Can't talk you into spaghetti?"

"Actually, I love their *fusilli bolognese.*"

"Sure you don't want spaghetti?" Matt put his hands on his hips.

"Hmm, come to think of it, I could go for a nice *cavatelli amatriciana*, or maybe *ricotta gnocchi.*" I crawled into Bertha, settled into heaven, and smiled at Matt sweetly.

"You're just trying to annoy me," he said.

"I'd keep at it, but I've officially exhausted my Italian."

"Mine was pretty much used up at spaghetti," Matt replied. "Oh, wait: *linguini.*"

"Anything you want to order is fine with me," I said, smiling and pulling off my shirt. "Even if it's just spaghetti."

"You're doing that snob thing again."

"You're just trying to pick a fight."

"I have to admit, the makeup sex makes it all worthwhile." Matt grinned, grabbed my folded shirt from me, and tossed it on the bed. He climbed next to me and started running his hands over my body, but I stopped him before I changed my mind about dinner in bed.

"Spoil sport!" Matt gave my body one final caress and planted a tender kiss on my forehead.

"Sorry," I apologized, "but I'm thirsty, hungry, and emotionally drained. Not to mention the proud owner of one enormous, devoted dog. Cater to my wishes, and leave me the hell alone, or you'll have to deal with her!" I pointed to Ellen, and she slowly stood and came over to me. She laid her head in my lap and rolled her eyes in Matt's direction.

Matt laughed, held his hands in the air, and backed away. "No need to get Ellen on my case! I'll go order dinner and send her down to collect the takeout when they get here. I bet we'll get a nice discount."

I AWOKE EARLY Monday morning and quietly made my way downstairs to check on Maggie. I hadn't slept well; I was anticipating the arrival of Henry with trepidation and relief, somewhat odd emotional partners. I had no idea how Maggie was going to react.

Having Matt around had been great—and at times necessary—but I was beginning to feel the added pressure of managing an unexpected relationship in addition to worrying about Maggie. I knew Matt only wanted to help, and I did enjoy his company, but I also knew that I was beginning to rely on him as if our relationship were permanent. I was accustomed to marriage—the give-and-take in a committed relationship was my comfort zone. I wasn't pretending that our relationship was more than it was, but I wasn't exactly putting up any boundaries, either. I feared I might be headed for trouble.

"Cavanaugh, I think we're headed for trouble," Matt said, who appeared behind me as I was standing in the hallway outside Maggie's door. "I think Henry's here—he's coming up the walkway." Matt sidled up to the front door and peered through the window.

The doorbell rang just as I was turning the knob on the French door to see if Maggie was awake. I was dressed in sweatpants and a tank top without a bra, and Matt was in his boxer shorts.

"Yikes!" I said. "Is the clock upstairs wrong? I thought it was only six a.m.!"

"You're right," Matt said. "Henry's early. *Really* early. Have fun—I need coffee." He turned and ambled down the hall toward the kitchen, scratching himself and rearranging his shorts as he walked.

The noise had awakened Maggie. "Who the hell's here!" she demanded, then, after a couple of beats, added, "Good God, it's six o'clock in the morning!" Ellen, who had been sleeping with Maggie and Stogie, suddenly appeared and pushed past me, heading for the front door.

"Oh, *gur-reat...*" I muttered. I followed Ellen and gently nudged her aside. I couldn't decide what to do about my outfit, but I was in a cranky, what-the-hell mood, so I grabbed the knob and swung the door open.

The man standing on the porch was nothing like I had expected. I imagined Henry would be tall and wiry, and middle-aged at most. What I got was Henry, short and squat, and a hundred years old. At least. Nice comb-over, big moon face, low-set ears, and the most bulbous nose I had ever seen. He smiled, and I was greeted with a mouthful of crooked teeth. He choked back the smile at the sight of Ellen.

"Good morning," I said, looking down at him. "You must be Henry Bujnarowski."

"And you must be Grace Cavanaugh." His eyes darted from me to Ellen and back again.

"She's harmless," I told him, and stepped back and waved him inside. "Do you have any idea what time it is?"

He entered carefully, clinging to the wall as Ellen's nose met his, and answered in a very small voice. "It's eight o'clock."

"Henry, it's *six* o'clock in the morning," I replied. "It's *six a.m.*"

"Oh, dear," Henry said. "My bad."

"Right. So—I haven't had any coffee, the doorbell woke up Maggie, and I have to get her to the bathroom. Excuse me."

By the time I helped Maggie from her bed and headed with her to the bathroom, Henry had managed to make friends with Ellen and was waiting for us in the hall. He snapped to attention at the sight of Maggie.

"Good morning, Mrs. Reilly," he said and took her left arm. "I'm Henry. I'm here to do your bidding. Sorry I'm a little early today. Must have reset my watch in the wrong direction last night after getting back from the poker tournament in Vegas. It has a great little alarm, gets me right up, no problem. Want to hear it?"

"Who the hell are you?" asked Maggie as we all shuffled together toward the bathroom. "Gracie girl, who the hell is this little man, and what is he doing in my house?"

"Well..." I looked down at Henry and sighed.

"Jesus, Mary and Joseph!" cried Maggie. "He's *the nurse!*"

We both looked down at Henry, and he shrugged. I could hear Matt choke back a laugh in the kitchen.

When Maggie and I emerged from the bathroom, Henry hurried over to help. "At your service, ma'am," he said to Maggie, and held out his arm. "You're in good hands. I'll provide you with excellent health care and meet all of your other needs as well."

"What other needs?" Maggie shot me a look. "What the hell is he talking about? Would you please tell Shorty here that I'm eighty-six years old, and I do not *have* so-called *other needs.*"

"I'm sure that's not what he meant," I said, stifling a laugh. Nevertheless, I was afraid to release Maggie to his care, and I clung to her other arm as if my life depended on it. I'd only just met the man and had no way of knowing if he was even competent. If the last fifteen minutes were any indication, we were in trouble.

"What I mean," Henry said, "is I prefer to think of my clients as more than just patients. I like knowing their interests—their likes and dislikes."

"Bourbon and seltzer," Maggie said.

Henry's smile didn't waiver. "I beg your pardon?"

"Bourbon and seltzer."

"Jack Daniels? Jim Beam?"

"Yes," Maggie said. "Gracie's upgraded me from Jameson, but it still works in a pinch."

"Good to know," he said.

We finally reached the doors to Maggie's bedroom. "So, tell me, Gorgeous, how do we ditch the clingy broad?" Henry motioned toward me with his enormous round head.

Maggie looked down at Henry, over to me, and then back to Henry. She took her arm away from mine, slipped it through Henry's, and favored him with a throaty laugh.

"Good grief," I said. "Not a problem. The 'clingy broad' is in desperate need of caffeine. Maggie, you are *way* too easy."

She just looked at me and shrugged.

I left Maggie in Henry's care, made straight for the kitchen, and poured myself a cup of coffee. I sat down, took a sip, and looked at Matt. He was smiling. "Good thing you bought her new underwear," he said.

)≪⟨

THE PORCH FURNITURE finally arrived the following day, but even though Henry tried to coax "Gorgeous" into joining Matt and me for a bit of fresh air, he was unsuccessful. The July weather was stifling even in the early morning hours, and Maggie couldn't handle the heat or the humidity. The old house didn't have central air conditioning, so Matt and I went to Home Depot and bought several window units to keep it cool.

Henry and Maggie spent most of their time in the living room watching TV and taking naps, the dogs at their feet. Henry sat in the new chair I had purchased for Maggie and made the occasional trip to the kitchen for fresh ice water. He gently encouraged Maggie to move about in bed between naps.

During the first week, Maggie refused to allow Henry in the bathroom with her, or to help her dress or undress. She finally relented the following week. When she was feeling too sick to get out of bed, she let Henry help her use a bedpan. He was kind and gentle with her, and she trusted him enough for me to leave the house on occasion. He was a good nurse.

I called and thanked Dr. Cunningham for hooking us up with Henry, and we shared a good laugh when I described the look on Henry's face when he first caught sight of Ellen. Dr. Cunningham arranged for one of his staff to check on us weekly, and he encouraged me to call whenever I needed.

Matt and I continued to spend a lot of time together, but when it was clear that Henry had Maggie's care under control, he stopped spending nights at the house. At first, I was a bit relieved at the thought of reclaiming my space, but then I grew lonely when he disappeared in the evening.

It was an odd time for me emotionally. I had vivid dreams about Michael most nights; the following mornings I'd lie quietly in bed trying to keep myself in a dream state as long as possible in order to stay with him. I missed him more than ever, but he felt further and further away. Michael and Matt began to occupy some of the same emotional space in my heart, and I spent a lot of time in my head trying to sort it out.

MATT AND I were naked, our limbs entangled, when my cell rang and woke us from a deep sleep. I noted the time as I extricated myself from Matt's embrace. It had to be Henry. No one else would call me at 8 a.m. on a Sunday. I scrambled for my phone on the night table, and, in my haste, knocked it to the floor.

"Dammit!" I said, feeling immediate pangs of guilt for agreeing to spend the night at Matt's house even though Henry had assured me he would not leave Maggie's side. I reached for the phone. "What's wrong, Henry?" I asked, too groggy for the caller ID to register in my brain.

"Who's Henry?" a female voice asked from the other end of the line.

I was relieved when I recognized the voice. Kat Alexander was my Realtor and close friend. I fell back onto my pillow. "Are you wearing your watch, Kat?" I asked. "You know, that cute little number from Chopard that Bart gave you for your birthday?"

"I'm great, Grace," she said. "Thanks for asking. And you?"

"Call me back in a couple of hours, and I'll let you know."

"Late night?" she asked.

It *had* been a late night. Matt and I had eaten at Tony and Marco's and gone out for a long drive afterward. I had counted on sleeping in. I ignored her question, and said, "I'm awake now—what's up?"

"I've been working with a family from L.A. They're relocating to Greenwich. They've fallen in love with your house. They're begging to go inside."

"Hmmm," I said.

"Honey, you've got to let them in or shoot me. I'm tired of telling people your house is on the market, but they can't buy it."

I gave a mental sigh. I had hired Kat because she and her husband were loaded, and she didn't need the commission. That didn't prevent her from engaging in a little melodrama on occasion. "You promised not to push me," I reminded her.

"It's been on the market for over a year, Grace! How am I supposed to earn a living if I can't sell it? How am I supposed to pay Sammy's tuition at Eagle Hill? The poor kid will be forced to attend public school. Not to mention—my butt is in serious need of rearranging. These things cost money. Do a friend a favor and let me show your house."

"You and Bart could buy and sell Eagle Hill on a bad day, and your ass is gorgeous."

"That is neither here nor there," she replied.

"I never could figure out exactly what that meant."

"It's *irrelevant*."

"It's irrelevant that I don't understand?"

"No, 'that is neither here nor there'— 'it's irrelevant.' Same thing."

"So, my lack of understanding just doesn't matter to you any way you look at it?" I asked.

"Okay," Kat said, "now you're just trying to annoy me."

I laughed agreeably and ran my hand down Matt's sleeping back. "How do these people know they love my house if they've never been inside?" I asked.

"I let them peek in through the windows," she replied. "Their pathetic little nose prints are all over your glass. Even the second floor—I got a ladder. Please, pretty please, let me show them the house."

I silently calculated the risk of letting the family from California inside my house. Matt turned over and mumbled in his sleep.

"What was that?" Kat asked.

"Nothing. One of the dogs."

"You don't let your dogs on your bed."

"I'm not in bed," I lied.

"It's eight o'clock in the morning. On a Sunday. You're in bed."

"If you know my routine so well, why are you calling me at this hour?"

"Is he gorgeous? Cough once for 'yes' and twice for 'I got drunk and woke up with this yahoo in my bed.'"

I cleared my throat once.

"I hate you, Grace Cavanaugh." She paused. "Um...I've been meaning to call to see how things are going. Didn't mean to stay out of touch for so long. How's your aunt?"

"*Great* aunt," I corrected. "She's not doing well."

"I'm sorry. And I don't really hate you."

"Of course you don't. Call me back in a couple of hours, okay?"

"Sure—get your evil ass to church!"

"Say 'hi' to Bart, Sam, and the twins." I hung up before Kat could tease me any further.

"What was that all about?" asked Matt, rolling on his side and propping his head in his palm.

"Nothing I want to think about this early on a Sunday morning." I turned to face him, sighed, and ran the back of my hand down his chest and abdomen. I hooked my thumb in the waistband of his boxers when I ran out of skin.

He planted a kiss on my nose. "You okay?"

"Bad people want to invade my personal space."

"Just point them out to me, and I'll give them a sound thrashing."

"They want to go into my house and touch things," I told him.

"That was your real estate agent?"

"Kat Alexander."

"Wife of Bart Alexander. Nice watch, great ass, three kids."

"You're very good at connecting the dots early in the morning, half asleep," I observed.

"I'm an audilegenic savant," he informed me.

"You just made that up."

"You got me there."

I extricated my thumb from his shorts and rolled onto my back. "Kat wants to show my house to a family from L.A."

"Aren't you trying to sell it?"

"Yes."

"So, what's the problem?"

"I don't *want* to sell it."

"That *is* a problem."

"Yes, it is. It is *the* problem, the Big Kahuna of problems." I stared up at the ceiling, and watched a spider work its way along the perimeter of the room.

"What can I do to help, short of assaulting a nice family from California?" Matt asked.

"I don't know—I can't figure out what to do about a lot of things lately." I turned and looked at him, pulled his face to mine, and kissed him briefly on his mouth. When I released him, he just looked at me, searching my eyes. He gently tucked a stray hair behind my ear.

"If you're referring to *me* as one of those 'things,'" he said, "maybe it would help to know that you and I are probably on the same page when it comes to our relationship." He continued to watch me carefully.

"What page is that?" I asked.

"We're great friends, Cavanaugh. I adore you—you adore me—but…" he smiled and ran his hand up my naked thigh.

"But what? We're great friends—that's it?" I asked.

"No, of course not."

"Let me guess: we're great friends who have sex."

"God, you are so smart!" Matt's hand continued to explore my body.

"I'm no audiowhatchamacallit savant," I said.

"Clearly. It's *audilegenic* savant."

"You can't correct me if you just made that up."

"Hey, I know what I am," he said, gently circling my belly button with his index finger.

I thought we needed to talk more about the page we were supposedly on in our relationship. I wasn't certain we were in agreement, and I didn't believe that Matt just thought of us as friends. Before I could speak, though, my cell phone rang again. I picked it up, tapped the screen, and put the phone to my ear.

"Good grief, Kat, I thought we agreed on a couple of *hours*, not minutes." When I didn't hear her voice, I quickly checked the screen and saw that it was Henry calling. "Sorry—Henry?"

"I really didn't want to bother you this early, but Maggie's had a bad night," he said. "Really bad. I figured you'd want to know."

11

i only have eyes for you

MATT AND I threw our clothes on and headed next door. We cut through the backyard and entered Maggie's house through the little back porch. The dogs were in the kitchen pacing, a sure sign that they needed to go out.

"Matt, please take the dogs out for a quick walk," I said as Henry came down the hall to meet me.

"She's not good." Henry sadly shook his big head. "Not good at all. She didn't get much sleep last night. I stayed on top of her meds, but they didn't seem to do the trick. She needs to be on something stronger."

I hurried into Maggie's room and found her lying on her side, pillows tucked beneath her waist and legs. She was breathing slowly.

"We've been working on breathing techniques to help with the pain," Henry said, "but it's not giving her any relief."

"*Yur gadam wight!*" croaked Maggie through ragged breaths, shifting her body uncomfortably.

I sat on the bed by her side. "It's pretty bad, huh?" I asked.

"Do you want me to get you to the hospital? If it's 'yes,' hum a bar of *Someone to Watch Over Me*, if it's 'no' make it *I Only Have Eyes for You*." I gave Maggie a little smile and squeezed her arm. "I'm sorry, really bad joke. I'll get right on the phone with Dr. Cunningham and have him call in something that works."

Maggie looked at me, tried smiling, and actually hummed a few tuneless notes. When the humming ended in a grimace, I gave her a long hug, and carefully climbed off the bed.

I motioned for Henry to join me.

"Jesus, Gracie," he said as we stepped into the hallway. "Would you mind if I hit the head real quick? It's been hours."

I nodded wordlessly and he hurried down the hall to the small bathroom near the kitchen. Matt returned with the dogs and asked for an update.

"She's in terrible pain," I said, keeping my voice low. "We have to do *something*."

I heard the toilet flush and water running, and Henry's stout little body reappeared. He suggested we chat in the kitchen, so the three of us headed down the hall.

"Sorry for not calling you sooner," he said. "I tried to talk Maggie into letting me call you hours ago, but she wouldn't hear of it. You know how she is."

"Tell me about it," I said. "It looks like we're going to have to get her some serious medication for pain control. I know Maggie would prefer staying here, but will that limit our options?"

Henry shook his head no. "I can administer whatever Dr. Cunningham prescribes."

"Like morphine?" Matt asked.

"Yes. I would recommend something for anxiety as well."

"What do you guys think?" I asked. "Admit her to the hospital or take care of her ourselves?" I looked from Henry to Matt and back at Henry.

"I'd hate to move her," Henry replied, shaking his head and hiking up his pants.

I looked at Matt, and he put a sympathetic hand on my shoulder. "If you want my opinion, I say let her stay at home as long as she can. We'll take turns so one of us is always in the room with her."

"It's going to be a lot of work." I was touched but not surprised by his kindness.

"Hell, what's a little work among friends?" He smiled briefly and gave me a reassuring wink.

"Okay," I said. "We'll keep Maggie here as long as we can, and I'll ask Dr. Cunningham for stronger pain medication." I pulled my phone from the pocket of my shorts, scanned through my contacts, and punched the screen.

MAGGIE WAS SLEEPING soundly for the first time in hours.

Dr. Cunningham had prescribed morphine and an anti-anxiety medication in the form of a compounded cream and asked me to stay in touch with frequent updates on her condition. Henry was familiar with the application of the drug, applying it to Maggie's wrist and covering the cream with a gauze wrap.

Matt took the first two-hour shift so Henry could go home and shower and change his clothes. He encouraged me to occupy myself elsewhere, so I would be rested when it was my turn to sit with Maggie.

"I'll let you know if I need you," he said.

Once Henry returned, the three of us took turns throughout the day. By early evening, I finally sent Henry home again under great protest. He was exhausted, and I knew he needed sleep. When darkness finally fell, I spent the night sitting with Maggie while Matt slept upstairs in my bed.

MAGGIE SPENT THE rest of the week in and out of a morphine haze. She stopped eating, but we continued to push small amounts of water and other liquids on her to prevent dehydration. I slept very little, getting by on a few dream-laden hours at a time; I relied on Matt and Henry to help me get through the day. To pass the time, Matt brought a card table from next door and set it up in Maggie's room and Henry taught us the finer points of poker.

Quinn made an occasional appearance after work. He sat with Maggie, watched TV, and hung out with Ellen, who quickly became enamored with him. I suspected Quinn reminded her of Michael; he had a way of grabbing her and hugging her with his big arms that was so similar. Ellen nuzzled him like a lovesick puppy, and after watching them together the first few times, I finally had to leave for my room whenever Quinn showed up.

When Maggie was awake, I tried to communicate with her as best I could, but she couldn't sustain conversation for long, and without her dentures, I found it hard to understand much of what she said. Still, it was clear she didn't want to be alone. "Gwath," she said more than once, "Ah canna sleep if no uns ere wif meh," and she would reach for my hand. After spending most of her adult life keeping her own company, she now feared being alone.

Clearly, the simple act of holding her hand comforted her. We made certain someone was always with her.

Father Brian visited most evenings after Mass, and I could tell it meant a lot to Maggie to have him near. Sometimes I sat with the two of them in her room and listened to Father Brian as he spoke to her quietly. I couldn't always make out what he was saying, but I could see his presence was that of an old and trusted friend. Once each week, he brought a small vial of oil, and gently rubbed it on her forehead and hands. I asked him about the ritual, and he told me it was a sacrament to help Maggie find peace with her illness. "It's a gift of love from God, lass," he told me. "It's meant to be a comfort."

Twice, at Maggie's request, he brought a small bag with a vial of wine and a piece of unleavened bread from Mass, and touched them to her lips and consumed them in her stead.

I RENTED A portable twin bed with a lumpy mattress so I could sleep by Maggie's side at night. The old mahogany bed she slept in was the same one she had shared with her sister Anne thirty thousand nights ago, and our hands crossed the space between my bed and hers each night until she fell asleep. Maggie and I shared the same sister comfort when we were growing up, and it made us feel safe.

One night I talked about Michael until she fell asleep, but she didn't seem to remember anything the following day. It felt good to talk about him, anyway.

Matt was wonderful through it all. There were times when I thought he was the nicest man I'd ever met, and I was beginning to regret our good friendship even given its benefits. Sometimes I wished we didn't keep each other at a slight distance emotionally, and that we agreed there was something more between us. Even Michael would have smiled at the attention I was getting: every morning, it was fresh coffee, fresh orange juice, and a full breakfast made to order; lunch was usually homemade soup and a salad. Dinner was sometimes takeout, but usually freshly grilled meat and a vegetable from next door. Matt had said he didn't know how to cook, but he had lied.

When Matt wasn't sitting with Maggie, he was walking the dogs or running errands for me. He took more shifts with Maggie than I, and sometimes kept Henry company when we weren't all together playing cards or watching TV.

Henry was the consummate professional, and he was extremely vigilant about managing Maggie's medication and her ongoing needs. He helped me dress and undress her, change her bedding, and give her sponge baths. He changed her diapers, which were necessary now, and he put up with Maggie's complaints without comment.

When Maggie was awake, he told her long stories until she fell asleep. Sometimes I would slip into the room to listen. The routine felt familiar and I was drawn to it. My father was a great storyteller, and often told my sisters and me elaborate bedtime stories to help us fall asleep. From time to time, sitting with Maggie and Henry with the drapes drawn and the house quiet, I would close my eyes and imagine I was a young girl again—safe in my room, my father close by—my life unblemished by loss and pain.

Spending all of my time with Matt, Henry, Quinn, and Father Brian made me realize how much I loved men, how much I still wanted one in my life. I began to believe that surviving Michael was a possibility, and that life could go on without him.

When I wasn't sitting with Maggie, eating, playing cards or taking catnaps, I cleaned. I went through the house from top to bottom, and it smelled like lemons and lavender. The old washing machine in the basement worked nonstop as I laundered everything in the house: clothing, bedding, scatter rugs, and towels.

I ventured into the attic and basement to take inventory of the generations of belongings that needed to be organized and disposed of, and decided that I would hire someone to handle what would be a daunting task.

I refused to fool myself. Maggie was dying, and it wouldn't be long before she was gone. I had thought we would have more time together and I feared her passing, but I didn't let that get in the way of doing what I felt she needed most from me. I refused to give in to death, and it felt good. I spent a lot of time on my laptop, making lists and getting ready.

ALTHOUGH KAT AND I had spoken briefly since the early morning call on Sunday, once Kat learned that Maggie was in her final days and required around-the-clock care, she had backed off for a while. Which was why I was a bit surprised when she called me one Saturday morning to let me know the family from California had returned to Greenwich for the weekend, and they were even more desperate to get inside my house.

"Honey—just let them in to get a closer look at the place," she said. "They may decide it's not for them, and they'll be able to move on."

"What if they love it?" I asked.

"Of course they'll love it."

"So, you're just 'managing' me?"

"Whatever it takes," she admitted. "Look, these poor people are at their wit's end. If you saw the hideous McMansions that are dominating the market this summer, you'd show them some compassion. They're a close-knit family; they'd like to bump into each other occasionally. They're not looking for ten thousand square feet."

"I don't know, Kat."

"By the way, how's your aunt?"

"*Great* aunt. You're trying to soften me up by taking a personal interest in my life."

"I'm your friend, Grace, I'm allowed." Kat waited patiently on the other end of the phone.

"Yeah, a friend who's trying to let a family of strangers take over my home." I sighed.

"It hasn't been your home in over a year, Grace," she said gently.

"It's still where my heart is."

"Honey, I think your heart needs to move on."

I was sitting by myself in the kitchen, my mind focused on Maggie's worn linoleum floor. A piece of it had rolled over on itself by the back door, and I worried that someone would trip on it. I really needed to make a trip to Home Depot and buy some glue.

"They can go inside, but don't promise them anything," I finally said. "Please make sure they don't touch any of Michael's things."

"I'll keep a close eye on them," Kat assured me.

)≪≪

SURPRISINGLY, MAGGIE SEEMED to be doing a little better over the weekend, so, after consulting with Dr. Cunningham, we decided to lower her morphine intake a bit. He advised us to try to get her to drink more liquids. She was able to sit up and watch TV with Matt and me, and we made a Saturday night of it with an on-demand movie and popcorn. I sent Henry home, with a promise to call him immediately if we needed him.

Matt and I had gone the whole week without making love, so when the movie was finished and Maggie was sound asleep, we left her with the dogs and went upstairs to Bertha to get a little relief from the efforts of the week. Matt was particularly responsive and tender with me that night.

"I have something I want to say," I told him afterward.

"Don't you always?" He said, amused.

"This is important. It's about us."

"Oh."

I struggled to find the right words. "Maybe our physical relationship is only temporary, but…"

"But?"

"I'll never forget what you've done for me and Maggie. I think the world of you. I value our friendship, and I hope I never lose it."

He was quiet for a few minutes, but finally said, "Cavanaugh, you couldn't get rid of me if you tried. If I didn't think I was part of some process you're going through, I would probably try to make a play for something permanent."

"You told me we were on the same page," I said warily.

"We are. I'm just maybe on a different paragraph tonight."

"Hmm."

"Don't freak out on me. I'm only saying you're terrific, and I know it." The light in the bedroom was dim, but I could see that he was smiling.

"You're being nice because you just got laid," I replied.

"Okay, you got me there. I never give you enough credit for how perceptive you are." Matt laughed and moved toward me. I gave him a gentle push, and he grabbed me and pulled me to him.

"Hmm, maybe you should do something about it," he murmured in my ear. "Put me in my place, pin me down and hurt me…"

"God—you are such a loser," I said.

He offered to spend the rest of the night with Maggie, but I wanted to be with her, even though the portable bed was uncomfortable. It didn't help that Stogie was snoring loud enough to wake the neighbors. I finally hauled myself out of bed around three a.m., grabbed a dog treat from the kitchen, and coaxed him upstairs to sleep with Matt. When I returned, Ellen was sitting next to Maggie's bed. "Come here, El," I said, and settled her on the floor near my narrow bed. "The little noise box is gone, let's get some sleep."

I passed out at some point in the night, and I was still out cold when Henry arrived the next morning at eight. The sound of his cheerful voice, as he greeted Matt in the kitchen, woke me. I could hear Matt getting our breakfast ready, and the smell of freshly brewed coffee pulled me out of bed. Maggie was still asleep, so I motioned for Ellen to follow me. I sent her down the hall, and Henry let her out the rear door while I made a quick pit stop in the bathroom before heading to the kitchen. Matt had a hot cup of coffee in front of me before I sat down.

"I love you," I said, making kissing sounds to his backside as he returned to the stove where he was frying hash browns.

"Maggie's not the only one around here who's way too easy," he replied over his shoulder.

"Something smells good," Henry said. "I think I love you, too."

IT WAS EIGHT-THIRTY Wednesday morning, and Maggie hadn't had a conscious moment since late the previous day. I had sat on her bed the entire night, hoping she would respond to my company, but by morning it was clear to all of us that she wasn't waking up any time soon.

Matt, Henry, and I had a pow-wow, and they voted to keep me in charge. "Thanks a lot, guys," I said. I realized it was up to me to decide what was best for Maggie at that point, but I honestly didn't know. I felt overwhelmed by the responsibility.

Maggie had asked me to use my best judgment regarding her care, so I called Dr. Cunningham and apprised him of the situation. I needed his help in deciding what to do. I was considering sending her to the hospital because I wasn't ready to let her go. I wanted to do whatever I could to help her. I didn't know if I was more concerned about her needs or mine, but I decided that Maggie wouldn't mind my taking us both into consideration.

"I can't give you any guarantees, Grace," he said, "but I might be able to get her stabilized and conscious again if you admit her to the hospital. But it will only prolong the inevitable. I know it's painful, but when a dying person lingers it's hard to decide whether or not—or when—to intervene."

He stopped talking and waited for me to reply. When I didn't say anything, he continued. "You have to try to balance your need to keep her here with her need to move on. It's natural to want to hang on to someone you love, but there's nothing you or I can do to prevent Maggie from dying."

I didn't speak for a long moment, and then I asked him what he was wearing. I sensed his smile on the other end of the line. "White shirt, blue tie with little pink whales on it. A gift from my girls last Valentine's Day. Not my usual uniform. Hope you can handle it."

He wasn't even a little bit insensitive, he said it kindly, but I knew he was waiting for me to laugh or at least respond with some humor of my own. Instead, I drew in a quick breath, and told him something I had never shared with another human being. I told him about the night I lost Michael—how it was swift and brutal and completely unexpected.

I told him how Michael had died in the emergency room forty-seven minutes after he woke me at 2:00 a.m. with a violent headache. How he had vomited in the bathroom while I dialed 911, how he had lost consciousness on the floor while I threw on my clothes. How I had slipped and fallen in his vomit, fracturing my wrist. How I had tried to give him CPR. How I had completely lost it before the ambulance arrived.

"I'm so sorry, Grace," he said.

IT WAS TEN a.m. when a bright white ambulance with red lettering pulled into the driveway. A blazing August sun had already climbed to the top of the sky, and the air hung thick with humidity.

Two EMTs entered Maggie's sanctuary in the living room, their movements quick and efficient as they prepared to transport her to the hospital. Even though I had personally made all of the arrangements, it all seemed surreal as I stood and watched.

Maggie had seemed to be doing so well over the weekend, and earlier in the week. She'd had many lucid moments, and we even shared a few laughs. I had hoped she would level out, maintain altitude, hang in there.

I was beginning to find comfort in our odd little family, stitched together by want and need. I liked being surrounded by all of the warm bodies. I might have been happy staying there on Cleveland Street, giving sponge baths, playing cards, watching TV. It was more than I had back in Greenwich now, more than I had anywhere else. I realized it would be hard to let it go, and no one was more surprised than me.

Once the technicians had Maggie strapped to a gurney, they quickly wheeled her out to the porch. Matt, Henry and I trailed behind them, staying until Maggie was safely tucked inside the ambulance and on her way to the hospital. We watched as the ambulance took a right turn and disappeared from view.

I turned to Henry, knowing it was time to say goodbye, even though he had promised to keep his schedule open through the following week in the event Maggie improved enough to return home.

"I don't know what we would have done without you," I said, "Thank you for everything."

"Please let me know how she's doing." He shook his head sadly. "I'll stop by the hospital tomorrow if you don't mind."

I gave him a long hug, he and Matt did a silly and complicated hand jive that had been their thing, and then he was gone.

I briefly considered going to the hospital by myself, but Matt made it clear I wasn't going anywhere without him. He considered Maggie as much his responsibility as mine. I felt a little pang that I hadn't fully realized how much Matt loved Maggie, and that she would be another loss for him. She had certainly been a bigger part of his life than mine over recent years.

I was worried about leaving the dogs since I had no idea how long we would be at the hospital. Matt called his brother with an update, and they chatted briefly. "The dogs are covered," he said once he hung up. "Quinn will walk and feed them when he gets home from work if we're still at the hospital."

"We need to get going." I grabbed my bag and cell phone. "Maggie will wonder what's taking us so long."

"Yeah, they'll probably have her conscious and complaining about what they're serving for lunch when we get there." He took me in his arms, gave me a long, hard hug, and walked me to the Beemer.

We rode in silence, following Cleveland Street to its artery, the artery to the highway, and the highway to the exit for the hospital. It was only a few miles, but it seemed to take forever. I pulled into an empty space in the visitor's parking lot.

"I hate hospitals," I told Matt before turning off the car.

"Join the club. Does anyone really like them?"

"Probably a few sickos out there who want to be here."

Matt's tense face settled into a small smile. "Well, can't really blame *them*."

"I don't want to see Maggie here. It's not how I saw it all play out." I fished the Beemer's electronic key out of a cup holder and grasped the set of slim keys collected on the key ring. There was a silver one I didn't recognize. It finally registered with me that it was an old key to my apartment on Greenwich Avenue.

"You wanted her to stay at home." Matt watched me finger the key.

"Yes. It would have been better for her. This is my fault—I'm just not ready to let her go."

"Nothing's your fault," Matt said. "It is what it is, and you're doing the best you can." He gently took the keys from my hand, reached across my lap, and opened my door.

Once inside the hospital, we headed to Dr. Cunningham's office where he had told us to meet him. He was busy, so while we waited, I stood and stared out his window since I was too anxious to sit. When he finally arrived, I introduced him to Matt and the two men shook hands.

He motioned for us to sit. "Maggie's settled in—we have her hooked up and monitored. But honestly, Grace, I wouldn't expect much."

I nodded. "I know. We'd like to see her now—I don't want her to be alone." I looked at Matt, and he took my hand.

"One of us will spend the night," Matt said. "As long as she needs us, someone will be here for her."

Dr. Cunningham opened Maggie's file, made a note, and picked up his phone. He identified himself as Maggie's attending physician and instructed someone to move a reclining lounge chair into Maggie's room. "Make sure there's an extra pillow and a couple of blankets," he said.

"Is there another bed in her room?" I asked once he hung up.

"There is," he replied.

"Can we use it if no one else needs it? I'd be willing to pay for it."

"Let me see what I can do."

⟩⟨⟨⟨

IN SPITE OF the hospital staff's efforts, Maggie remained unconscious throughout the day and into the evening. They kept her on fluids and monitored her vital signs, moving quietly and efficiently in and out of her room. I sat on her bed and talked to her from time to time, but she remained unresponsive.

As the evening wore on, Matt and I decided that we would both spend the first night with Maggie. The other bed in her room was available, so I crawled into it and Matt took the recliner. It was hard for us to sleep because of visits from the night nurses and light from the corridor.

"Are you awake?" Matt whispered to me from his chair around one in the morning.

"Pretty much." I yawned and turned, trying to get comfortable. A stiff top sheet and thin blanket wrapped themselves around my legs, and I kicked them loose.

"Wanna cuddle?" he asked.

"Seriously?"

"I'm always serious on the subject of cuddling."

"Well, if only we were alone, in my bed—or, hey—yours—or in a nice hotel, even—with a teeny, tiny bit of privacy..."

"So, the circumstances are less than ideal for you," Matt said. "Copy that."

I snorted a sleepy laugh and tried to fall back to sleep. After a few minutes, I heard Matt's gentle breathing, and I began to drift off. I hadn't been asleep long when another nurse came into the room to check on Maggie and woke me.

It was a long night.

By morning, Matt and I were both ready for a shower and

a cup of coffee, so after saying good-bye to Maggie, we headed home for a quick breakfast and a change of clothing.

"Grace, you can take a break if you'd like," offered Matt when we had finished showering, and were working on our second cup of coffee. "I'll go back to the hospital for the rest of the morning, and you can stay with Maggie in the afternoon. It's going to get pretty boring."

I took Matt up on his offer, and spent the morning emailing and calling relatives, informing them of Maggie's condition and prognosis. It was a little awkward with many of them, since they didn't know I had been staying with Maggie and hadn't seen me since Michael's funeral. One of my cousins hadn't heard about Michael's death until after the funeral, and he was painfully apologetic about not getting in touch with me.

"It's okay," I assured him. "I really didn't want to talk to anyone. Even if you had called or written, I doubt that I would have responded." It was true, and our conversation made me acutely aware of how thoroughly I had shuttered myself away from the world after Michael died.

Emily was glad to hear from me, but she was concerned that Maggie's eventual death would be too hard on me. She offered to come to Springfield, but I convinced her I was fine and had plenty of help.

This, of course, led to speculation and prying questions on her part, and I almost left her speechless when I finally caved in and told her about Matt.

"Yes, he's adorable, Em. He looks like a cuter, younger Colin Farrell—he's been wonderful to Maggie and me. He's with her at the hospital right now."

"Good Lord," Emily said. "When you finally move on, you *move on*."

"It's nothing permanent. We're just friends."

"Well, if he gets tired of an older woman like you, let him know you have a younger sister. A cuter, younger sister who looks like Kate Hudson."

"Yeah, with two kids, a husband, and a rich fantasy life," I pointed out. "Plus, you're only eleven months younger than me. Hardly counts."

"Details."

"I have to get back to the hospital," I said. "Would you call Laura for me, and let her know about Maggie? Don't mention anything about Matt."

"Yeah, right—mum's the word." Emily laughed and hung up.

I made one last call to Father Brian, who promised to stop in to see Maggie as soon as he could. I walked the dogs, gave them a treat, and packed a tote full of magazines, books, and snacks. I went upstairs and filled a small overnight bag with clothing and toiletries. Once packed, I straightened Maggie's room, made her bed, and opened the drapes.

I took a last look around and stepped into the front hallway. I just stood there listening to the quiet of the house, wondering if Maggie would ever make it home again.

The drive to the hospital took ten minutes, another five to get to Maggie's room. Matt was sitting in the lounge chair, watching an old boxing match on ESPN Classics and snacking on corn chips and vanilla pudding.

"Yum," I said. "I bet you'll never want to leave. Sports and junk food."

Matt looked up and smiled when he saw me. "It *is* quite the life."

"How's she doing?" I sat on the arm of his chair and watched Maggie closely.

"Same and same," he replied, sadly. "Nothing that resembles consciousness. The doc stopped by about an hour ago, asked me to have you call his office from the nurses' station when you got here."

"You want to take a break and go home? I've got enough stuff with me to amuse myself for a while."

"Nah, I'm fine staying here with my junk food and my girl." Matt slipped an arm around my waist and gave me a squeeze.

"Didn't know I was 'your girl.'"

"I could call you 'my woman,' but that seems a little risky."

"Sounds a tad possessive," I agreed.

"Seems to make a point about your age, too." He squeezed me again and smiled.

"Talk about risky."

"Yes—I will, in fact, change the subject. Would you like a chip?" Matt extended the bag in my direction.

"Thanks, but I need to make a phone call. Staying on the subject—why don't you just continue to refer to me as Cavanaugh? I like it." I kissed Matt on top of his head, stood, and headed for the door.

"Anything you say, *Cavanaugh*," he replied agreeably. "Anything at all."

I paused. "God, what's *not* to like about you?"

"Keep that in mind at my annual review," he replied, raising his voice a little as I walked out the door. "Don't forget I offered you chips, too!"

I called Dr. Cunningham's office, but he was attending a hospital staff meeting, and wouldn't be back for an hour or more. His assistant told me that she would have him stop by when he returned.

I returned to Maggie's room, where Matt continued his junk-food-and-sports fest, and I pulled an armless chair next to Maggie's bed. I watched her and held her hand for a few minutes, hoping her sleep was a peaceful one. The light over her bed was unforgiving. The flesh on her face and arms resembled wafer-thin parchment paper in a milky-gray hue. She had grown so thin over the past few weeks that her skin sagged, exposing bony ridges and sharp angles.

It had been too long since I had taken her to get her hair cut and colored, and her hair made a pale, fuzzy halo around her slack face. I felt that I had let an important little detail slide; I wouldn't want to be lying in a coma with bad hair. I spent a minute trying to figure out how to get her hair done in her hospital bed, before I realized I was being ridiculous. Maggie had bigger fish to fry.

I finally pulled John Irving's *A Prayer for Owen Meany* out of my tote, and I began reading aloud. I had read it many years ago, enjoyed it immensely, and wanted to read it again. Matt turned off the TV, and when I tired of reading, he took over. I fell asleep to the sound of his voice.

When I opened my eyes, Matt was gone, and it was late afternoon. Dr. Cunningham stood at the foot of Maggie's bed reading her chart. He looked tired.

When he saw that I was awake, he apologized for the delay. Shortly after his meeting, an elderly patient had gone into cardiac arrest. Attempts to revive him had been unsuccessful.

"Please don't apologize," I said. I motioned to the recliner next to Maggie's bed, and offered him a seat, but he remained standing.

"I was hoping Maggie would regain consciousness," he said. "She must be doing worse than I thought. I'm so sorry."

"There you go apologizing again," I said. "If you were God, you'd have some explaining to do."

"What—I'm *not* God?" he replied. "Darn it, when did that happen? Take one quick vacation to the Cape for the weekend, and they pull your creds." He gave me a weak smile, and, once again, I pointed to the chair.

He slowly walked over to it and sat down heavily. He was quiet for a moment, and then said, "I never get used to losing them." I heard the weariness in his voice, noted the lines on each side of his mouth.

"Loss is—" I paused, trying to think of how best to describe it, at least from my perspective. "It's a real bitch."

He nodded. "Yes, it is."

"Must be tons of fun being an oncologist."

"It's a riot," he replied, smiling. "Kind of like working for Cirque de Soleil."

"I remember when I first met you, and I was sitting in your office, I noticed from your photos you were married with kids. I was glad to see you had a family. I think, for someone in your position, it's very important to have loved ones waiting for you at the end of the day."

"My life would be a disaster without Cecelia and the girls." He looked at me. "It also helps when one of my patients has a nice family member," he added and smiled. "About Maggie," he began, his voice serious. "Her vitals aren't as good today as they were when she arrived. They're only going to deteriorate from here on out. I'm sorry, Grace."

I was touched by his gentle tone, even though it rode the coat tails of the worst possible news. He didn't have to say the words; Maggie would be gone soon, and nothing more could be done. "I see no reason to keep her here," I said. "She'd rather be home."

"You would be taking on a lot," he said.

"I have help—I won't be alone." I knew that I could count on Matt and Henry.

Dr. Cunningham hauled himself from the chair. "I'll take care of the arrangements." He smiled, did a quick take on a high wire act across the room, and disappeared into the hallway.

>‹‹‹

I SAT ALONE with Maggie for another forty-five minutes, waiting for Matt to return. I knew I had several messages on my voice mail, but dreaded checking them. I couldn't keep putting it off, though, so I pulled out my cell phone. The oldest message was from Kat. She had called me on Saturday evening after the family from L.A. had toured the inside of my house. They were wild about it and had made a full-price offer. Kat had emailed me a document specifying the terms. Although they had given me plenty of time to think about it, my time was running out.

Kat had left three other voice messages since Monday, casually asking me to get back to her when I could find the time. "No big deal, but the clock's ticking," she said on her final message. "If you don't want to sell to this poor, pathetic, homeless family, just say the word. Hey, maybe I'll let you tell them yourself. Just kidding. Call me, Kiddo."

I sighed, and erased the messages. I knew it wasn't fair to drag it out any longer, so I dialed Kat's number. She answered on the second ring.

"Hey, Grace."

"Hey, Kiddo," I replied.

"What? *I'm* not 'Kiddo,' *you're* 'Kiddo.' It simply doesn't suit me."

"You *said* to call you 'Kiddo.' I quote: 'Call me Kiddo.'"

"I meant 'call me, Kiddo.' Not 'call me Kiddo.'"

"I did. Call you 'Kiddo.'"

"You're giving me a headache, Grace Cavanaugh," she said.

"That's the thanks I get for complying with your wishes?" I knew Kat heard the smile in my voice.

"God, I miss you, Grace. Most of my friends are very mature. You're a breath of fresh air. Please come back to Greenwich," she pleaded. "I need you!"

"If I do return, it's going to have to be somewhere besides Lake Avenue." I blew out a long breath. "I'm going to sell the house."

Kat was quiet for a minute, and then said kindly, "Good for you, Grace. Well, good for *me*, but really, it's the right thing to do. When I took them through your house, Michael was everywhere. *Everywhere.* I can understand why you couldn't stay. I can see why it's been so hard to sell, too. The place actually still *smells* like him."

I thought I was beyond feeling physical pain when it came to Michael, but I was wrong. It felt as though an enormous fist had plunged itself inside my chest and taken hold of my heart, squeezing it so tightly I couldn't breathe. I barely managed to say, "I've got to go, Kat," before abruptly hanging up.

When Matt arrived twenty minutes later with takeout from Tony and Marco's, I was lying next to Maggie, tears streaming down my face, my arm thrown across her frail body. He quickly put the food down on a table and ran to us.

"Oh God!" he said, "I'm sorry I took so long! I should have been here."

I sat up, swung my legs over the edge of the bed, and grabbed a handful of tissues from a box on Maggie's nightstand. I blew my nose, grabbed another bunch, and wiped my eyes. I looked at Matt and gave him a wan smile.

"Maggie's fine," I said, waving the wad of tissues in her direction. "Well, not fine, but not, you know—gone." I whispered the last word.

"Oh, thank God!" exclaimed Matt. *"You're* not fine, though?"

"I'm-selling-my-house-and-it-still-smells-like-Michael," I blurted, and hiccupped loudly. *"Jeez—sorry!"* Another hiccup erupted, and I clapped my hand over my mouth and slid off the bed. Matt took me in his arms, and I burst into tears again. He held me tight, tucked my face in his neck, and murmured in my ear. "Everything's going to be okay."

He eventually reeled me in, and my hiccups softened to quiet gulping. He grabbed more tissues and handed them to me. "Wow, I turn my back for five minutes and all hell breaks loose," he gently teased.

I dried my tears, blew my nose, and apologized for the meltdown. "I'm definitely going to sell my house," I said, and took a deep breath. "And I've decided to bring Maggie back home. I'm trying to keep it together, but it's a lot to deal with. It's going to be hard, you know—all of it."

"You know I'll be there for you," he assured me.

"I do." I looked at him and tried to smile. "I keep thinking I'm making progress with losing Michael, but I guess I still have a way to go. Sorry about the drama."

"Cavanaugh, you don't have to apologize to me for missing your husband. Anyone who deserved you must have been pretty special. Hell, I miss him, and I never even met him." He smiled at me, reached into the takeout bag, and pulled out a bottle of red wine. "A little something from Tony. I wasn't sure you'd want to crack open a bottle in Maggie's hospital room, but I'm guessing you probably wouldn't mind right about now."

Just as I was about to respond, the evening shift arrived in the form of a very tall nurse named Cindy. She eyed the bottle. "Hmm, thinking of drowning your sorrows with a nice Cabernet?" she asked.

"Actually, it's a pretty decent Chianti," replied Matt. "To go with our pasta." He held up the bag of takeout.

"Did you remember to bring a corkscrew?"

"Of course," Matt said. "I was a Boy Scout."

"Very well, then. At ease, Scout." Cindy checked Maggie's monitors, straightened her pillow and blanket, and quickly exited the room.

Matt pulled a multi-purpose tool out of his pocket, opened the bottle of Chianti, and pulled two plastic cups from the bag. He poured wine into each cup and handed me one, and held his glass out to touch mine.

"It'll be okay," he said. "All of it."

After eating dinner and sending Matt home, I fell asleep in the bed next to Maggie's. Late in the night, I dreamed of my house on Lake Avenue. Michael and I were having breakfast in the garden, tossing bits of scone to a flock of mourning doves. Beneath a sun-drenched sky, the crab apple trees were in full bloom; their delicate, pearly white flowers hung in the air like miniature clouds. It felt so good to be there with him; I wanted to capture that one perfect moment in the palm of my hand and hold on to its sweetness. I was sleeping lightly, though, and before I could reach out to touch Michael, my mind sorted through the layers of consciousness and realized it was just a dream.

Disappointed and awake, I got out of bed and checked on Maggie. The light from the corridor found its way under the door, making elongated shadows of chair and table legs, fading before it reached the outer wall. I could see my feet as I walked, and a small length of leg, but the rest of me navigated in darkness.

A bit of light reflected from the metal on Maggie's bed, creating a ghostly outline. I stood and listened to her quiet breathing, felt for her hand in the dark, and took it in mine. I squeezed it gently, willing her to squeeze back.

My feet grew cold as I waited, so I finally returned to my bed feeling very much alone.

I AWOKE SEVERAL hours later and took a quick shower in Maggie's bathroom. I called Dr. Cunningham's office to discuss getting her home. I was told he was making patient rounds and would arrive at Maggie's room within the hour.

Matt showed up while I was drying my hair and applying make-up in the bathroom and placed an enormous Styrofoam cup of coffee on the sink next to my girl stuff. "Thought you might need this." He put his hands on my waist and kissed my neck. "Mmm, you smell sexy."

I met his gaze in the mirror and shook my head sadly. "Only a man could get turned on in a wheelchair-accessible hospital bathroom, surrounded by bedpans and antiseptic wipes."

"What's your point?" He nibbled my neck, clasped his hands in front of me, and pulled me into his body. I could feel myself responding to him and became a little alarmed. I unclasped his hands and squirmed away, knocking over some of my makeup. It cascaded into the sink bowl and settled in the bottom of the wet basin.

"Honestly, behave!" I said. "People are dying here and stuff."

"And I bet all of them would vote for us having sex right here and now, if they could." Matt sighed, carefully removed my makeup from the sink bowl, and placed it back on the rim. He motioned to my makeup. "Sorry I interrupted you." He put the lid down on the toilet, sat, and waited while I finished.

"Can I take you to breakfast?" he asked, as I stuffed the makeup in my bag.

"Maybe later," I said. "I'm waiting for Dr. Cunningham."

He followed me out of the bathroom, and we pulled the chairs close to Maggie's bed and sat. "She doesn't look good," I whispered. I reached for his hand, and he held it, squeezing gently.

"You better bring her home soon."

"What happened when your mother died?" I kept my voice low. "Was she at home? Were you ready?"

Matt looked at me, and then down at his hands. "She was at home. We had hospice caretakers, but Quinn and I were there with her pretty much twenty-four-seven. She didn't recognize us toward the end, but she knew where she was. We knew she was going, but—" he paused and blew out a long breath. "No, we weren't ready."

We were both quiet for a few minutes. I was lost in my thoughts, and I could tell he was somewhere else, as well. I wanted to comfort him, but I didn't know what to say. It was Matt who finally broke our silence.

"I think she would have fought harder and longer if my dad had been around," he said sadly. "She lost interest in life after he died, and when the cancer hit, I think she just gave into it. She was only fifty-nine." He looked at me with a mixture of pain and sympathy in his eyes. I had to look away.

"Do you think Maggie knows where she is?" I straightened her covers and rested my hand on her arm. "I'm sure she'd rather be at home. I feel like I've let her down, all this moving back and forth."

"Cavanaugh, you haven't let Maggie down. She couldn't have asked for more." Matt scooted his chair close to mine, gently took my hand, and pressed his lips to my palm.

Dr. Cunningham arrived half-an-hour later with two interns in tow. He introduced them to Matt and me, gave us an apologetic look, and launched into a description of Maggie's history and vitals. The interns took turns giving Maggie a brief examination, made a few comments to Dr. Cunningham, and went back into the hall.

"Sorry about that," Dr. Cunningham said. "It's part of the job."

"It's all right," I said.

"I've made arrangements for Maggie's discharge." He reached for her chart, took a pen from his coat pocket, and made a few notes. "When do you want to take her home?"

"Soon. I was thinking first thing Monday morning."

"No problem. Please call me any time with questions or concerns." He put his hand out, and I took it. He held my hand briefly, and then he and Matt shook hands.

"Why don't you both go home and get some rest?" he advised. "I know from experience that you don't get any real sleep at a hospital. You're going to need to be rested when she comes home."

"Thanks," I replied. "That's probably a good idea. You're right—sleeping here hasn't exactly been easy."

"There's a reason we have everyone here on morphine," he said.

12

just the two of us

I WAS SITTING on Bertha, my cell phone, laptop, and notepad spread before me, checking messages and taking notes. Several relatives had called to see how Maggie was doing and I returned their calls, letting them know I was planning on bringing her home as soon as possible. Kat had left a long, apologetic message on my voice mail. I knew I had to call her; she had never meant to hurt me by talking about Michael.

Ellen and Stogie were sprawled on the floor, pretending to sleep. They took turns checking on me, making certain I wasn't going anywhere. My incarceration was fine with me. As soon as I finished retrieving all of my messages and returned a few phone calls, I was going to follow Dr. Cunningham's orders and take a nap. It was early afternoon but felt like it had already been a long day.

I called Henry to let him know I was bringing Maggie home and needed his help. I let his cell phone ring several times and was just about to hang up when he answered.

"Hello?" he said.

"Henry, it's Grace. Hope I didn't interrupt anything important—what's with the noise?"

"Oh, that." He chuckled. "It's the casino 'buzz' they pipe in to keep us all lulled into complacency—I'm playing poker at Mohegan Sun. Winning, by the way."

"Good for you. I don't want to spoil your fun, but I'm calling to let you know I'm bringing Maggie home."

"Oh." Henry said.

"I'll need your help."

"Of course," he replied. "Don't worry, Grace, it'll be all right. I'll take good care of her."

"I know, Henry. I'll be glad to have you back." I listened to the background noise for a minute, told him to win big, and hung up.

I called Matt next and gave him a quick update. He was at home planning his schedule for September, when he would return to MIT. Despite all he had been doing for Maggie and me, he had also been consulting for a tech firm in Boston over the summer and had a minor deadline before the end of the week. He tried to explain to me what he was doing, but my brain was too fried to follow him. He finally gave up, and instead we made plans to spend the night together if we weren't both too exhausted.

I WAS FEELING the insistent pull of a nap, but I wanted to get my phone call to Kat out of the way so I could relax and sleep. She answered on the third ring, and I could tell she had me on her speakerphone in her car.

"Hey, Grace."

"Hey, Kat. Sorry it took me so long to get back to you. Maggie's still in the hospital, and she's not improving. I've been staying there, sleeping there—it's been hard to make calls."

"If you're trying to make me feel even worse, it's working."

"I know you well," I informed her.

"You manipulative little bitch," she replied.

"You know *me* well." We both laughed.

"Honey—I'm so sorry about our last conversation," Kat said. "I wanted to talk to you about the house, and about Michael, but I never meant to make things worse for you. I just wanted you to know I understand."

"It's getting easier."

"That's my girl."

"You sound like Maggie. I'm going to miss her a lot."

"I can't open my mouth without putting my foot in it, can I?" Kat said, and added, "You're going to make me pay for my indiscretions, aren't you?"

"Sure, we can start by talking about your ridiculously high commission."

"Oh, fine, now you're picking on my poor little Sammy and his special educational needs."

"Not to mention your sagging ass."

"Not to mention."

"Actually, I think you've more than earned your paycheck on this deal," I told her. "I'm sorry I've been such a mess. No one else on the planet would have put up with me. Tell the nice people that they can still have the house, but it won't be right away. I don't know how long I'll be taking care of Maggie."

"No problem. I've found them a nice month-to-month rental in town. They'll be thrilled to hear you're willing to sell."

Before we hung up, I promised updates on Maggie's condition. The dogs were sound asleep, so I snuck downstairs for a bottle of water, and returned to a little rest and relaxation with Bertha. I set my alarm for four o'clock and adjusted my pillow. Five minutes after I pulled the down comforter over my tired body, I was out cold.

I would have slept straight through until my alarm went off had Ellen not felt the need to check on me. Her chocolate stare penetrated my dreams, and I awoke to find her head resting on the bed just inches away from my face.

"Hey, girlfriend," I said, yawning. "You've been missing Momma, I guess." She pushed her face to mine and gave it a polite bath with her gentle tongue. I groaned and wiped my face. "I guess I'm up now," I said, and scratched her head. "Want to go for a walk?"

The dogs were thrilled to have me home, and I felt bad knowing I had to leave them again, but Maggie needed me. I had no choice. I knew Matt would feed and hang out with them until I returned.

I took a long walk around the block with the dogs. We visited a few neighbors and I updated them on Maggie's condition. I told them I was bringing her back home. A few of the old Catholics had been lighting candles for her at Stan's, and Father Brian had held a special Mass for her the evening before. I was touched by their thoughtfulness and told them I would let Maggie know she was in their prayers.

Back home, I gave the dogs fresh water and a treat, and tossed a few snacks and my book into my tote. I called Matt but got his voice mail, so I left a message letting him know I was heading back to the hospital.

When I arrived at Maggie's room, it was clear that her condition hadn't changed. Her face was pale and drawn. Her dentures had been removed upon her arrival at the hospital, and her sunken mouth was slightly open. Her breathing was weak. I put my hand on hers, told her I was there, and I watched her eyes closely, hoping for some sign that she heard or felt my presence.

I closed my eyes and tried to imagine the darkness that enveloped her, and the thought saddened me. I tried to cheer both of us by sitting on the edge of her bed and giving her updates on Henry and the dogs. I told her I had decided to sell my house, and that I was slowly coming to terms with losing Michael.

"It hasn't been easy, Mags" I admitted, "but being with you has helped. You've been such a trooper—I realize I need to stop feeling sorry for myself."

I got up and closed the door, and dragged the recliner next to the bed. I sat down and reached for her hand, and I held it as the sun fell away and the room grew dark.

Once the other patients had been served dinner, and the last of the visitors said their goodbyes, I finally left.

It was a pleasant August evening, warm and slightly humid, so I drove with my windows down. When I reached Cleveland Street, several neighbors were sitting on their porches, and I waved to them as I drove past. I pulled into Maggie's driveway; a lone light burned in the living room window. The rest of the house was dark, and I realized how much I missed having Maggie at home.

I locked the car and walked up the new bluestone walkway. It was already eight-thirty; fireflies and a bright, low moon illuminated the night. I paused and touched a fat white bloom on one of the oversized hydrangeas planted on each side of the steps.

Two had convinced me they would be a better choice than the boxwoods I had specified. "It'll be worth looking at those spindly sticks in the winter when you have gorgeous blossoms in the summer," he'd said. I agreed it had been a good choice.

The dogs greeted me as I came through the front door. They followed me to the living room where Matt was watching a sports channel in Maggie's chair with a cold beer in his hand.

"Honey, I'm home," I said. "Did you miss me?"

He set his beer on a table, got up, and took me in his arms. "Not only did I miss you, but I couldn't get you off my mind," he murmured, kissing my neck and gently biting my ear lobe. "You hanging in there?"

"I'm as fine as I can be. I didn't want to leave Maggie, but I'm exhausted, and I know I need a good night's rest."

"Too tired for dinner?" he asked. "I made a nice roasted chicken and salad."

"I'm never too tired for your cooking." I held him tightly. "And, just in case you're wondering, I'm not too tired for a little piece of you, either. Spend the night, okay?"

"Even if it just involves some spectacular spooning, I'm in." He gave me a gentle squeeze.

We had a quiet dinner at the kitchen table with a bottle of wine Matt had brought. I got up to clear the table when we were finished, but he gently pushed me back into my chair. He poured me another glass of wine and began putting our plates and utensils in the sink.

I surveyed the room. "Doesn't look like I'm ever going to get the chance to renovate this kitchen. Maybe they can turn it into a museum. Let the kiddies see how people lived in the good old days."

"It certainly is a time warp." Matt turned the faucet on, and the plumbing screeched momentarily before spitting out a stream of water.

"I've actually grown a little fond of it. Hearkens back to a simpler time, a simpler life."

"Hearkens?" Matt poured detergent into the sink.

"Yeah, you know, refers to a former period of time."

"Oh, I know what 'hearkens' means, Cavanaugh. I just didn't realize anyone actually still used the word. At least anyone under the age of . . ."

"Hey, don't even *try* to mess with me," I said. "Just because you made me dinner and you're doing the dishes, well—you know—don't even try."

"After that pithy comeback, I bet if I tried, I'd win." Matt grinned and flicked water in my direction.

"Pithy? I think that makes us even."

When everything was tidy downstairs, we went upstairs and took turns getting ready in the bathroom. Matt went first, washing up and brushing his teeth; and then I went through my girl routine: removing my makeup, applying moisturizer, flossing and brushing my teeth—while Matt sat on the toilet lid and watched.

"Are you developing a new hobby?" I pulled out my magnifying mirror, plucked a few errant eyebrow hairs, and put a light glosser on my lips.

"I just enjoy watching women do their thing. It's an interesting process."

"Bit of a voyeur in you?" I brushed my hair and worked a dab of argan oil through the ends.

"Call it what you want. I like to watch." He leaned back, propped an elbow on the sink, and smiled.

I pumped some body lotion out of a dispenser and rubbed it over my arms and legs. Matt's eyes followed my every move.

"Well—show's over." I put away my supplies, gave a little curtsy, and headed to the bedroom with Matt in tow. The dogs had been waiting patiently in the hallway and followed us.

"Sorry, kids, Momma and Uncle Matt need a little privacy," I said when we reached the threshold. I closed the door, and the dogs settled down in the hallway after a little shuffling and sighing.

I snapped off the bedroom's harsh overhead light, lit the scented candle that I kept on my dresser, opened the rear windows, and closed the drapes. Matt sat on the edge of the bed with his arms and legs crossed, smiling. "Setting the mood?"

"And you say *I* have a one-track mind." I smiled back at him. "Maybe I just like ambiance for the sake of ambiance."

"That would be a bummer."

I laughed and took Matt's hand in mine. "I'm glad you were here waiting for me when I got home. It felt good to know I wasn't alone in the world. Thanks."

"And now—to show your appreciation—you can slip into something a little more comfortable."

IT WAS PAST midnight when Matt got up to blow out the candle and let the dogs into the room. I was about to fall asleep when a thought that had been banging around in the back of my brain finally surfaced. I quickly sat up in bed.

"Matt—I almost forgot! It's our birthday on Monday. Maggie's and mine. We can have a little party when she comes home."

"Hey, that sounds great. A little weird, but great. How old are you going to be?"

"Don't worry, it's not a major birthday. I did say *little* party."

"So, how many candles should I buy for your cake?"

"A whole lot fewer than the ones we need to buy for Maggie."

"How many fewer?"

"Give it up, Matt," I said. "Frankly, I don't want any cake, and Maggie can't have any. There will be no cake and no candles."

"Fine. It's your day. What gift is customary for your age?" Matt gave me an innocent look.

"Nothing. You're confusing birthdays with anniversaries."

"If you were an anniversary, what would be the appropriate gift for you?"

"I said, give it up." I plopped back into my pillow and sighed. "I used to love birthdays when I was a kid. Doesn't seem quite fair that the enjoyment you get from a birthday is inversely correlated to the number of candles on your cake."

"Yeah, you can't enjoy your dependent variable independent of your independent variable," Matt agreed. "Doesn't work that way."

"Jeez, I hate that." I pulled my comforter up over my shoulders.

"Yeah, it sucks." Matt moved his hand under the comforter and found mine. "But you're right. We should have a little party."

"Maggie and I used to go out on our birthdays together and have sundaes."

"Sounds nice."

"It was. Seems like a million years ago. Seems like yesterday."

WHEN I AWOKE the next morning, Matt was gone, but he had left a carafe of coffee on my nightstand. Sitting next to it were a pitcher of half-and-half and a sugar bowl. My favorite mug and a spoon rested on a paper napkin along with a delicious-looking cinnamon scone. In my world, it just didn't get any better than that.

The dogs were nowhere to be seen, so I assumed they had gone downstairs with Matt and he had let them out in the backyard for their morning potty break. I briefly considered trying to get a little more sleep, but the smell of fresh coffee slowly filled the room. Once my mind started to anticipate the pleasure of a caffeine buzz, there was no turning back.

After visiting the bathroom, I opened the bedroom window, crawled back into bed and poured myself a mug of piping hot coffee. Matt must have nuked it in the microwave before putting it in the carafe since he knew I liked it good and hot. What a guy.

I sipped in silence and enjoyed the fresh morning air. It was a little humid, so I kicked off the comforter and stretched out my legs over the cool sheets. I looked out the window and thought about our backyard on Lake Avenue. When Michael and I finished renovating our house, we had landscaped our small lot and found room for a pool. During the summer months, we spent early weekend mornings sitting by it dressed in our pajamas. We enjoyed our coffee and newspaper together and watched the neighborhood swallows feast on gnats that swarmed above the water. I recalled pieces of the dream I had in Maggie's hospital room and felt Michael's presence.

I missed everything about my life with him. I suppose I could have kept pieces of it intact—continued living in the house and enjoying the pool with Ellen and Stogie—but even after three months of living in Springfield, the thought of being there without Michael was still unbearable. If I couldn't have all of my old life back, I wanted none of it.

I finished a second cup of coffee and started wondering what Matt was up to. I reluctantly slid out of bed, pulled on a pair of shorts and a T-shirt, and went back into the bathroom to wash my face and brush my teeth. While pulling my hair into a ponytail, I heard the front door open and close, followed by footsteps coming up the staircase. Matt entered the bathroom, sweaty and shirtless from his morning run.

"Pretty day out." I smiled at his reflection in the mirror.

"Gorgeous—but hot already." Matt moved behind me and wrapped me in his sweaty arms. "Hope you don't mind, but running gets my juices flowing, you know what I mean?"

"Your 'juices' are getting all over my T-shirt."

"Sorry."

"It's okay, I haven't showered yet." I had finally hired a plumber to install a showerhead and enjoyed its simple luxury. I was learning not to take certain things for granted living in Maggie's old house.

"How 'bout we take one together?" he asked and nuzzled my neck.

"I wash your back and you wash mine?"

"Something like that." He smiled at me in the mirror. "Although I would find the front more interesting." He slid his hands under my T-shirt and cupped my breasts.

"So, you're a breast man," I said.

He removed his hands from my breasts, slid them down to my bottom, and gently squeezed. "Well, now I'm confused," he said.

We stripped off our clothes and got into the shower. The water pressure wasn't very good, so we jockeyed for position, trying to get the best spot. We tried to have a little fun in the process, but the tub was too slippery. Finally, Matt turned off the water, stepped out of the tub, picked me up dripping wet, and carried me into the bedroom. He tossed me onto Bertha, retrieved our towels from the bathroom, and took his time drying my body. When he was done, I returned the favor.

We spent almost an hour enjoying each other, but once the passion haze cleared, I noted the time and felt immediately guilty. "I should have been at the hospital long before now!" I said and scrambled to get dressed.

Matt looked amused as he climbed from the bed and searched through a short stack of clothes he had left in my room. He threw them on and headed out. "Give me five minutes and I'll meet you in the driveway," he said. "We'll head over to the hospital together. You, Maggie, and I will plan the party."

We had a hard time finding a parking spot when we reached the hospital. It was the weekend, and the halls were crowded with anxious relatives and friends. The room next to Maggie's was packed with people visiting an elderly patient who was new to the ward. They were practically shouting at the woman who appeared to be the patient's wife. A middle-aged man looked in our direction when we walked by the room. "Sorry about the volume," he said. "My mom's hearing isn't great."

"Please don't worry," I said. "My great-aunt isn't conscious—you're not bothering her." Matt and I entered Maggie's room, closed the door, and pulled two chairs beside the bed.

"Hey, Mags," I said, running my hand up and down her arm. "Did you have a good night? I hope the racket next door didn't interrupt your morning nap." Maggie's gaunt face remained expressionless; I took her hand and squeezed it tenderly. "We're taking you home tomorrow. You'll be back in your own bed, and Matt, Henry and the dogs will keep us company." Maggie was pale and silent. " Matt wants to plan a birthday party for us. Nothing big, mind you. I think we should keep it simple."

"Don't listen to her, Maggie," Matt said, sitting down on her bed and taking her other hand in his. "I'm going to buy a gigantic cake, so it can hold all the candles, and then I'm going to invite the whole neighborhood."

I gave Matt a droll look. "Hmm, yeah, or maybe *not*."

We sat quietly for a few minutes, listening to the din in the hallway, and the muffled shouting from the room next door.

"We have to get Maggie out of here," I finally said.

"Tomorrow," replied Matt.

The visitors in the adjacent room finally left, and we spent a quiet afternoon with Maggie. Dr. Cunningham stopped by late in the day and asked us to step into the hall with him. We discussed the process for getting Maggie back home the next morning.

"Do you think I'm doing the right thing?" I felt as though I was second-guessing my every move, but I couldn't help myself.

"If bringing her home is what you want to do—do it. There is no right or wrong decision. Maybe you'll rest easier having her there. Maybe that's reason enough."

"I think she'd rather be surrounded by family and friends."

"Who wouldn't?" he responded kindly.

It was late—a few minutes past visiting hours—when I asked Matt to drive me home. On the way, we stopped at a restaurant for dinner, but neither of us had much of an appetite.

Once we were back at Maggie's, Matt walked the dogs, and

then disappeared upstairs. I changed the sheets on Maggie's bed and fussed about the house getting it ready for her to come home. When everything was neat, I went through my nighttime routine—a hot shower, flossing, brushing, moisturizing—and found comfort in how ordinary it felt. Finally, I went into my bedroom and climbed into bed. Matt was already gently snoring, so I gave him a tender squeeze and then promptly fell asleep.

I GOT THE call at 3:00 a.m., on our birthday.

Cindy, the night nurse, apologized for waking me but thought I should know that Maggie probably wouldn't make it through the night.

"I'm on my way," I said and hung up.

The phone had awakened Matt, and he turned on the lamp. "What's up?" he asked.

"It's Maggie." My feet hit the floor, and I hurried to the closet. "She—" I blinked as hot tears began to form in my eyes. "She doesn't have long." I yanked a skirt and top from the closet.

Matt climbed from the bed and reached for his clothes. I put my hand on his arm. "No—*please*," I implored. "I've got to do this alone."

"What?" He rubbed both eyes and squinted back at me. "Why?"

"I don't know—I just think I need to." I didn't know, not really, but I thought I needed to face death alone with Maggie. Just the two of us, in the end.

"Let me go with you," he begged. "I don't want you going alone. Not at this hour."

I felt a tear slide down my face, and I wiped it away. "I'll take the dogs," I said. "They'll keep me company. Please don't take this personally. I just need to deal with this—with loss—and know that I can get through it on my own."

His expression softened, and he reached out and gently squeezed my hand. "Okay, Grace, if that's what you want. I'll wait here for you."

I HEADED OUT the door and went to the cube with the sleepy dogs trailing behind me.

"We're goin' for a ride," I told them. They piled into the car quietly, and Ellen settled down in back for more sleep. Stogie sat in the passenger's seat and yawned. I wished I could take them into the hospital to be with Maggie and me.

Traffic was light, with only an occasional pair of headlights streaming past us. I felt alone in my mission and reached out to Stogie and placed my hand on his warm little body. He stirred, shifted his head, and blew out a sigh.

The cube's clock read 3:46 a.m. when I pulled into the deserted parking lot at the hospital and parked in a space near the lobby. Bright security lights illuminated the night hovering above us but faded abruptly into darkness where the asphalt turned to grass. I rolled down the windows, said good-bye to the dogs, and entered the hospital alone.

It was clear Maggie had taken a turn for the worst in my absence, and it broke my heart to see my bony Amazon lying so utterly still. Cindy informed me that Maggie had experienced cardiac arrest around two a.m. and had barely survived. The attending physician didn't think she'd last more than a few hours. Her vital signs were not good; it was close to the end.

I sat in Maggie's room next to her bed. Muted conversation drifted down the hall and I could hear the soft rustling of nurses at work as they moved in and out of rooms. My fingertips moved lightly up and down Maggie's pale, dry arm. I held her hand. Her fingernails were too long. I brushed a translucent hair behind her ear.

I imagined her in her garden, waving her trowel, talking to the dogs. I imagined her a young girl, skipping down the sidewalk on Cleveland Street in the spring, wearing a new dress and shiny new shoes.

Gray dawn and blue morning appeared in sequence, and I was still holding her hand long after she was gone.

13

jmj

I spent the morning of my birthday calling relatives with news of Maggie's death and making funeral arrangements. I had a long list to work through before Father Brian came to the house. He had offered to help me write Maggie's obituary and plan her service at Stan's. I was feeling a little overwhelmed by everything that needed to be done, but I was determined to get it all right for Maggie.

One of the last calls I made was to an older cousin of Maggie's—Catherine Murray—who had sent her several lovely cards in recent weeks. When I gave Catherine the sad news, she started crying. Maggie's death hit me like a dark wall when I heard pain and loss on the other end of the phone; I had been coasting along in an emotional daze, and it was as if she flipped a switch in me. I started crying with her and shared my grief with a woman I hadn't seen in years. When we both finished crying, we sat and listened to each other breathe for a silent minute until I finally said good-bye and hung up.

I found out that Maggie had been a fixture in many relatives' lives. I knew that she and I shared a special bond, but it was nice to learn that she had a broader emotional circle than I had imagined. I listened to a lot of Maggie stories that had me both laughing and crying, sometimes at the same time. Several of us decided we must have "Jesus, Mary and Joseph" T-shirts made for her service.

I had told Matt we were still going to have a party; not to celebrate the birthday Maggie and I shared, but to celebrate Maggie's life. It was going to be a beautiful summer night, and we would have the party in the backyard.

Matt, Henry, Ellen, and Stogie were out inviting everyone on Cleveland Street to Maggie's party. (God bless Henry—he had showed up at six o'clock that morning to get the house ready for Maggie's homecoming.) Once they finished with Cleveland, they would hit Jefferson, and then it was on to the rest of the presidents. Tony and Marco were closing the restaurant for the evening and bringing aluminum trays of pasta and salad. They planned to leave a sign on the restaurant door inviting everyone to Cleveland Street for our celebration.

I finished making all of my calls, including those to Emily and Laura, both necessitating Matt updates. The calls had been tiring, but I knew that Maggie would have appreciated my effort. It felt good to be there for her even though she was gone.

I sifted through several pictures I had taken of Maggie, and took one to a nearby photo store where I asked an employee to blow it up to almost life-size. It was the one I'd snapped on our trip to Quabbin Reservoir. Maggie was reclining on the Hudson Bay blanket, dogs at her side, polyester pants a bit twisted, with a contented smile on her face.

With Maggie's mega-sized photo glued to poster board, I bought a black marker so I could be the first to autograph it: *"From your great (or grand?) niece, who already misses you. Love, Gracie girl. JMJ, what will I do without you?"*

I finished my last-minute errands for the party and arrived back at Maggie's, where I found Father Brian sitting on the front porch with Stogie and Ellen. He was having a friendly conversation with them about dogs in the Bible.

"I don't remember a whole lot of biblical dog stories," I said as I joined the three of them. "At least not very flattering ones."

"I admit ta takin' a little poetic license." Father Brian gave Ellen an affectionate pat on her hairy head. "The Good Book can be a little harsh regardin' these poor beasts."

"How do you like this picture of Maggie?" I leaned the poster against the porch wall.

"Ach, I'll miss that woman, I truly will," he said, shaking his head sadly. "What a shame, her dyin' on her birthday, and all."

"So, you know it's her birthday. Mine, too."

"Of course it is." Father Brian smiled at me.

I opened my mouth in surprise.

"You were one of her favorite people," he said. "She talked about you a good bit. I saw the Christmas photos every year, and she always mentioned you on her birthday."

"Is that why you encouraged her to ask me to come to Hungry Hill?" I asked.

"Oh, no, lass—I had nothing to do with it. Maggie took me aside after Mass one day and asked me to stop by her house so we could talk. She gave me the bad news about her cancer." Father Brian shook his head. "I asked her what she was going to do. I was very worried. She told me not to fret about the situation, that she would be all right. She was going to ask you to come and stay with her."

"She told me *you* insisted she call me," I informed him. "According to her, you were being a real pain in the ass about it— pardon my language. I didn't entirely buy the story, though."

Father Brian threw his head back and laughed. "Oh, yes, that sounds just like Maggie! I can only imagine the things I've been blamed for over the years."

"My mother got involved, too, and told me Maggie had no choice. You'd keep after her until she called me." I smiled at the thought of my mother falling for Maggie's manipulation. Or maybe they were co-conspirators. It could be hard to tell with my mother.

"I'll admit to having some sleepless nights over it," Father Brian said. "I asked her what she'd do if you couldn't come, and she said she'd figure it out." He looked at the picture of Maggie for a long moment. "She knew you'd come. Now that I've gotten to know you, I can see why. You're a special person, Grace, and you've always been close to her heart whether you knew it or not." He put his hand over mine and squeezed. Ellen tolerated the show of affection briefly before shoving her nose under our hands.

It came as a surprise to me that Maggie was so fond of me. I had assumed that she had asked me to take care of her simply because I seemed to be the most available family member. I didn't have much of a life to maneuver around. I told Father Brian it hadn't occurred to me that our early connection had remained so tangible to her.

"Oh, Maggie wasn't overly sentimental," he said, "and she never would have intruded on your life, but you mattered to her just the same."

"I'm glad I came. I really am. The whole thing has been okay."

"You've been a fine little trooper, lass. Maybe Maggie knew

what she was doing, asking you to come here. Maybe it was as much about you as it was about her."

"Maybe." I thought about Maggie's way of giving to her family, and knew after spending so much time with her recently it involved more than new shoes and ice cream sundaes. I could feel her presence on the porch and couldn't help but smile.

"Since you know it's my birthday, would you like to help me celebrate a little?" I asked.

"What might ya have in mind?"

"How about a little bourbon and seltzer with lots of ice? I've almost acquired a taste." I smiled.

"It *is* a pretty hot afternoon, but I have ta be sharp for Mass at six."

"Just do the whole thing in Latin—no one will know if you screw it up." I winked at Father Brian and he laughed.

"I'll have ta give that some consideration while we have ourselves a little drink. I can cut Mass a bit short, too, so I can get back here to Maggie's party. I think my flock will understand. Especially if they're invited," he added.

IT WAS A beautiful summer night when we celebrated Maggie's life. One hundred and forty-seven people showed up (according to Henry). Most were from the surrounding neighborhood and Stan's, but a dozen people who stopped for dinner at Tony and Marco's joined us, and there were a few people driving by who stopped to see what was going on. They included four Springfield cops who were patrolling the hood.

We went through three cases of very good Chianti supplied

at a discount through our local grocer, seven bottles of bourbon, and two cases of seltzer. There were a lot of takers for "The Maggie"—one-part bourbon, three-parts seltzer. Many neighbors brought coolers full of sodas and water, and everyone shared. We put dozens of candles in glass jars and circled the yard with them until the night glowed like a warm embrace.

Vinnie and his cousins helped transport the food and alcohol in their pick-up trucks, and they stayed through the evening to help serve and clean up. Two neighborhood teenagers brought a portable speaker and were impromptu deejays. The driveway was our dance floor, and the blinking summer stars our disco ball. Ellen was the official bouncer, but she didn't turn anyone away.

THE MORNING OF Maggie's funeral was a summer scorcher. Most of the mourners at Stan's were dressed in light-colored casual clothing, so it didn't look like a funeral crowd. Father Brian performed the Mass, of course—mostly in Latin—and the lovely old cathedral was nearly full by the time relatives joined the neighborhood and parish crowd.

I was glad to see that Maggie's funeral was properly attended. Even young couples from Cleveland Street who barely knew her sat in the pews. I had been to the funerals of elderly people that could have been held in someone's living room, which only made their passing so much sadder. When half of Greenwich showed up at Michael's service, it meant the world to me. I would always make an effort to attend funerals, knowing what I knew about being left behind.

My parents had taken a red-eye flight from Greece and arrived just in time for the service, and Emily and Laura had flown in from their respective homes in Philadelphia and Atlanta. It was a relief to have them all there with me, and I experienced that supremely odd conflict of emotions that occurs when you're sad and happy all at once. My dad sat next to me at Stan's and wrapped his big, warm arm around my shoulders, and I felt myself slowly giving into the comfort of having him there. Eventually, everything got very quiet in my head, and I felt a great peace wash over me.

When the Mass was finished, and Maggie had taken her place in the parish cemetery along with her parents, my grandfather, and her sister Elizabeth, we returned to the house. I enjoyed catching up with family news, and I realized how much I had missed everyone. I was able to share a few happy moments talking about Michael, finally, and it felt good.

My sisters spent the entire afternoon vying for Matt's attention. Occasionally, Quinn and I would attempt an intervention. We eventually gave up and parked ourselves in a corner of the parlor passing a "Maggie" between us while socializing with the rest of the crowd. It was wonderful to see everyone, even under the circumstances.

After most of the relatives and guests had left, a small group of us headed over to Tony and Marco's for dinner. Henry joined us and had us all chuckling about Maggie and her antics.

"She'd talk to the dogs about me behind my back," he told everyone. "Make stuff up. It was a different story every day. Once, she told them I was holding her hostage. Another time, she told them she suspected I was slipping something into her drinks. I was. It's called *water*."

He bonded with my dad over a mutual respect for Vesper martinis (shaken, not stirred), and my mother pumped him for information on Las Vegas because she and my dad were planning their first trip there during the winter. He played several impromptu rounds of poker with two of my cousins and Father Brian, even though Matt warned them not to get involved. "You might as well just hand over your wallet," he told them. One of my older cousins, a senior insurance executive at The Hartford, eventually ended up paying for dinner after he lost his fifth and final hand against Henry.

My parents and sisters left for their hotel, but promised to come back to the house in the morning for breakfast before leaving town. They had taken an Uber to the church, so Quinn had offered to drive them to the hotel and pick them up in the morning. It had been a long day, and I was exhausted. I said goodnight to everyone, and Matt took me home and tucked me into bed.

"Those sisters of mine are something else," I said to him after he turned the lights out and crawled into bed.

"They are indeed." I could hear the smile in his voice.

"They're also both very married," I added for the record. "What are you grinning about?"

"How do you know I'm grinning? It's dark in here." Matt felt for my face and traced a finger over my lips.

"Not that dark—and your teeth are pretty white—plus I know you."

"Okay, so I'm happy to be in bed with you. You've found me out."

"Hmm." I wasn't buying it.

"You doing okay?" Matt asked, changing the subject. He slipped his arms around me and pulled me to him. We gravitated to our favorite position in one easy motion: my left leg inserted through his legs, my right leg riding his left thigh, our bodies pressed together. It was a good fit.

"Yeah, I'm pretty good," I admitted, and pressed my lips against his neck.

"Oh, Cavanaugh, trust me, you're better than 'pretty good.'"

"So, if you had to choose between Emily, Laura, and me, you'd choose me?" I asked and nibbled on his ear lobe.

"You must think I'm a total idiot," he murmured, and pulled me closer.

"Not a *total* idiot, but you did ignore me most of the day."

"Only because I knew you would have me all to yourself tonight. Have to spread the love around a little."

"It's pathetic that you need so much attention."

"I do have my faults." Matt kissed me and ran his hand down my thigh.

"Hmm, yeah, faults..." I mumbled, losing my train of thought.

THE REILLY FAMILY had owned the house on Cleveland Street since 1918—just over one hundred years, almost a record in the city of Springfield. No one in the family was interested in buying it from Maggie's estate, so as her executrix, I met with a real estate agent the week after the funeral to put it on the market. It seemed a shame to sell it, but I couldn't think of a good reason not to—I wasn't staying.

Emily asked me if Cormac and Natalie could have a few pieces of Maggie's furniture, since they were moving into an apartment together the following spring. I picked out a few of the better pieces, including Maggie's old mahogany bed, and had them cleaned and delivered to a storage facility in Springfield. I was glad to put them to good use; it made it easier to get rid of everything else. I found a buyer on Craigslist for Maggie's vintage refrigerator and stove, which were still in good condition, and gave an old laundry mangle to a gay couple on Jefferson who thought it would make a cool garden ornament.

I hired Vinnie and his two twenty-something sons to help me go through the rest of the contents of the house and prepare it for sale. It was quite a project, given the age of the house and the generations of accumulated possessions. We started in the attic and worked our way down and out into the backyard, where we sorted through everything. Much of it had no value and went immediately into a large dumpster. Items that might be of value were placed in neat piles in the garage.

At the end of each day, we put useable items in the front yard for the neighbors to pick through. Everything was free with a dollar contribution to the "honor bar"—and the late afternoons turned into cocktail parties on the front porch. Maggie's poster board picture always attended, and the autographs grew until they covered every inch of it. Several artistic neighbors added accessories to her picture: jewelry, a fur coat, and a full set of luggage; she eventually looked like she was ready to set sail on the Queen Mary. ("Hey," said one slightly drunk neighbor, "hope she's goin' someplace *nice*.")

Maggie made the local paper, the Springfield Republican, in a special interest story on the history of the Hungry Hill area. Ellen and Stogie became minor local celebrities since they were mentioned in the article as "surviving next of kin" by the dog-loving journalist who did the interview and story. People stopped by to reminisce about growing up in the neighborhood, and several of them brought treats for the dogs and bottles of Irish bourbon. I wished Maggie could have been around to see what a fuss everyone was making over her.

WE PUT SEVERAL boxes full of old photographs and albums in the front hallway, and I went through one or two of them every night with Matt after cocktails and dinner. He was due back at MIT the following week, so we tried to spend as much time together as possible.

I didn't want him to leave, but I couldn't ask him to stay. *I* wasn't staying, and we were headed in opposite directions. Matt had a life in Boston, and I had one in Greenwich that needed sorting out. I couldn't ask Matt to change his plans for me and join me in Greenwich—I had nothing to offer him except my need for his company.

It was late Friday night, and our daily cocktail party had finally concluded. Matt and I cleaned up the porch and disposed of the trash, and I made a light dinner since there had been more than a little junk food at the party. We took our plates and sat on the floor in the hallway going through the last box of photographs. I wanted to cull the best ones, scan them, and make them available to my family.

There were a few great shots of family gatherings that included my immediate family. I set them aside so I could later have them duplicated and framed. I knew Emily and Laura would love them.

In the bottom of the box, there was a blue album with pictures of Maggie and me. The first few pages had photos with "August

6th" written in Maggie's scrawl beneath them, with the year added. I was very young in the photographs.

"Take a look at this," I said to Matt, handing him the album. "I don't remember any of these pictures being taken. Maggie looks so young. I don't remember her ever being that young."

"You were just a little peanut," Matt said. "A very cute little peanut."

"Couldn't help myself. I was born adorable."

"This sure proves it." Matt flipped through the pages slowly, watching me grow into a twelve-year-old. "You look like a little colt in this one." He laughed and pointed at my legs.

"Better long and lean, than short and stubby," I replied, defending my skinny legs and rather knobby knees. "Besides, that period didn't last long. It was all uphill and gorgeous from there." I smiled at Matt and pointed. "I do remember that picture being taken. Look at the shoes—I remember getting them from Maggie's store for my birthday."

Matt continued to look through the album, and in the middle found a picture from my wedding day. Michael and I were at our table, toasting each other, all smiles. Maggie hadn't attended, but I had sent out Christmas cards that year with the photo.

"You were beautiful," Matt said. "Really, really beautiful. Michael wasn't bad, either."

I took the album back from Matt and studied the photo. The original sat on Michael's desk in his office at our home, and I thought briefly about what was waiting for me in Greenwich. I slowly went through twenty-one more years of Christmas photos we had sent, and Maggie had kept, and my chest felt tight. I had never seen them all together at once. Michael had always insisted on having quirky, fun candids taken of us with the dogs, and they provided a micro history of our wonderful life together. The earliest ones included our first dog—Jack—another handsome wolfhound. His dark brown eyes gazed at Michael in the photos, his adoration obvious and complete.

The final photo in the album was from our last Christmas together. We were all wearing silly ski hats—Michael and Vertigo had Viking horns attached to theirs, and Stogie's had a skull and cross insignia. "Gotta let the men be men," he had told me, "and the girls be girls." Ellen and I had matching knitted pink hats with long, yellow braids. Stogie had taken to his hat immediately, but Vertigo and Ellen had merely suffered through the photo shoot. The tightness in my heart moved into my throat.

"Yeah, we were a pretty cute couple," I said quietly, closing the album.

"You still miss him," Matt said.

"I miss *him*, I miss being *married*—I miss our life together. Sometimes, I wake up thinking he's still around, and get my heart broken all over again."

"I'm really sorry, Grace," he said gently.

"Hey," I said, "I thought we agreed you'd call me 'Cavanaugh.'" I blew out a long breath.

"That does sort of keep you at arms' length, doesn't it?" he replied sadly. "Like we're just buddies."

I didn't know what to say. I didn't want to hurt him. "It helps me remember who you are. Michael never called me that." I looked at Matt and offered a small smile. "I don't mean to keep my distance. It just seems safer keeping the two of you separate."

"Not that I could actually compete," he responded, smiling tightly.

"I don't want you to even try. You're very different from Michael, but I still like every square inch of you." I leaned over and planted a kiss on his cheek.

"Is that just a polite way of calling me a geek? If you only knew about my fan club in Boston, you wouldn't go there." He put an affectionate headlock on me, and gently held me until I wiggled my way out. "*Cavanaugh*," he continued, "I know that you think if we talk about 'us' it means we have to come to some conclusions. I'm not asking for that. I just don't want to head to Boston not knowing if I'll ever see you again."

I didn't want to say the wrong thing. It was too important to give Matt something of myself without implying there was more to come. I didn't know where my life was heading, but I cared about him. A lot. I didn't want him disappearing from my life any more than he wanted me to walk away.

"You mean you don't want to feel like I've just fallen off the face of your earth?" I asked. "This may not clarify things, but does it help you to know that I'm going to miss you like crazy?"

"I like the sound of that," he replied. "You promise you'll miss me?"

"Like a crazy person."

"I guess I can live with that. Can I see you once in a while?"

"As long as your fan club doesn't object." I sighed, took Matt's hand, and led him upstairs.

THE WEEKEND WOULD have been wonderful if it hadn't been my last one with Matt on Cleveland Street. I finally had a chance to relax without my demolition crew around, and Matt and I had decided to take a break from hosting nightly cocktail parties. We slept in late on Saturday morning, and Matt made me bacon and eggs on the old stove. A delivery service was picking it up the following Monday, along with the refrigerator, and we watched the fry pan like it was our last meal.

The house was almost empty except for a few pieces of furniture and the TVs. I had told Quinn he could have the enormous TV in the living room if he wanted it—that was a very brief discussion—and Matt agreed to take the one from my bedroom along with Bertha. "They belong together," I said. He was moving into an unfurnished apartment in Cambridge and promised to give them a good home. I had a house full of TVs and beds in Greenwich, and the last thing I needed was more of each.

The kitchen was empty except for a few necessary utensils and pans, and it echoed while Matt cooked. I thought about how the kitchen must have sounded eighty years ago at dinnertime with my great-grandparents and their four rambunctious children. I imagined Maggie in the center of the bustle, and I missed her.

Matt and I talked about the weather and his plans for the coming semester. We were polite but tiptoed around each other emotionally. I knew that Matt wanted to talk about us, but I kept our exchanges light and made it hard for him to bring up the subject. I knew it wouldn't take much for me to cave in and ask him to remain a part of my life; I was so afraid of going forward on my own.

Ellen and Stogie wandered around the house all morning taking naps in patches of sun on the empty hardwood floors. They were unsettled by all of the activity over the past two weeks, and obviously missed Maggie. Stogie spent a lot of time napping in the living room next to where her bed had been. Each time I saw one of them wandering aimlessly, I felt a pang of sadness at the thought of moving again.

Taking them back to Greenwich was going to be difficult. I knew they would be thrilled to be back in the house, yet confused that Michael and Vertigo weren't there waiting for us. Once I packed up the house, I would have to move them again to another strange place.

We were all in the same boat, though. All I had to do was think about it and my heart raced.

"WHAT'S GOING ON in that little head of yours?" asked Matt, after a particularly long spell of quiet between the two of us.

"Just thinking."

"I already knew that. I'm interested in the subject matter."

"It's been a long time since anyone cared about the crap banging around in my head."

"I doubt that." Matt smiled at me and turned the gas off underneath the fry pan.

"Do you really want to know?"

"Of course." Matt wiped his hands on a towel and looked at me expectantly.

"I was thinking about how miserable I'm going to be next week. You're moving on to continue your MIT adventure, and I'm heading back to Greenwich to face my demons." I knew I was courting everything I had spent the last few hours avoiding, but I couldn't help myself.

"Doesn't sound fair," he said. "Sounds pretty epic, too."

"Tell me about it."

He was quiet for a moment, and then said tenderly, "You don't have to do anything you don't want to. You have options."

I knew he cared about me, probably loved me, but my feelings toward him were complicated. It would take time for me to sort them out. Until then, I risked hurting the wonderful man who had helped me make it through the past three months.

"I don't have any that feel, um, tenable." I swallowed, and mentally kicked myself for being a jerk. I should have just made light of the situation, and not put pressure on Matt to rescue me from my lonely future.

"Tenable's a big word." He put a plate of bacon and eggs in front of me. "Sometimes you just need what you need. Not everything in life can be easily justified." He placed his hands on my shoulders, and slowly ran his thumbs down the vertical line of my back.

"I'm sorry. I shouldn't have said anything. You're being too nice." I stared at my plate, feeling pathetic. "I don't know what got into me."

"Maybe you shouldn't be so hard on yourself." Matt kissed me gently on my head.

Breakfast was cooling on the plate in front of me, but all I could do was stare at it as tears welled in my eyes. I was overwhelmed by recent losses and didn't have the courage to face a new one. I got up from the table, carefully pushed my chair back in, and went upstairs.

We didn't talk about Greenwich again or about any of my options that afternoon. I didn't invite it, and whenever Matt looked at me and tried to hold my eyes, I immediately looked away. It wasn't how I wanted to end our time together, and I was upset with myself for putting him in a position where he felt he needed to offer me something.

I could only guess about his intentions, but I assumed his logic was no less convoluted than mine. I was pretty certain that a future with me wouldn't resemble the one he had planned for himself. Maybe I was imposing my vision of a perfect life onto him: marriage, children, and white picket fences. A life with someone that started at the beginning. I didn't know how I felt about marriage, and it seemed a little late for children. There was a lot at stake between us, and I wasn't ready to figure it out. Not yet.

We had a quiet dinner together at the wicker table on the front porch. I had decided to let the porch furniture stay with the house—it belonged there. It was a beautiful evening, and the August humidity was finally giving way to a few crisp breezes that felt like autumn. When we were finished, I asked Matt if he'd like to take a walk with the dogs and me.

"Yeah, I'd enjoy one last cruise of the hood for the summer," he said. "I think I'll head to Boston tomorrow morning, if you can bear the pain of losing me a couple of days early." He looked at me and briefly caught my eye.

"I hope my whining hasn't scared you off," I said.

"No one would ever call you a whiner, Cavanaugh."

"This isn't the way I wanted it to end here, Matt." I reached out and took his hand.

"Oh, I know. Not what I wanted either." He sighed.

"I was hoping I could be brave, suck it up, and send you back to Boston a happy man." I laughed a bit.

Matt laughed, too, and squeezed my hand in return. "So much for the best laid plans," he said.

"I think you mean 'the best lay plans,'" I replied, smiling.

"Well, I guess I could stick to my original schedule. I'm willing to give you a second chance for a memorable send-off."

"Aren't you a good sport. So, did you have any big send-off plans for me?" I asked.

"Oh yeah: big, big plans!" he said, and grinned.

"Like what?"

"Do you really want to know?" He slowly ran his finger along the ridge of my nose.

"You could always *show* me."

"Okay, but some of what I intend to do with you could be dangerous," he said, lowering his voice to a confidential level. "Very, very dangerous—it's not for the faint of heart."

"Hey, they don't call me 'Evel Knievel' for nothing," I replied.

"What's 'evil neevil'?" Matt asked and slipped his hand under my shirt. "Sounds kinky."

14

easy for you to say

I HATE GOOD-BYES. They rank right up there with root canals as far as I'm concerned. Leaving Cleveland Street and all it represented was hard, but leaving Matt was harder. I had a lot to wrap up in Greenwich, and he had his obligations at MIT, but I knew I would miss him. That was probably why I agreed to loan him the Beemer.

Sheila had gasped her last breath just before he was supposed to leave for Cambridge, so I let him borrow my car until he found a replacement. I would miss my luxury wheels but decided the payoff would be worth it—Matt had promised to show up on demand whenever I called so I could inspect my vehicle for dings. I wasn't worried. I knew it was in good hands.

Going back to my house was the last thing I wanted to do. I wished I could hire a moving company to pack up my life there and put it all into storage, but that would have only delayed the inevitable. Eventually, I would have to go through everything. It would be horrible opening up box after box—in a hideous

Pandorafest—not knowing what part of Michael I would find. I had to deal with it now, even if I dreaded it.

I left Hungry Hill on a bright Monday morning after handing Vinnie a set of keys to Maggie's house and putting him in charge of painting the interior and making light renovations. I could almost see Maggie rolling her eyes at me, but I wanted to leave the place in good order.

I loaded the dogs into the little cube, backed out of Maggie's driveway, and watched the house on Cleveland Street grow ever smaller in my rearview mirror. I turned right at the stop sign, and it disappeared. Before I knew it, we were on the interstate south of Springfield, and then on the Merritt Parkway in Connecticut, hurtling toward our destiny in the comical little box.

Stogie sat up front with me, paying close attention to the greenbelt lining the parkway, waiting for me to shout "Deer!" when I caught sight of any white-tails munching on the roadside turf. Occasionally, he would show off by barking frantically at the window as he spotted a few of his own.

The late summer foliage flashed by in a green-and-yellow blur, and one stone bridge after another passed overhead. As we got closer to our destination, I couldn't help but dredge up memories of my life in Greenwich after Michael died, and they made me sad and anxious. Moving out of our house into the apartment on Greenwich Avenue had been a neat little psychological trick. I convinced myself of a thousand different scenarios there, and none of them included the fact that Michael was gone.

I had spent over a year in that sad place, with the barest of necessities: a mattress on the floor, a sofa, a TV. A small kitchen stocked with too much wine and cheap paper plates. Three dog dishes and one enormous water bowl. I had tried to make sure

I changed the water every day, but sometimes didn't realize that the sun had risen and set again. The only exercise I got was walking the dogs around the neighborhood. I never got lost, but sometimes it felt like I did; when that happened, Vertigo would take charge and get us all back to the apartment. One day, we had walked halfway to Lake Avenue before I realized that Vertigo was going home instead.

Leaving Greenwich and spending time with Maggie had helped me put my life and circumstances into perspective. Loss still loomed large but driving back to Greenwich finally seemed like the right thing to do. I didn't feel ready to pack up my house, but I knew I could do it and survive. The tiniest bit of resilience grew in me like an early spring flower—hidden below the frozen surface but pushing toward the inevitable warmth of the sun.

WE PULLED INTO the driveway at noon sharp and sat in the car with the engine idling. I finally turned the car off reluctantly. We sat for a while longer, the dogs pressing their faces to the windows. Finally, Ellen let out a low whine.

"All right, already," I said. "Just give me one more minute." Stogie placed a hairy paw on the window and turned to look at me.

"It's no big deal? Sure, it's easy for you to say." I sighed and unlatched my seatbelt. "Okay, here we go." I opened my door and got out. Stogie was right behind me and made a beeline to the rear door of the house. Ellen whined again from the back seat, and I let her out.

"You're sure you're up for this?" I asked. She ignored me and pushed past me. I grabbed my tote and dug around for the house key, pulled it out, and stood motionless looking at the house. Even with the gardens past their prime the grounds were gorgeous. Gabriel had weeded and mulched the beds and trimmed the shrubs and hedges. He had planted healthy lavender-toned annuals in the two large urns that flanked the glossy chocolate brown antique front door—the one that Michael and I had stripped, sanded, and repainted together.

I sighed again and headed for the back entrance. The dogs waited impatiently while I put the key in the lock and turned it. I hesitated, and then pushed the door open. Stogie went in first, followed by Ellen and then me. The house alarm beeped gently, waiting to be acknowledged. I entered Michael's birthday month and year.

I expected the house to be stuffy and dark, but the air conditioning was set at a comfortable seventy-four degrees and the blinds and drapes were all open. A fresh vase of flowers from my garden sat on the kitchen island with a note propped against it in Kat's singular scrawl:

"Dearest Grace, Welcome home! I ran into Gabriel when I stopped by to check on the place, and he cut you a bouquet of flowers. I may steal the dear man from you...Love, Kat.

P.S. Call me."

My cell phone was tucked inside a small pocket in my tote, so I pulled it out and tapped my way to Kat's number. She answered on the third ring.

"Hey, Kat," I said.

"So?" she replied.

"So." I said.

"You're at the house?"

"I'm at the house."

"You okay?" she asked.

"Never better."

"Do you need me to come over?"

"Nah, I'm okay. Really. You can come over later, if you want."

"You sure you want to pack up that big house all by yourself?" she asked.

"I'm having boxes delivered tomorrow morning. I need to go through everything myself. I need to know what goes in the boxes so I can compartmentalize."

"Compartmentalize?" Kat waited for an explanation.

"Yeah, put my new life in boxes marked 'Grace's New Life,' and put what I want to keep of my old life, in, you know, boxes marked 'Grace's Old Life'—Michael's stuff I want to keep."

"You're going to do that all by yourself?" Kat didn't sound convinced that my plan was a good one.

"No, no—I have a friend coming tomorrow to help me."

"A friend?"

"Henry. Looks like Mickey Rooney on steroids. He has a great attitude, and a certain, um, charm."

"Surely you're not *sleeping* with the man!" she said. "I'm envisioning a geriatric Caucasian midget sumo wrestler!"

"I don't believe that adjective is politically correct." I suppressed a laugh.

"Which one?" she asked.

"Uh—*midget?* Maybe others. Of course, I'm not sleeping with him!" It felt good to laugh. "Sometimes I don't know who's more ridiculous—you or me."

"Trust me, *you* always had the corner on that market. I just try to humor you." Kat and I laughed together, and she made little snorting sounds.

"You're snorting," I said.

She laughed and snorted some more, and then we settled into silence.

"I'm sorry I couldn't make Maggie's funeral, Grace," Kat finally said. "It was a bitch getting the twins settled at Georgetown."

"It's all right, Kat. You can make it up to me by coming over this evening and keeping me company."

"Sounds like a plan for redemption. Can I bring anything?"

"No, not necessary. I'm going to head out and load up on food. There's nothing in the house, and I have to feed Henry."

"As long as that's all you do for the little man!" she said, snorting again.

"God, you need to get that fixed. Forget your ass."

I SET MY cell phone on the kitchen counter, girded my loins, and took the dogs on a nostalgic post-traumatic tour of the house.

My first stop was easy: the wine cellar in the basement. I retrieved two bottles of my favorite pinot gris from an enormous wine refrigerator and put one of them in the ice drawer of the Sub Zero in the kitchen to get it nice and cold. I set the other bottle on the kitchen counter and fished out a corkscrew from a drawer near the sink. I didn't use the hydraulic bottle opener in the butler's pantry because I had never learned how to use it. Michael always did it for me.

"This is going to be fun," I told the dogs. "A regular little sentimental journey."

After pulling out the cork, I poured myself a glass of wine

that stopped just short of the rim. I sipped carefully for a minute, bracing myself for the rest of the tour.

The dining room was just off the kitchen, toward the front of the house, and the family room was in the rear next to the kitchen. I briefly appraised the emotional quotient of both spaces before deciding the dining room would be the safest room to venture into next. It was a lovely space, but not too many items of a personal nature resided there. It was a sort of United Nations of furniture: Michael's paternal grandmother's enormous French walnut dining table was surrounded by black leather Breuer chairs we had bought in Milan. A stunning Irish cupboard from a pub took up a whole wall and was loaded with my collection of English pewter.

"I bet the nice family from L.A. gets rid of my charcoal toile wallpaper," I said to the dogs. "They'll probably go mid-century or something in here."

Ellen looked at me.

"Well, they're from California."

I hesitated before continuing into the front parlor, which we had designated our "formal" living room, although nothing about our beautiful house was really formal but its fine bones. The room was extravagantly trimmed in layers of elegant molding, and the original owners had gone wild with the fine craftsmanship of the nineteenth century. In spite of its formality, the room was one of the most comfortable in the house. I had upholstered all of the furniture in cream linen so it wouldn't distract from the room's beautiful proportions and details. The fabric was washed and relaxed, and all of the seating was upholstered with down filling. A high-gloss indigo covered the walls, and decorations were kept to a minimum.

Michael had found a large collection of antique watercolor botanicals on a business trip to London, and they filled a wall over the largest sofa. The elaborately carved fireplace surround was the focal point of the room; above it was a simple gilded mirror we had found in Austria when Michael had joined me at an international convention for architecture and the decorative arts.

"No memories here," I commented to the peanut gallery, as my eyes wandered. They stopped at collection of exotic vacation photographs of Michael and me that were clustered on the walnut baby grand piano near the wall opposite the fireplace. Michael's green eyes watched me from a dozen different angles. "I don't know what I'm going to do with these," I said, and picked up a favorite and fingered the simple black frame. "What do I do—put stuff like this in a box, tape it up, and try to forget?" I looked at the dogs, but they didn't offer any useful suggestions.

We returned to the kitchen, and I felt bolstered by the fact that I wasn't decompensating. My emotional response to being back home was strong, but I was okay. I decided to keep myself on an even keel and finish the tour later, after I had tossed back another glass or two of wine with Kat on the back terrace.

The dogs and I headed out to buy enough food to keep Henry fueled and happy through the next few days. We stopped at the grocery store on Putnam Avenue for staples, and then continued up the road to the organic specialty store for fresh produce and meat. The process was such a familiar one, repeated hundreds of times in a former life, but it felt strange to be finally doing it again. I had survived on takeout menus and food from the little convenience store on Greenwich Avenue for a long time. When the meat guy at Whole Foods said, "That all, Mrs. C?" like no time had passed, I almost had an out-of-body experience with the weirdness of it all.

Back in the cube, I told the dogs how strange everything felt, but they just looked at me and waited for the little treat they always got from the meat counter.

"You two haven't really bothered to process the time and space continuum," I lectured. "Must be nice."

WHEN I WOKE up the next morning, it was because my head was pounding. I was tired and had a headache. Two Advil only put a dent in my pain. Kat and I had put away a lot of wine—she spent the night in my guest bedroom even though her house was less than two miles away. It had been good to have her company my first night back, even if I was paying for it with a throbbing skull.

Henry showed up right on time; thank God it *wasn't* six a.m. Once I let him through the front door, my life was in his capable hands and it made me feel better. He offered to make coffee and walk the dogs while I dug around in the medicine cabinet for a non-existent hangover cure. I took another Advil and drank a lot of water.

Henry returned to the house with the dogs, and I heard him talking to someone. I looked out my bedroom window to the front driveway, and saw a small white van bearing a moving company logo. A moment later, the driver began unloading boxes and carrying them to my garage.

I took a long, hot shower, so Kat beat me to the kitchen once the aroma of coffee made it to the second floor. She and Henry were old friends by the time I headed downstairs a half-hour later. I was sure the moment she met him, she realized my attachment to him was emotional, not romantic, but I could hear her teasing Henry about our odd relationship anyway.

"So, Hank, what's the deal with you and Grace?" I heard her ask.

"I think I remind her of her dad."

"Her dad is tall, dark, and, um..."

"Yeah, he's a pretty nice guy."

"YOU'RE LOOKING AWFULLY chipper for a woman who did better than match me drink-for-drink," I complained when I walked into the kitchen and saw that Kat was already showered and dressed and her usual pulled-together self.

"I can't help it if you're an amateur," she said.

"Amateur? I drank like a fish."

"We are talking *wine*, you big wuss. Try tossing back a half-dozen martinis with the club crowd, and *then* waking up early for an open house."

"Fine," I said, and yawned. "You win."

Henry put a cup of coffee in front of me: a little bit of sugar, a little bit of cream.

"I love you," I said.

KAT AND I said our good-byes after breakfast, promising to get together for lunch once the packing was finished.

Henry let the dogs out again while I tidied up my bedroom, and once I had the room squared away and neat, I gave myself over to the chore of packing. I can't say it felt great, but I did experience a small seed of relief that made it worthwhile.

Henry spent a lot of time holding my hand the first day, and a little less the second. Packing up Michael's office was the hardest task so we saved it for last, and I found out a few things about Michael I never knew. He saved every paper clip that landed on his desk in an old cigar box, and all of the pictures of me I hated were in a neat little bundle in the bottom drawer of his desk. I was pretty certain I rated more than the paper clips, but it didn't matter. It was nice to know Michael found it so hard to let go, too.

GRATITUDE

Because I'm an extremely slow writer, there's a cast of thousands—or at least, certainly dozens—of individuals who deserve thanks for their support while I was working on *Hungry Hill*, my debut novel. In particular, I'd like to give thanks to an enthusiastic and supportive Charlotte Hughes—my editor and mentor throughout much of the process. I learned invaluable lessons regarding the craft of writing fiction from Charlotte, and her many contributions are scattered throughout my novel.

My two book clubs—in Connecticut and Florida—provided early feedback and support, for which I'm grateful. It was early enthusiastic readers like them who kept me at my writing. A big shout-out, too, to my family and friends, many of whom also served as beta readers.